BUMPS
IN THE
NIGHT

BUMPS
IN THE
NIGHT

AMALIE HOWARD

Delacorte Press

Text copyright © 2023 by Amalie Howard
Jacket art copyright © 2023 by Matt Rockefeller

All rights reserved. Published in the United States by Delacorte Press, an imprint of Random House Children's Books, a division of Penguin Random House LLC, New York.

Delacorte Press is a registered trademark and the colophon is a trademark of Penguin Random House LLC.

Visit us on the Web! GetUnderlined.com

Educators and librarians, for a variety of teaching tools, visit us at RHTeachersLibrarians.com

Library of Congress Cataloging-in-Publication Data is available upon request.
ISBN 978-0-593-64587-1 (trade) — ISBN 978-0-593-64588-8 (lib. bdg.) — ISBN 978-0-593-64589-5 (ebook)

The text of this book is set in 11.25-point Adobe Caslon Pro.
Interior design by Jen Valero

Printed in the United States of America
10 9 8 7 6 5 4 3 2 1
First Edition

For my son, Noah, the most
"Trini-to-the-bone" of my kids

ALL SKIN TEETH EH LAUGH.

*—Trinidadian expression meaning that friendly appearances
can be deceiving, and some smiles should not be trusted*

1

PRIDE AND PUNISHMENT

Airports have to be the first places to go in an apocalypse. From the plane's window, I watch a five-year-old pick his nose a few feet in front of me before using those same wet, goopy fingers to grab the handrail as he and his parents exit down the rollaway stairs. I cringe, reach for the hand sanitizer attached to my backpack, and squeeze out a large dollop. I wrinkle my nose at the people swarming the aisle to leave the airplane, where they'll be touching that same booger rail. It only takes one infected person and—*bam!*— mass contagion. That kid could be patient zero and within seconds everyone's hungry for each other's brains.

Instant zombie apocalypse.

Not that zombies exist, but a girl can't be too careful.

Stepping through the rounded plane door, I blink at the thick, bleary heat blasting into my face at the top of the stairs. Holy melting Skittles farms, the Caribbean is hot. Not like bone-dry summer hot, but sticky, humid, take-a-dozen-showers-to-stay-cool hot. Already my armpits are sweating into the cotton of my tank top, and I've only just arrived at the destination indicated on the plane ticket tucked in the front pocket of my backpack.

Port-of-Spain, it reads, the capital of Trinidad and Tobago.

Might as well say Port-of-Prison. Because that's what Granny's house will be—my jail cell for the next three months. It'd been her idea when my dad called her a month ago out of frustration. I had been written up for vandalism—*again*—though no charges had been pressed against me by my school, thank goodness. But I'd been royally grounded.

No phone. No drawing tablet. No anything.

I couldn't text friends. I couldn't sketch. I couldn't even use my computer to game. And now I've been banished to another country for the whole summer without any of my stuff. To be fair, I knew this was coming—this was *the last straw*. Those words replay in my mind in Dad's grim voice and my heart squashes in my chest. I could have done my homework, gotten better grades, stopped cutting school, and not drawn on public property.

Stop feeling sorry for yourself, Rika, I tell myself. *Three months is nothing. Get over it.*

Sure. Three months of trying not to die of boredom.

And who knows what Granny has planned? She is a weathered battle-ax who lives on an estate in the middle of nowhere, grows her own fruit in a massive orchard, sews her own clothes, and is just . . . *weird*. I used to think she was made of magic when I was younger—that she had eyes in the back of her head that saw everything.

She'd tell me stories about witchcraft that would have my spine curling and my blood crawling. Myths of monsters and jumbies, creepy lost children called douens whose feet faced backward, and a shape-shifting woman called la diablesse who came in the night to steal the souls of children, only she said it like "la-ja-bless." I remember shivering in terrified delight when Granny teased that kids' bones were always soft and delicious.

I used to live for her tales. But I guess they're about as real as zombies.

Now I can only think about the fact that Granny has no internet. I'll be cut off from everything and everyone. And by the time summer ends, in this heat, I'm probably going to dissolve into a sad puddle of melty goo that no one back home will even recognize.

On cue, a hot gust steams into my entire body like it's cackling in the face of my epic pity party, and I sigh. Even the weather is against me. I give a half-hearted wave to the airline representative waiting at the base of the rollaway stairs and force my legs to move. It feels like I'm moving through syrup in the heat.

"Miss Lovelace-Rose?" the woman says when I reach the bottom.

Mom always said names have power, and apparently ours does, so *Lovelace*-Rose it is.

I nod. "That's me."

Unaccompanied minor and future goo puddle.

Unwanted miscreant and trouble with a capital *T*.

"Welcome to Trinidad and Tobago," she says, her accent soft and musical. *Tania*, her name tag reads. That starts with *T* too. I wonder if she ever got sent away by her dad to some strange place when she was younger. She's beautiful, tall with brown skin several shades darker than mine and a red-lipped smile that's so wide, it makes you want to grin back. I'm not ready to stop sulking, so I mumble noncommittal responses to her friendly questions about the flight and whether I'd been to Trinidad before.

"Yes, it was fine." *I don't want to be here.*

"Once, a few years ago." *My life officially sucks.*

After we get through the lines in immigration, where my passport is scrutinized and stamped, Tania eyes me. "It says here in my packet that a Mrs. Lovelace will be meeting you?" she asks.

"My grandmother."

"Okay. Let's get your luggage, then wait for her."

This airport is much smaller than the one I left from in the United States, and the large open windows let in a warm breeze that smells of a rainstorm and fresh-tilled earth. Colorful brown-green foliage sways in the distance, a rise of darker purple-hued mountains looming behind it. A plump lizard sunning on one of the sills catches my attention.

No, not a lizard, more like a baby iguana. As long as my forearm from elbow to wrist, it's a brilliant green with black tail markings and looks like a miniature dragon, without the wings. For an instant, its eye connects with mine until a long pink tongue slicks over it, which is somehow simultaneously gross . . . and kind of adorable.

Keeping my face stoic, I look away. I don't want to be charmed by or like anything about this place—not the cool reptiles, not the fresh smells, not the friendly, smiling faces like Tania's.

Last time I was here, I was nine. More than three years ago. Before Mom left. Before Dad got remarried to Cassie. Before my stepbrothers, Max and Theo, came. Before *everything* in my life went downhill.

I stare at my scuffed sneakers, feeling sorry for myself again, when the hairs on the back of my neck stand up. Shuddering and resisting the urge to rub my nape, I glance over my shoulder. My gaze instantly snags on a thin-faced but gorgeous woman, with her hair scraped back beneath a wide-brimmed hat, sauntering through the crowd.

My adrenaline spikes, like when you enter a pitch-black room and can't find the light switch or right before the jump scare you know is coming in a scary movie. As she sails past me, her floor-length red gown way too fancy for the airport, my skin crawls.

Something about her feels *off.* A strange noise fills my ears, like a swarm of buzzing flies . . . or the faint rattle of chains. Stomach rolling, stark terror grips me in a giant fist. My breath stutters in my throat, and I drop my eyes. *Don't look at me, don't look at me, don't look at me,* I chant silently.

On instinct, I shift so I'm hidden behind Tania's ample form, out of the woman's sight, though I can still see her. Her flowy old-style dress reminds me of a fancy ball gown and her face is so still it's unnerving. Those wide-set eyes don't blink and her mouth doesn't move in that gruesome rictus. I narrow my gaze. Her chest doesn't move either, for that matter. *Why isn't she breathing?*

Is she dead?

UNDEAD?

When a pair of milky eyes sweeps in my direction, every muscle in my quaking body locks up. Oh my gosh, why can't I move my feet anymore? I feel a sticky, soupy energy reaching for me like a dozen pairs of tentacles with long twisty feelers that are going to grab me and gobble me whole.

Trolleys clang behind me and I nearly jump a foot into the air.

I let out a small gasp, and that's enough for her to swing around. My heart thrashes behind my ribs as the sensation of a hundred spiders scuttles across my skin, and fight-or-flight kicks in a half-second too late. Everything feels foul. I want to scream for help, call my dad and beg him to bring me home. Offer up anything—eternity in my room, babysitting duty for Max and Theo forever. I just want *out of here.*

But my shoes are glued to the floor.

My body is frozen in a trance, legs like iron weights, dread thickening in my throat with each manic thump of my heart. I stay close to Tania and try not to breathe or attract any more notice . . . but the sound of those chains rattling nears. Coming for me.

Suddenly, something bright green launches across my vision, breaking through the weird spell holding me in its webby grip. As my limbs gracelessly loosen from their corpselike hold, I see a familiar black-and-green-banded tail swish out of sight. My breath whooshes out. *Thanks, little guy.*

The slimy sensation eases as the woman strolls in the opposite direction, eyes probing the crowd, probably looking for her next meal. Waiting to strike when you least expect it, like a monster that hides in the closet or sleeps under the bed.

Monsters aren't real, Rika.

But even after reminding myself of that rational fact a few more times for good measure, my pulse won't quit racing. Reminiscing about Granny's old stories and the shape-shifting spirit who eats people's souls had gotten under my skin. I suppress a quiver. That woman had definitely looked like she'd enjoy a good soul buffet with a serving of soft, fresh kid bones on the side.

A snicker of nervous laughter bubbles up in me and I shake my head. "Get a grip, girl."

"Did you say something, dear?" Tania asks.

"Nope," I mutter.

"Flight 1214 from Denver, Colorado, on carousel two," a nasal voice announces through the airport speakers. As we head that way, the ground beneath us abruptly starts to rumble. People around us shriek and Tania grabs hold of me, but the quake is over before I can fully flip out.

"What was *that*?" I yelp.

A man next to me with dark-brown skin and the longest locs I've ever seen clutches his arms to his chest and gives a loud moan. "Is because Papa Bois run an' gone."

I blink my confusion, more at the thick Trinidadian dialect

than the words, but Tania sniffs. "Blame climate change for these earthquakes, not folklore."

Curious, I ask the man, "Papa Bois?"

"King a de forest. The obeahman say someting wrong, an' we payin' for it."

Tania tugs at my arm with a scoff. "Come, dear, don't waste your time with him. Some people will say anything to explain away science." She sucks air and saliva through her teeth, making a vexed sound that Granny says people here call a *steups*. "Is not obeah, is *people* killing the planet."

But even with Tania's logical explanation, I can't help but shiver at the man's choice of words. Now that I think of it, Granny had also mentioned Papa Bois, the protector of the woods who was a shape-shifter with horns and a beard of leaves. And even I know that the premonition of the obeah-man, a master of witchcraft, is something islanders here take seriously.

My mind immediately hitches on the milky-eyed woman and whatever spell that had come over me. What if she was actually one of *them*? One of the folklore come to life . . . a monster in disguise, hunting in plain sight.

Or . . . maybe your brain needs a snack and a nap, Rika! Chill.

We head over toward the baggage carousel, and when my suitcase finally appears, I yank it off the belt, eager to put some distance between me and the eerie strangers in here.

"Okay I've got my luggage," I tell Tania, my skin still crawling. "Can we leave?"

She smiles. "I bet you're excited to get out of this crowded airport and see your grandmother. Let's go."

I swallow a snarky reply that I'd much rather get back on the airplane and go home to Colorado, then follow her in silence. While we make our way through the space jam-packed with people yelling about their bags and piling carts tower-high with suitcases, I make sure to keep my body angled close to Tania's, just in case.

Thankfully, we pass through customs in a flash since I have nothing to declare. The only contraband I've stashed is a dozen bags of assorted candy for personal consumption. We hustle out of the airport into the waiting area beyond, and there's my grandmother, front and center, with a huge smile on her weathered face, holding a big cardboard sign saying *Welcome, Darika Lovelace!*

Guess she forgot the Rose.

Despite last seeing her when I was nine, she looks the same: tiny, fierce, and striking. Her thick curly hair is tied back, her brown face open and kindly, dark eyes twinkling. She confirms her identification with Tania and signs some paperwork before turning to me.

"Rika-love."

"Hey, Granny," I say, smiling at the old nickname as she gathers me into a rib-crushing hug.

The familiar scent of her—sweet spices, sunshine, and baby powder—is instantly comforting, making my eyes wet once more with stupid tears. Hesitantly, I wrap one arm awk-wardly around her small frame. At least someone in my family wants me around.

"Come, let me look at you, doux-doux darling," she says in that deep singsong voice I love, holding me in front of her by the sides of my arms and twirling me around. A smile tugs at my lips at the Trinidadian endearment for *sweetie*. We might not have seen each other in years, but she does call for my birthday and other holidays and makes sure Dad buys me presents from her every year. "Chile, you're bigger than me now. How old are you these days?"

"Nearly thirteen," I say. Hooray for an end-of-summer birthday, which always makes me the youngest in my grade. *Not.*

"You resemble your father, but I see my Dulcie in you, too." She grins, the lines bracketing her mouth and eyes crinkling as she scans my hair and tugs fondly on an unruly lock that looks just like hers. Like my mom's too.

Granny reaches for my suitcase with one hand and grasps my palm firmly in the other. "Come, come. Becks is waiting with the truck outside."

"Who's Becks?"

"My foreman and handyman around the place. You name it, he does it."

We head through the wide exit doors. Standing next to the truck is the biggest man I've ever seen, wearing a singlet tank top and faded overalls. His dark-brown shoulders are hunched slightly as though he wants to make himself smaller and less noticeable. It doesn't really work—even his muscles have muscles, and his arms are as thick as my waist. "Miss Darika, pleased to meet you."

"Hi, Mr. Becks," I greet him, feeling instantly at ease seeing his warm smile. I wonder if he is also a bodyguard or something—not that Granny would need one—but still, he is practically a mountain. "Nice to meet you too."

10

"Is just Becks, Miss," he says. "Mr. Becks was my pops."

For a moment, his cheery tone makes me forget my sulkfest as I climb into the back seat of the old truck and wait for him to stow my luggage in the trunk. I can't believe Granny still drives this. Last time I was in it, we rode up over the mountains to my favorite beach here, Maracas Bay, on the north side of the island. Powdery white sand with awesome waves and some of the best shark-and-bake sandwiches I've ever eaten.

My mouth waters at the thought of food. I decide to ask if we can stop for my favorite Trini street food, called *doubles*—two round soft pieces of fried dough with curried chickpeas between them—when the crawly sensation of spiders races over my skin again. Granny is standing at the passenger door, her body immobile, tension coiling over her. I turn in slow motion to see her stare locked on the woman in the hat and flowing dress.

My pulse thunders in my ears and I dig my fingers into the car seats.

Did she *follow* me?

Recoiling, I hold my breath as time contracts and drops to a crawl. My grandmother's lip curls ever so slightly, the sound of a snarl so soft that no one else would have heard it escape, and I feel the menace unroll in the pit of my stomach, like two alpha predators facing off in the wild.

Wait, does Granny *know* her?

I squint, staring boldly at the woman in red now that I'm safe in the truck. Glittering pale eyes crash into mine, and in that moment, I realize how wrong I was earlier. She's not scary; she's friendly! Her face is so lovely that I actually sigh with longing. I'm overwhelmed by the biggest urge to run over and give her a hug. I want her to like me more than anything! She smiles, and I instantly smile back, delighted that I've caught her attention.

"Go now!" Granny hollers at Becks, swinging her lithe frame into the front seat, and the odd eye contact between the woman and me breaks. I blink rapidly, my brain foggy as though I'm waking up from a deep sleep, and I swear I could hear a shriek of rage on the wind.

"Who was that, Granny?" I mumble, feeling disoriented. "The lady you were staring at. She was so beautiful."

Her piercing gaze swivels to mine. A puff of air escapes Granny's lips, alarm flashing in her stare for a hot second before she turns back around, fingers toying with a bracelet of red and black beads she's always worn for protection around her wrist. "She's no one. Forget her."

I flinch at the sharp rebuke, but shrug it off. *Yeah, whatever, Granny.*

Blowing out a sullen breath, I distract myself with the landscape. Some of the roads look familiar as we leave the airport, driving past open tracts of land filled with neat rows of sugarcane and thatches of bamboo. A new gas station and what looks like a strip mall come into view. At the main intersection, we take a left and get on the highway.

Compared to the six-lane interstate I'm used to in Colorado, this one is tiny, and we swerve madly to avoid the gigantic potholes in the road. Now, those I remember. My mom used to joke about losing half your car in them and that driving here when she was a girl was practically a survival-of-the-luckiest obstacle course.

As we drive, I can't help noticing that a lot of the green fields seem brown and withered, almost like the island had suffered a dreadful drought. It makes me think of the earthquake and what Tania had said about climate change. Or the missing Papa Bois . . . who might be responsible for it all, according to that man at the airport anyway.

My dad's a researcher for the United States Department of Agriculture, so he's always firing off facts about climate change and how we're destroying the world with our eyes wide open. He insists the government should be more active about slowing down its effects, and I bet he'd be tickled to know some people here were blaming global warming on local folklore.

Biting back my own snort, I stare at the passing neighborhoods, noting how other things have changed. Bigger buildings dwarf little ones, and shantytowns are huddled in between upscale housing developments and the rural areas with wide-reaching sugarcane fields. A huge mountain range swells to the right, cradling the pockets of towns that we pass through, and before too long, we are pulling into the long driveway leading up to my grandmother's expansive property in the mountains called the Northern Range.

"Look, we reach home," Becks says, the truck rolling to a stop in the cobblestoned courtyard with a crumbling old well at its center. I can't believe it's still standing. When I was small, I used to dump my mom's spare change in it every day

13

in exchange for wishes. Back when I used to believe in things like magic.

But everyone knows wishes are useless.

If they weren't, Mom would still be around. Maybe she might have taken me to New York and I'd be living with her, not banished here. Maybe I wouldn't be so messed up and life would be perfect. I bite my lip and drag a fist against my chest, rubbing the ache there. Sighing, I exit the car and stretch my sore legs, stuffing my sadness down to where it doesn't hurt quite so much. Dredging up old memories about Mom won't help anyone, but my brain doesn't listen, caught up in them.

Mom dancing with me in this same courtyard . . .

Mom telling mc to make a wish . . .

Mom being . . . my *mom*.

With a sniff, I fish for a coin from my backpack and toss it in. *I wish you were here.*

Despite my efforts to hold back the tears, moisture leaks from the corners of my eyes. My plea will never come true. None of this matters anyway because Mom's been "taking a break" for two years, according to my dad, and she's probably never coming back, no matter how much I hope she will. I swipe an arm across my face.

"Are you okay, lovey?" Granny asks, coming to stand beside me next to the old wishing well.

I tug on the frayed rope attached to the rusty bucket. "I guess I just . . . miss Mom."

"We all do," she says. "But now that you're here, I'll bring her back soon."

That frustrated steups sound escapes her and I peer up

at her with a curious frown. It's the exact same sound Tania made, and Granny looks furious with herself, which means she's said something she hadn't meant to say. My heart begins to pound. Last Dad told me, Mom was in New York . . . but what if she's *here*? "Granny, is Mom in Trinidad right now?"

Her face tightens as she stalks away, leaving me in a state of stunned disbelief. She didn't say no. My mother, whom I haven't seen in years, might be on this very island. At the same time as me. My brain trips trying to process the information. Does Dad know? Is that why he sent me here? A tiny seed of wonder unfurls in my chest, making my banishment suddenly not seem so horrible, because if Mom's around, that changes *everything*.

Hope and excitement burst inside me like twin flames.

"Wait, Granny, where is she?" I ask, hurrying to where she's hauling bags of groceries from the bed of the truck and muttering to herself. She looks vexed, but I press on. "Can I see her?"

"No. Forget I said anything. It's complicated."

I growl and grind my back teeth. I hate that word: *complicated*. It's the one adults use when they think you're too silly or young to understand. As Granny marches toward the house, my hands curl into fists and raw determination roars through me. I can be stubborn too.

Because if my mom is anywhere on this island, I don't care how complicated it is, I'm going to find her.

2

GAME PLANS
ARE THE BEST PLANS

The sprawling ranch house with its huge wraparound porch and graceful columns looks the same as it did last time I visited, though there've been a few improvements, like a new roof and a whole addition to the right wing of the house. The faint echo of what sounds like high-pitched childish singing reaches me at the entrance from the orchard, and I cock my head, straining to listen. I hear the same tinkling notes again and the ripple of children's laughter.

The eerie notes of a nursery rhyme my mom used to sing filters through on the breeze. I notice Becks stiffening, but he doesn't say anything. Does he hear the sounds too? I turn toward the citrus grove, ears on alert. *Tra la la la la . . .*

If I recall, Granny's neighbors were miles

away from her enormous estate. Well, except for one. When I'd stayed years ago, Granny was mentoring a local girl around my age and teaching her how to sew. The girl—Monique or Mona or something—hadn't liked me from the start. An old forgotten memory drifts through my brain.

A vision of my much smaller self, standing on this very porch in front of a surly girl with high cheekbones and dark hair in neat braids, rises to the forefront.

"You don't even know of the trinity, do you?" Monique had taunted.

"The what?"

She'd sneered. "Never mind."

At the time, I dimly recall being annoyed with her smug attitude, like she knew something I didn't. Something secret. Something *special.*

"Is that my granny's bracelet?" Younger Me had demanded, staring at the shiny shells and beads around her wrist that I recognized from seeing it in Granny's drawer.

Monique had clutched it to her chest. "She gave it to me."

"Why would she give *you* her bracelet?"

"Maybe because I deserve it." *And you don't* had been more than clear in her reply.

Jealousy had been quick to surface and I remember seeing red, wanting to get the bracelet back because there was no way my grandmother would give that away. The altercation was a blur, but the fragile string of beads had caught and scattered in the scuffle. Granny had hugged me as I'd burst into tears after breaking her treasured bracelet, and told the two of us

17

that she'd make another. Monique had looked as though the world had ended.

Huh. I hadn't thought about that in years. I'd had too many other things on my mind, with Mom and Dad's split and everything that came after.

I wonder what Monique would be like now. Would she still be haughty and horrid, talking down to me any chance she got? Honestly, I'd take her attitude if that meant I didn't have to spend this entire summer alone.

"Are there other kids nearby?" I ask Becks as he hefts my suitcase to follow in Granny's footsteps up to the house. A flash of bright green in the truck bed catches my eye, but disappears before I can tell what it is. Another iguana, maybe. Or worse, a snake.

Becks frowns. "Nah, man. Most a them still in school."

I love how he says the *th* sound like a *d,* and drops all the verbs when he talks in his cool Trini dialect. Becks is right. Unlike in Colorado, which starts summer break in May, kids in Trinidad get out the last week of June. Still, I know the noises I heard. "Didn't you hear the singing? Over in the trees?"

"No. Doh go in them woods, you hear?"

I instantly look to the green hills rising beyond the orchard, watching the wind dance through the lush treetops. "Why not?"

"The devil over dey. He calls, laying his traps with tricks."

O-kay, then. I fight a giggle. He could have just said it was dangerous or off-limits. I sneak a furtive glance toward the swaying trees and feel a weird tingle creep down my spine.

Whatever. Becks's warnings are the least of my worries. "Is Granny upset with me?"

"No. She have plenty on her mind these days with your mother, and after what happened at the airport with Ushara, is no wonder she gone quiet." He shakes his head and scratches his chin.

"Ushara? Who? The pretty lady in red?" I blink, his words registering like a hammer to my overactive imagination. "Who was she?"

"Doh mind that."

"Who, Becks?" I insist, hurrying along beside him. He doesn't answer, and then we're at the entrance to a bedroom, where I expect I'll be staying the next few months. "Let me guess, she's the bestie of the devil in the woods."

I mean it as a joke, obviously, but something close to alarm flashes in his eyes. His voice lowers. "She is someone you should stay away from, Miss Darika. She means Dulcie—" He breaks off with a flustered expression and then he hustles down the corridor, leaving me more confused than ever until I connect the dots. My eyes widen. Dulcie's my *mom's* name, and clearly the two of them are related somehow.

What had Becks been about to say? A person either means well or means harm. After running into Ushara earlier, I'm betting on the second. Does she mean my mom harm?

"She means Dulcie what?" I yell after him.

No answer.

Great, more secrets.

As if that'll deter me. I'm the queen of ferreting out secrets. I'd found out about my planned summer banishment weeks earlier while I'd been snooping on Dad's computer and saw the messages from Granny telling him to send me there for the summer to keep me out of trouble. Sadly, no amount of my begging or groveling had gotten him to change his mind. But more silver lining—it definitely seems like my mom's here too.

A knot forms in my throat. What're the chances I could find her?

And if I did, would things be different for me at home or at school? Would I feel less alone? Probably. When my mom was around, I felt special and seen. I could tell her anything and she always knew the right thing to say. We'd talk for hours about what was going on in class, about my art and soccer and insecurities, or whether I had any new friends or crushes. We would have movie nights with popcorn and our own special just-the-girls dates that we did together on the weekends, rain or shine. One weekend, we'd take a beginner hip-hop class, the next we would go hiking in the mountains because we both loved trying new things. She just *got* me.

After my parents' divorce, I'd floundered. My sense of belonging disappeared, like I was left adrift on an open sea. When my parents split up, Mom moved out and Dad moved on with a new wife and new kids. A brand-new family. And I simply stayed . . . me. A strange puzzle piece from an old set trying to fit into his perfect life. Don't get me wrong, my stepmom loves me, but she's just not *my* mom.

No, my mom stuck around for a year and then disappeared when I was ten without a word. It was as though she'd sort of vanished off the face of the planet. Dad had assured me that she was fine and working out a few personal things on her own in New York, so I knew she was still alive and well enough. I had thought she'd been in the United States all this time, but maybe she'd come back to her home country.

But why hadn't she ever called or texted?

I'd always thought it was me. Something *I* did to make her go away. And then it hurt to think of her too much, so I stuffed my feelings down where I couldn't feel them. I suppose a part of me always believed she'd come back one day—*what kind of mom leaves their kid behind without any explanation?*—but she never did. Two and a half years and counting.

My brain ticks over a thought that hadn't occurred to me until today. What if she's in serious trouble and *couldn't* get back to me? That would explain why she never got in contact. And if she is in trouble and we're now in the same country, maybe I can help. My pulse picks up again, a rush of adrenaline making my ears hot.

Holy purple Skittles, if I'm doing this, if I'm going to find Mom, I need a plan. The most important step is to get more information. Forewarned is always forearmed.

Buoyed by this strategy, I head into my room. A row of windows occupies two of the walls, golden sunlight streaming through the big glass panels, causing prisms of light to dance on the polished wood floor. A door on one side leads into an overgrown garden, bright green vines climbing and twisting over a metal trellis gate.

The garden is lush with multihued wildflowers and hanging feathers tied together with wind chimes blowing at intervals in the breeze. This time, I can't help my laugh. Granny's a big believer in her protections. Pouches of various roots and herbs are laid out in bunches to guard against jumbies, another word for monsters, and maljo—what she calls "bad eye."

She wants to make sure no one can put a hex on her home or nothing evil can enter her spaces. Some things never change. Maybe I should ask her to weigh in on whether *she* thinks Papa Bois is responsible for all the environmental havoc. I'll bet my right eyeball she does.

A flash of emerald and onyx scurrying across the lawn catches the sunlight. Another tiny iguana? Or maybe the same one? I frown, then shake my head. There's no way it could be the same reptile from the airport. Hundreds of geckos and iguanas must be around, and besides, the airport is miles away. I better get used to the wildlife, all the different kinds of flora and fauna here. Some are pretty and others are pretty deadly. Like the manchineel tree, the most dangerous tree in the world, which bears a fruit called poison guava that can kill any human. Wicked!

Dropping my stuff, I retrieve a notebook and pen from my backpack. Time to outline MISSION DARIKA UNDER-COVER.

> a. Where is Mom?
> b. Is she in trouble?
> c. Who is Ushara?
> d. What does she have to do with Mom?
>   Dad said that Mom went away to work
>   out some "private issues." Could
>   Ushara be part of that?
> e. Get enough clues to find Mom.

All of the questions above mean I need to get Granny talking by any means necessary. What better way to get answers than to engage the dragon head-on? And there's no time like the present. I grab my soccer ball from its sling in my backpack and kick it against the wall, causing a loud thud. I'm going to be in trouble for that one.

But how else will I confront my tight-lipped grandmother about Mom? I kick the ball again and again, the obnoxious thuds echoing down the hallway. Sure enough, before long, I hear the clack of brisk footsteps. I smash a particularly hard kick, wincing at the huge thump as the ball ricochets off the wall and knocks over a nearby wooden side table that looks like it might have been handmade and snaps off a leg. *Oops.*

The door swings open.

"No football in the house, Rika-love," Granny chides softly.

"It's soccer," I reply, exasperated, knowing full well it's called football here. "Football is a whole different game."

Deep brown eyes meet mine with a frown. "I know you're tired and have had a long flight, but there's no need to take that tone, young lady. No back chat. My house, my rules. If you want to play with *that* ball, take it outside."

"Sorry." Ears burning, I put the ball to the side and right the table as best as I can with its broken leg. "Granny, did you feel the earthquake after my plane landed? Some man at the airport said something about an obeahman. Do you believe in that stuff?"

Her mouth tightens. "Obeah is no joke."

"The man said the ground shook because Papa Bois was gone."

23

Granny's lips have flattened into a pinched line. "People like to run their mouths too much. Are you hungry?"

My stomach rumbles. "I could eat."

I follow her to the dining room, where she points for me to sit down at one of the two place settings. A mouthwatering scent wafts into my nose. Lifting my fork, I stare down into the savory stewed fish and dumplings.

"This is cascadoux," Granny says. "You remember the legend?" My brows scrunch together as she grins. "Those who eat the cascadura will, no matter where else in the world they go, choose to return and end their days here."

I don't return her smile. As if I need the reminder that I'm stuck here, now a dead fish on my plate is telling me my soul will live here forever. Great!

She lets out a brittle cough, a strange look flitting over her face before she pounds herself on the chest. I frown at the strange, dry noise that's probably rattling her rib cage. I wrinkle my nose. "What's wrong? Are you sick?"

She sips her water. "No, nothing like that. Allergies. Eat your food before it gets cold."

I peer at her. That cough had sounded sharp and painful.

Doing as she says, I use my fork to shift the hard-armored scales off the steaming catfish. Though the dish looks partly like an armadillo, everything my grandmother cooks is scrumptious. It smells spicy with a hint of curry, coconut, and tomatoes, and the dumplings are thick and fluffy. When I stuff a forkful into my mouth, flavors burst on my tongue, the fish succulent and tasty. I shovel in several bites to take the edge off.

"Granny, does that girl Monique still visit you?" I ask as innocently as possible. "Or did you get new neighbors? I heard singing."

Her stare narrows on me. I paste a smile on my face now and scoop up a dumpling, lowering my eyelashes to show nothing of my much-too-avid curiosity and avoid being thrown off the scent again. It must work because she nods. "She does from time to time."

The pressure of her gaze itches as if she can see right through me. "And no new neighbors, not especially close, but sometimes there can be poachers and wild animals. Don't go beyond the gardens unless someone is with you."

"Becks told me. He said the devil was in there."

Granny's brows lower. "He can be superstitious. Many of the old people on the island revere our folklore."

A weird shiver snakes up my spine, but I push forward. Granny is the key to getting the information I need about Mom and Ushara. I can't back down now. I'm getting the heebie-jeebies for no good reason. "So there's really something wicked in there?"

"Depends on your definition of *wicked*. Eat your dinner, Darika."

Momentarily stalled, I cram more of the delicious fluffy dumplings in my mouth, but my mind won't stop racing. Does she believe there's actual danger in the woods on her property? I mean, I can understand thieves and poachers, but I get the feeling there's much more to the story. I finish chewing my mouthful and straighten my spine, not one to give up so easily.

"Sorry, I thought I heard kids when I was in the courtyard."

25

I give a casual shrug as if it doesn't matter to me one way or another—I should really win an award for my acting—and fork another flaky piece of fish. "It sounded like someone laughing and singing that nursery rhyme that Mom used to sing about the brown girl in the ring. You know the one?"

Her posture stiffens. "The wind whistling through the trees makes strange sounds. The woods bordering my property can be dangerous. That's public property, and sometimes there are squatters. Keep to the fruit tree line and you'll be safe."

I hide my scowl. It wasn't the wind—Granny and Becks are just being extra cagey about safety. Why? Like warning me off isn't going to make a girl more suspicious. And besides, how is a tree line going to stop a squatter from following me? Those woods are getting more and more interesting by the minute. I push the rest of my food around my plate, my thoughts racing in multiple directions.

"Dinner's not good?" she asks with a sharp gaze from across the table.

Pulled out of my thoughts, I glance up and say the first thing that comes to mind: "It's not that. I guess I'm a little tired from the flight."

"You want to give your dad a call to let him know you've settled in?"

Eagerness swells in my chest before I remember that he'd banished me in the first place. I swallow my bittersweet feelings. "I'm good. He doesn't care."

"You know that's not true." Granny stares at me with kind but knowing eyes. "Eat your belly full and I'll get you some dessert. I have soursop ice cream or I made fresh sawine." She winks. "With extra raisins."

Um, yes, please! Sawine is made with thin noodles, almonds, milk, sugar, cinnamon, and raisins. I've helped her make it before, and it takes a lot of stirring to thicken the milk, but every step is worth it. "Thanks, Granny." If one thing is true, it's that Trini food is delicious. I'm full already, but I always have an extra tummy compartment for dessert. "Can I have some of both?"

She gives me a fond smile. "Of course you can, and then you can get a good night's sleep. Things will look better in the morning."

My joy dims and I roll my lips between my teeth. When I was little, Mom used to say that, as she tucked me into bed at night after I'd had a rough day. She was wrong, though, especially later on. Things never got better. They always seemed to get worse.

I let out a shallow sigh and scrape the last few bites of dinner off my plate and into my mouth. When I'm done, I stare at my grandmother. Maybe direct questions are better. I still need answers. "So why did you tell Dad to let me come here?" Unexpected pressure builds behind my nose. "Because you knew he couldn't wait to get rid of me too?"

My grandmother sets down her fork and studies me. "Is that what you think?"

"He sent me away for the whole summer!" Though I try hard to keep my voice gruff, it breaks. "My own dad doesn't want me around anymore. He's made that kind of obvious."

"You know he only wants the best for you. He loves you."

"No. He doesn't. He has Cassie and the boys."

Granny pushes her plate to the side. "You all needed a little space, doux-doux. I asked for you to come because I wanted to reconnect and for you to get to know yourself better. I also need a little help with some things."

"What kinds of things?"

She shoots me a look that I haven't forgotten. Granny has always been of the opinion that a little elbow grease never hurt anyone and that responsibility is a great teacher. I bet I'll be polishing wood floors with a dust rag or scrubbing old windows. "A special project," she says. "I'm cleaning out some of the old rooms and need your assistance."

"Great."

My grandmother doesn't speak for a full handful of seconds, her gaze heavy, boring right through me, *seeing* right through me with those shrewd, knowing eyes of hers. She always could, even when I was little. It seems like an eternity goes by before she rises, her chair squeaking back across the worn parquet floors. "Come with me."

Stiffening, I frown at her. "Now? Where?"

"It's a surprise," she says when I follow her to the far end of the room toward a pair of double doors. "Tell me about your art."

I blink at the out-of-the-blue question. "My art?"

"A little bird told me that you're quite talented." She grins over her shoulder, her teeth white in her lined, brown face. "When you're not defacing school property, that is."

"I didn't mean—"

She stops so suddenly that I nearly crash into her. She

quirks an eyebrow, an unexpected twinkle in her eye instead of the censure I expected. "You were going to say that you didn't mean to do it? That you accidentally spray-painted your rival soccer team's mascot on the bleachers before the game?"

My cheeks heat and I pin my lips together. I'm pretty sure I can guess who the *little bird* is. "Dad told you."

"Sent pics, too."

"They kicked me off the team," I mutter.

"And you were upset?"

I don't know how to answer that. I hadn't told Dad or anyone why. Sure, I was mad. But I was hurt too. It sucked that my coach hadn't fought to keep me. I was sad that I'd disappointed them. What did I expect? I'd skipped practices, and the truth is, if your grades tank, you get benched. Dad hadn't known that I got cut. I'd been too ashamed to tell him; he'd only see it as another cry for attention instead of asking me *why* soccer didn't make me happy anymore.

My throat squeezes and my nose prickles. "My team was my family," I say. "Well, my sports family . . . until I lost them too."

"Them too?" she asks, her warm stare holding mine.

"Mom," I whisper. "And then Dad."

"Lovey, you didn't lose your parents. I know my Dulcie. She would never leave you without a good reason. Never."

I swallow hard, shoving down the feeling of bitterness. "But she *did* leave."

"Not by choice, trust me."

A shadow crosses Granny's face before she starts walking again, and I keep pace with her quick-legged steps, hoping she'll say more. I blink and take stock of where we are. Another wing of the house. The older part. It smells musty and unused as though she doesn't come to this side often. No wonder she's planning an overhaul. Dimmed wall sconces light the gloomy corridor.

I'd forgotten how much this place is like a maze, full of narrow passages and alcoves all leading to different rooms. So easy to get lost in. When I was little and scared of losing my way, Mom had taught me a trick to never get lost—and that was to put my palm to one wall and never lift it until it led to an exit. Eventually, she'd said, I would find my way out.

She used to love this old house. I pick at the beds of my nails and purse my lips, eyes scanning the dark paneled walls of the hallway. Paintings cover them. They're mostly landscapes, flowers, and fruit, but a group of them look more abstract, covered in shadow and mysterious swatches of color that seem to shift with the guttering light.

"Who did all these?" I ask, my voice loud in the silence.

"Want to take a guess?"

Curious, I stumble to a halt in front of a gorgeous landscape with the sun dappling a grove of laden citrus trees. It's so detailed and the use of color is bold and powerful. I scan the painting. I find barely visible and faded letters in one corner, *Dulcie Lovelace*, and gasp.

I swallow hard, wonder racing under my skin. "Wait, did . . . *Mom* paint these?"

"Where do you think you got your mad skills?" Granny asks with a jaunty smile.

A giggle bursts from me. "I didn't know she painted."

Because, before she left, my mom had been a high school *math* teacher. On the weekends, she'd taken me to soccer games with Dad and we'd sometimes do paint-by-number watercolors for fun, but she hadn't been an artist. But then I think back to the wall mural of colorful vines and bracts—bougainvillea, she'd called them—in my room that had been there since I was a baby, so like these vibrant brushstrokes here, and I realize now that *she* must have painted it. I wonder why she'd never spoken about it.

Dazed, I blink. What *else* don't I know about her?

"Here we are," Granny says, unlocking a door to a room cluttered with boxes and covered in fluffy dust bunnies. It's a bedroom, from what I can tell, the walls a faded pink with more floral, hand-painted accents. Trying not to sneeze from the dust, I wrinkle my nose. "This was Dulcie's room growing up before the other wing was built. I thought that while you were here, you could help me decide what to donate and what to keep. A summer project, so to speak."

My eyes open in wonder as I take in the space with a fresh perspective. It's no longer just a messy bedroom. It's my *mom's* room. She would have been my age in here. Maybe there are clues that will tell me where she's gone and how I can find her. At the very least, I'm curious about who my mother was at my age, especially after this discovery that she'd been an artist. Like me. What else do we have in common? I nod eagerly at Granny.

There's no time like the present to get some sleuthing done.

Where did she like painting on the estate? Did she have

a secret grove in the garden? Did she take lessons in town? Could she have a secret journal hidden in here somewhere? All the questions are swirling in my brain. The urge to get closer to my mom any way I can is almost impossible to ignore.

There's a tug in my belly. A *knowing*. I'm getting closer.

3

MISSION KIND OF IMPOSSIBLE

It's been nearly a week and I can't stop sneezing, but I haven't let that stop me. I sweep the last of the dust off the parquet floors and feel a sense of satisfaction at a job well done. The floor had been filthy, covered in years of dirt, cobwebs, and neglect. Surveying the space that suddenly seems cheerier now that it's clean, I decide to tackle a stack of boxes and the half-empty bookcase next.

Granny must have half-started this job and gotten busy with something else. One box is full of old textbooks; another holds a collection of novels. I huff a laugh to see some old favorites that Mom and I have in common: *Little Women,* Roald Dahl, *Grimm's Fairy Tales,* and a few Judy Blume novels. Their covers are yellowed, dog-eared, and worn, obviously well loved.

I think back to the treasured copies on my own shelves at home. Though my tastes lean toward graphic novels and manga now, those stories will always have a special place in my heart. Granny has marked the box *Donate to a local school,* and I'm glad for her generosity. Some other kid deserves to read a good book.

I start emptying the bottom shelves when a thin, large dusty book with gold stitching on the spine calls to me. Settling my body into a cross-legged position, I pull the book from the shelf and open it in my lap. The letters on the cover are in some other language. Latin? My pointer finger traces the lettering and a prickle heats my skin. Weird. Must be static electricity.

When I open the book to the first page, I gasp. It's a sketchbook. Well, one with drawings as well as writing within. I frown. Is it my mother's? Or is it even older than Mom? Doodles of plants, animals, jewelry, and strange figures take up the pages. There's a ball of fire framing a haggard old woman that instantly gives me the creeps. The image is so detailed that it seems like I could reach out and feel the weathered texture of her skin.

My fingers hover over the image and the oddest sensation comes over me. They're warm as if I'm about to touch a hot stove. Bizarre. Pages of notes with annotations in the margins follow along with more drawings. Flicking to another page, I swear I can smell the odor of burning incense. When I turn over a few more, there are ingredient lists that look like recipes.

I frown. No, not recipes. I've never even heard of some of these things. Teas made from tree bark and ash. Cure-all remedies made of guava, citrus peel, sage, and soursop leaves. Notes about maljo, or bad eye, and how to ward against it using garlic and camphor. Chants to guard against the spirits that go bump in the night. Instructions to collect an enemy's footprint from dirt, put one in a bag, and stick pins into it to cause an infection. Yikes, that's some next-level revenge.

A shudder snakes up my spine. Maybe this book belongs to Granny and I shouldn't be messing with it.

But I can't seem to help myself.

I keep flipping. On one of the last pages, there's a tree. A family tree with Lovelace names going back centuries drawn in dark red ink. With a tentative sniff, I touch one of the upper names with a fingertip, and when nothing happens—no heat or weird smells—I trace the lines. I don't know any of the names, but I feel a connection with them.

When my finger reaches my granny's, Delilah Lovelace, my heart swells, a clear image of her face forming instantly in my brain. But as I drift down to my mother's, the image is weak and grainy, as if she's not even there at all. I press harder into the paper as if that can help make her come into focus, but nothing happens.

Names have power and hers feels weak. Very weak.

My name is written beneath hers, a faded, barely visible line connecting them. A sense of alarm makes my finger pause. What will I see when I touch my own name? There's only one way to find out, but the hesitation is real. What if I start vanishing too?

"Come on, Rika!" I whisper. "It's an ordinary book with names. You're being totally paranoid."

Is it silly to be cautious? My inner voice isn't wrong, but I've always had a more active imagination than most. Case in point: Ushara was probably just some old lady looking for her family. Maybe she and Granny have some bad blood, but that doesn't mean she's a monster. I wrinkle my nose. So what if this is some kind of witch's book? Grimoires, I think they're called. Granny might be a witch, that wouldn't surprise me, but no way my mom is.

I'm safe. My grandmother would never let me in here if I was in any danger.

Before I lose my courage, I jam my finger onto my name and feel my spine arch as if I've stuck my finger into an electrical socket. My eyes roll backward. This can't be real, but the images filling my unseeing vision are no dream: names etched in blood, a generational history always in threes—the matriarch, the mother, and the child—scenes of rot and decay. Granny's face, Mom's face, *my* face. Auras blossoming like bruises. Shadows creeping like mold over an enormous tree nearing death.

Darika, find the Minders!

The voice in my head is not mine. It's male, and it sounds feeble. Desperate.

Sorry, who on earth are the Minders? And how exactly does a disembodied voice know my name?

With a strangled yelp, I yank my hand away and slam the grimoire shut. My wired brain goes blissfully blank once the connection is broken. Shaking my head to clear it, I throw the book into a nearby box. For an instant, I have the unnatural urge to clutch the tome to my chest, but I force myself to shift away. None of what just happened is normal. I'm hungry—that has to be the explanation. I probably need a snack.

Breathing hard, I reach for the nearly empty bag of Sour Skittles in my pocket and swallow a mouthful of the candy. After I devour the rest and feel better from the sugar rush, I decide to resume my work. There are no more strange grimoires calling to me, so I let the boring monotony of the activity take over. It isn't long before the big cardboard moving box is filled and I glance around for another, at least for the remainder of the books.

Rolling my neck, I stand and stretch, and then head over to the side toward a large open box that's still open. I peer in and recoil at the creepy collection of dolls, some staring up at me with sightless glass eyeballs. My blood curdles—that's a whole lot of nope right there.

One or two dolls remind me of Ushara, in their old lacy dresses. I'm glad Granny added these to the donate pile. I reach to close the box, stuffing down all the dress frills while cringing, when I see something glint near the bottom, and I rip my hand back with a shrill scream.

The something is *moving*. A pair of beady eyes stares back at me as a creature uncurls and slithers loose, making the flounces ripple. I gasp and rear back. What *is* that?

Both Granny and Becks come running down the hallway. "Darika, what's wrong?"

Shaking, I point to the box. "Snake."

Becks peers gingerly into the box and uses the nearby broom handle to push the dolls apart. Smart. If it is a snake, it could be venomous. Letting out a stream of air through his teeth, he reaches in, and I hold my breath when he pulls his palm out, a coiling gray and brown body wrapped around his fingers.

"Is only a harmless grass snake, Miss Darika, doh fear." I know he means don't be afraid, but I'm not a fan. He smiles, holding the little fellow out as if to offer it to me. I step back. No, thank you. "See the yellow mark on the neck?" he says. "This one's not dangerous."

Suddenly, the pungent odor of garlic reaches my nose and I plug my nostrils with my fingers. "Ew, what is that smell?"

"That's a defense scent from the snake's anal glands, since it's not venomous," Becks explains.

I gag. "That garlic smell is from its butt?"

He grins at my expression. "The odor eh go kill you, just run you off."

Good job, little snake, your powers are working! I wave energetically for Becks to yeet the little creature to a land far, far away.

"More of them are coming into the house," Granny murmurs in a low, thoughtful voice as Becks walks past her to take it out into the yard. "Seeking refuge."

"Refuge?" I ask, frowning. "From what?"

Her answer comes in a grim whisper. "The woods."

"Isn't that their natural habitat?"

Troubled brown eyes meet mine. "Our forest is not safe anymore." She shakes her head. "But that's not for you to worry about. Good work so far in here."

Pride fills me as I look around. Most of the junk has been removed and all the surfaces have been wiped down. It took a while—full days of scrubbing—but Mom's desk is next.

Drawers always hide the best secrets. At least, mine back home do.

Locating a thankfully snake-free box, I make quick work of the remaining books and then Granny helps me drag the empty bookcase out into the hallway. I wonder if I should mention the weirdness with the witchy sketchpad and then clamp my lips shut. She'll probably brush me off, like she has with everything else.

Me: *Hey, Granny, who is that lady?*
Granny: *She's no one to you.*
Me: *Is Mom here?*
Granny: *No. Forget I said anything.*
Me: *OK . . . Also, I found a strange book with creepy old spells, written in what I think is most likely, almost definitely, blood, and had a bunch of wild visions flash through my brain.*
Granny: **Insert blow-Darika-off dismissal here.**

Hard pass. Weird things are clearly happening, but I'll have to muddle through them on my own. My fingers prickle with heat and I shove them into my pockets.

When we return to the bedroom, I point to the walls, the real beauty of the forest mural showing now that the huge mountain of clutter has been lessened. Three are covered in a pretty woodland setting with overladen fruit trees; birds, like scarlet ibis, hummingbirds, and ravens; as well as manicous and agoutis. But one wall is completely blank. "She never finished," I murmur.

Granny clears her throat. "I was hoping you might want the job."

"I—I couldn't," I stammer. "I'm nowhere near as good as she was."

"You won't know until you try, will you?"

I feel my shoulders rounding, my ears heating, but a trickle of excitement at being able to create again unfurls in my chest. I've missed it, especially my electronic stylus and my tablet that Dad took away, but there's nothing like the smell of paint and the swish of a brush. "We don't have any paint or supplies or anything."

As if summoned, Becks returns from his trip to the garden pulling a small wagon behind him. My eyes fall to the neat stacks of cans, realizing they're tins of paint. Almost every single color under the sun. My gaze drops to the folded painter's cloth and the wide selection of brushes resting next to it. "Wait, you're serious?" I ask my grandmother in confusion.

"Yes, chile. This wall is yours," Granny says with a wave of her arm. "Think of it as your canvas. I want you to create anything your heart desires on there. It doesn't have to be the same as the rest. Just let it out, whatever's inside."

"But why, Granny?"

"Why not, Rika-love? You and Dulcie are part of each other. Isn't this a way to find everything it is you've been looking for in all the wrong places? What's the worst that happens? You paint something and hate it? It's easy to erase, doux-doux, with a simple coat of white."

Emotions welling, I rush over and fling myself into her

wiry arms. She pulls me close, the smell of powder, citrus, and clean laundry filling my nostrils. Granny kisses my forehead. A blush warms my cheeks as I recall my earlier fears. "I thought you were going to make me scrub toilets or pull weeds the entire summer."

Her dark eyes twinkle when she peers down at me. "Oh, sweet chile, that's for later."

I must look horrified because she laughs. "No, but don't worry. Once you're finished here, I have lots of other jobs to keep you busy. You're going to earn your keep while you're here and maybe figure out a *healthy* way to control your impulses." She grins. "But for now, all these art supplies are yours."

"Did Mom paint the murals for that reason?" I ask, curious.

"Yes. Art was the best outlet she could find." A sad smile flits over my grandmother's lips. "She always said there was something a bit rebellious about drawing on a wall."

I muffle my snort. Looks like I take after Mom in that, too. Not that she would approve of what I did back home.

Granny's lips compress as her eyes dart to the open window, letting in fresh air. I follow her stare. Outside, we can see just the tops of the trees and the purple-tinted mountain range rising in the distance. For the briefest moment, I wonder what's truly out there in Becks's so-called devil woods. If the baby snakes don't feel safe, what does that mean for everything else? A shudder rolls over me and I rub my arms. I don't plan to find out any time soon.

After Granny leaves to get lunch ready, I prop my hands on my hips, and survey my "canvas." I do have *a lot* of feelings right now . . . about my parents, Granny's secrets, all of it. And my fingers are itching to open those cans of paint and go to town without consequence. For once.

Mom's right—the act does feel rebellious.

As I bend to sift through the paints that Becks brought over, I catch movement out of the corner of my eye, something that looks like a tail. Panic surges—is it another snake? I squint and relax. Not if those are limbs. This time there's no mistaking the shape of the cute little iguana peeking in through the open window. Bumps and spikes, with a jowly, chubby face that reminds me of a green chipmunk, catch my eye.

I tiptoe over, careful not to scare it away, and scrutinize its sinuous green body and the sharp spines on its back. Its head tilts, one penetrating eye staring me down. I know there's a slim chance that it's the same iguana from the airport who'd practically saved my life, but something about the creature seems so familiar. Maybe the little critter had hitched a ride in the truck! I remember the flash of green I'd seen when Becks took out my suitcase, but I know that's highly unlikely. Wishful thinking, I guess.

"Shoo, before you get locked in here and then what will you do?" I say, flicking my wrists. His—at least, I think he's male based on size and the floppy chin flap—jaw parts, audibly chuffing. Is the tiny green beast *laughing* at me? "Go on, little lizard, scram!"

He chuffs again, a hind claw coming up to scratch at his side.

"You're not afraid of me, are you?" I grin when the creature gives a lazy shake of its head, though I'm pretty sure that's random instead of an answer to my question. I can see the mottled wrinkle of reptilian skin and the bumps across a blunt snout. He's a beauty as far as iguanas go. I lean in, watching him. "Fine then, first to blink wins!"

It's no great surprise when I lose.

A huge surprise comes, however, when I hear the words *I win.*

Yelping in fright, I fall on my butt and scrabble backward. I blink at the reptile. He blinks back. We blink a bit more . . . me in shock, him deep in lizardy thought. When my nerves return to normal, I creep forward and peer at him, squinting as though that might give me some kind of magical sight. "Did you just . . . can you talk? Or did I totally just space out and dream that?"

My new friend chitters, making his dewlap quiver. I might have imagined him speaking before, but I get the distinct feeling he's laughing at me. *Again.* With an attempt at one of Granny's steups that fails miserably and sounds like the air deflating from a balloon, I turn back to my wall and rub my hands together.

Finish the rest of this cleanup first, then start painting. If I can come up with the perfect design, that is, and get over the fact that there's no way I'm as good as Mom. I have ideas, but none of them seems right. Her use of color is like nothing I've ever seen, her brushstrokes confident and bold. I don't want to wreck the mural with something silly, not that it matters, as she might never even see it, but a part of me wants to measure up. Wants to be worthy of her.

Maybe I can think of a decent concept while I pack up the rest of these boxes. I glance up at my curious little friend, whose beady eyes are fixed on me.

"Hey, little buddy, any ideas?" I ask, hoping for a response but none comes.

Grinning, I scrunch my lips together and mimic my version of a squeaky baby lizard voice. "I believe in you, Rika!" He flicks his tongue over his eyeball, and I laugh at myself.

If there's any good time to paint, it's now.

You know, while my imagination's hot and I'm thinking iguanas can talk.

4

MY IMAGINATION
NEEDS A DO-OVER

Stretching my cramped body, I wipe the crusted sleep from my eyes and feel sticky drool clinging to my lips. I groan at the effort it takes to uncurl from my tight position. Ugh, *why* do I ache so much? The answer to that becomes clear as I slowly grasp that I've been sleeping on a very hard floor instead of a very soft bed. The texture of my fingers is rough, and I glance down, seeing them streaked in nine different dried colors.

Oh!

Blinking myself awake, my eyes focus on the result of my hours upon hours of painting, and I freeze. Horrified, I glance at the locked door and then the still-open window. My lizard bestie had taken off shortly after I'd started painting, once I'd finished up with Mom's desk. Nothing special in there, unfortunately, except for a bunch of pens, old paintbrushes, and some old photos of her in a plaid school uniform. Then again, after the interaction with the grimoire, I was kind of glad that was all I found.

Granny had swung by at various points to drop off sandwiches and snacks, but I'd been in the zone. I glance at the time on the wall clock and the setting sun outside. I'd spent an entire night and nearly a whole day in here. I'd cleaned and packed until midnight, then painted until dawn, only to fall asleep and wake up in my bed—had Granny and Becks carried me?—desperate to resume my mural that had only been bare bones and abstract color.

I remember inhaling some stewed chicken with red beans and rice for lunch, and then rushing back to Mom's room as if compelled. Granny had let me, though her face had been hard to read. And then I'd crashed hard for a few hours in the afternoon in the hammock on the patio, exhausted, but my idea of a mysterious glade was beginning to come together. Good thing I'm alone now.

Because *this* is something out of a nightmare.

An enormous painting of a tree takes up most of the wall in shades of shadowy gray, as though trapped in bands of moonlight. Flecks of paint like falling ash sprays across the entire width of the mural, giving it an otherworldly aura, like it's shrouded in strands of ghostly webbing. The tree itself gleams with dark-shaded hues, the silvered trunk shimmering. I've painted trees and flowers before, but never like this. Never so unnaturally eerie.

And that's not even the half of it. I don't want to look down near the gnarled roots, but I force myself to. Small creatures resembling children are painted there, hands clasped and circling the base of the tree, faceless, feet noticeably backward and dressed in threadbare shapeless shorts and ragged shirts. They're from Granny's stories. Douens, she calls them. Mischievous jumbies who lure children away from their unsuspecting parents to steal them forever.

Why on earth had I painted *them*?

And *that* tree! The one I'd seen in my head when I'd touched my name in the book had come to life in shades of charcoal and gray.

The tiny hairs on my arms stand straight up and a tingle slithers down my spine. The image is so real I can imagine stepping through the wall and finding myself there beneath its sprawling roots. A strange shimmer sweeps over the mural, and I blink, wondering if I'm still half asleep and dreaming.

I must be. Paintings don't move.

And yet, I could have sworn the douens shimmied just now and a gentle breeze had chased through the branches of the tree. Spine-chilling laughter fills my ears, and this time, I shake my head. *Hard*. Now I'm really imagining things.

Deep orange shadows glint at the midpoint of the tree and stretch outward, hinting at something inside, and for a heart-stopping second, I see movement again. Though not from the douens. I squint more closely as the orange orb flickers. Wait . . . is that a face? Why would I have painted a woman's face in the tree? I stare harder as the details brighten and the blood feels like it's draining from my head when recognition fills me.

What in the—! That's my *mom's* face!

Goose bumps erupt over my skin, a frigid chill winding around my wildly hammering heart. I squeeze my eyes shut and open them, wondering if she'll disappear because my imagination is on the fritz again. But there she is, staring at me. Pulse pounding with equal amounts disbelief and dread, I step closer.

Unbelievably, *impossibly*, her mouth moves as though she's trying to communicate. Rearing back with confusion, I rub my eyes in shock, but she's still there. Still *talking*.

But. Paintings. Do. Not. Talk.

Or move. Or act like windows to other worlds.

Still in a daze, I take another step, and a pungent sweet odor assaults my nose—the scent of overripe fruit that has just turned toward rot. I lift the fingers of my left hand to trace the outer edge of the trunk near her face and feel a sharp yank shoot up my arm as if something invisible is trying to drag me into the piece.

A buzzing sound fills my ears when a tugging sensation pulls at my belly button and then crawls over every inch of my skin like a spider's web catching hold of prey. Breathing heavy, I squeeze my eyes shut with a squeak, disoriented by what feels like movement even though my feet are firmly planted on the wood floor.

When I open my eyes, I'm in a narrow room, divided by a strange floor-to-ceiling glass panel. A person-shaped body is resting across a small cot. I'm pretty sure I am hallucinating or in a waking nightmare, but I'm much too curious not to find out who's on that bed.

Heart in my throat, I creep across the room. "Hello?"

The lump on the bed moves and then sits up, a woolen blanket falling away. A hand reaches up to rumple a head of thick curls that I instantly recognize, the person's eyes going wide.

I stare. "Mom?"

Brown eyes, like Granny's and like mine, flare with joy, followed swiftly by panic and dread as I rush to the see-through barrier, hands flat against the glass. She hobbles to the wall and presses her palms to mine. She's thinner than I remember and her face is lined with exhaustion.

In a daze, I pound on the barrier, making my fists ache. "Mom, are you hurt? How do I get you out? Mom? *Mom?*"

Her mouth opens but no sounds emerge before her eyes enlarge, and prickles race over my nape as a dark pressure descends as if some invisible beast is rising up behind me. The hairs on my arm stand on end, the sense of danger rising with each second, panic clawing up my throat. It feels like whoever—or *whatever*—it is will snatch me up in the next heartbeat.

"Run, Rika," my mom says, though I can barely hear her.

Try as I might, I can't move, caught like a deer in headlights . . . a well-fed fly in a thick spider's web. I glance over my shoulder and scream at the sight of the dark shadow eating up the light in the room and bearing down on me.

"Mom, help me!" I sob and pound on the glass, but she's stuck too, her face petrified, her mouth open and soundless.

Suddenly, nails dig into my calves. No, not nails, *claws* . . . and they hurt.

49

A wild roar fills my ears next, the sound of a monster intent upon feasting. Swallowing a scream of my own, my vision tunnels to the point that I can't see, and then I'm shuttled back to Granny's house. I crash to the floor as I gasp for air and stare at the painting of the tree—there's no evidence of any orange color, my mom's face, or anything out of the ordinary. Except maybe a bright green iguana that's clamped to my leg.

"Get off, get off!" I shake my leg and hop from one foot to the other, trying to dislodge the clingy little beast.

The lizard leaps off and gives me a reproachful look as if to say *A little gratitude wouldn't hurt.* Exhaling a shuddering huff, I guess I *am* grateful that he chased me out of that nightmare, because that was . . . grisly. I glance up at the mural and shiver, remembering the icky, hungry touch of the shadow monster that had almost caught me.

"What in the bananas was that?" I say out loud.

The devil nearly got you.

Fear makes my bones lock up and my stomach dive to the floor. I don't know if that's *my* inner voice, the lizard's, or someone else's, but all of this is too much.

What's with this place? Walls definitely shouldn't be able to yank you into them.

Moms don't appear in glass boxes in trees.

And monsters don't actually exist!

A frightening quiver rolls through me, and suddenly I'm huffing shallow, useless breaths as I shy away from the wall, wrench open the door, and practically sprint down the hallway to safety, wherever that is. Tiny shivers chase through my veins like I'm on the verge of an enormous panic attack. Am I in shock? Alarmed? Frightened? All three?

It's a miracle I make it back to my bedroom, but before the door even shuts behind me, I'm having a major meltdown. I know the rush of adrenaline and my fight-or-flight reflex is making me irrational because I can't breathe. Before I can stop myself, I dig into my backpack for my cell phone to call my dad, but the stupid thing is dead. I forgot to plug in my phone earlier to charge.

Sniffling, I stare at the basic flip phone—I'd lost privileges for my old smartphone months ago—and squash the urge to fling it across the room. If Dad really did love me, I'd be at home in Colorado, grounded like any other normal preteen.

Instead, I'm here, facing off against shadow monster hallucinations.

Would Dad even believe me?

I've put him through a lot. He'd been disappointed to learn about all the graffiti I'd done at the school. Unlike my mom's bedroom walls, those were "acts of vandalism." Painting was the only time I felt in control of anything . . . and the only time all the pressure in my head eased. *Get good grades, Rika. Be a good role model for your brothers, Rika. Don't mess up, Rika.* The school counselor had asked me if the vandalism was for attention.

Looking back, maybe it was.

Sensing a presence, I glance up to see my new green sidekick staring at me with his beady black eyes, his tail twitching as he hoists himself up to my windowsill to a patch of fading sunlight. Had he followed? Strangely, instead of being weirded out by a lizard stalking me, I am comforted by the sight of him. He did rescue me, after all.

"I should probably give you a name," I say, happy to focus on anything else. "How about Hulk?" I shake my head.

"Nah, you don't look like a big, green, smash-happy dude. You're too cute."

The iguana doesn't react—both his eyes are now shut.

"Fine, then. I'll call you Piku. It means smart and sweet in Hindi, I think."

But Piku is obviously in a sunny dreamland.

I wish I could zone out that easily.

Relaxation is now impossible as my mind returns to the inevitable. What was the deal with that tree and my bizarre dream, anyway? Everything seemed so real, even though I know—*rationally*—my imagination must be going haywire. But if it isn't, what then?

The experience was like entering some kind of magic portal.

Which is impossible; I know this! Portal magic only exists in books, video games, and movies.

But I can't *un*-know the sensation of being sucked into the orange orb in that painting like one would a Slurpee through a straw. I rub my ice-cold arms.

"Darika, come back. . . ." The voice is ghostly, making me jump, and is barely a whisper on the wind, but it sounds like . . . Mom. I clap my hands to my ears.

Stop, stop, stop!

Squeezing my eyes shut, I wrap a blanket around myself.

There is no voice. There is no tree. And even if there was, Mom's face in my day-mare had definitely communicated: *Stay away.* Whoever is speaking is not my mom.

With a groan, I breathe in the comforting, grounding scent of clean laundry, which smells of sunshine and safety, and focus on more mundane, real things. If rain doesn't fall, Granny will dry all her clothes outside on lines, giving them a very literal air of freshness.

It might feel like summer outside, but it's not. Unlike in the United States, this island only has two seasons: wet and dry. And right now in June, we're on the cusp of the wet season, though as I'd noticed from some of the browning vegetation, the island probably just suffered a hard drought.

Granny's garden seems to be flourishing, though.

I glance over at the neat sachet of herbs and dried lavender on the windowsill near Piku. Granny's a firm believer in her superstitions too. Shivers race over my skin—maybe she has reason to believe in them.

Face outward when entering your house so jumbies won't enter.

A butterfly in the house means good luck.

A blackbird outside your window means someone will die.

Always carry a match behind your ear at night to keep jumbies away.

My very quirky grandmother was a stickler for cleaning out her house top to bottom before New Year's Day to ensure good fortune. She wore protective stones, jet and jumbie beads, and copper bracelets to ward off illness and infection, and put herbs on the windows to ward off bad spirits. It's a wonder how she keeps track of everything. Years ago, I asked

Mom once if Granny was some kind of witch. Come to think of it, she'd never answered my question.

If someone did curse my mother into a tree, Granny would know.

She just wouldn't tell *me*.

Faint singsong laughter trickles into my room from beyond the window where Piku is dozing and I bolt upright to peer outside. Granny firmly said she didn't have any new nearby neighbors, but that definitely sounded like a group of kids. Maybe it's just Becks or some other workers, but anything will be better than being alone with my thoughts right now.

I'd take Monique at this point! Even if she still hates me.

Running a hand through my loose hair and wincing at the tangles, I give it a pat and throw on some sneakers. Piku opens one eye. "Want to come?" He tilts his head at his dwindling red-gold sun patch and then back at me. I laugh. "Don't get all excited or anything."

He looks so thoughtful that, for a moment, I actually think he's going to reply.

"Sure, Rika, I'm your new best friend," I say in my special baby lizard voice. I cough to hide my giggle. Piku hisses, his dewlap extending. Maybe he's not a fan of my fake iguana voice.

"Come on, let's go." I hold out a hand, palm side up, half expecting him to dash off as most lizards do when humans come near. But he doesn't.

To my utter surprise, he climbs onto my hand. He feels heavy for such a small creature, his tiny sharp nails pricking my skin and his striped tail wrapping around my pointer finger. Up close, the green color of his hide is almost neon against the light-brown hue of mine. I set him on my shoulder, unable to contain my grin. After he curls under the mass of my dark, tangled hair, I open the door leading into the garden and follow the sounds. I squint up into the light of the descending sun over the trees. Nighttime is coming soon, but I've stayed out late before.

Not here, a voice warns, but I ignore it.

The sweet scent of ripe mangoes and the tang of citrus mixed with fresh air reach my nostrils as I make my way through the weeds toward the orchard. I follow the echo of singsong voices that seem to come from everywhere at once.

A flicker of yellow fabric catches my eye around one trunk and I chase after it. "Hey!"

But it's no use. Whoever it is disappears with a trail of mischievous laughter. "Catch up, Rika," someone chirps.

Huh? Who'd know my name?

"Where are you?" I call out.

"There's a brown girl in the ring, tra la la la la . . ." Strains of that same catchy nursery rhyme that Mom used to sing filter in and I blink, the clearness of the memory halting me in my tracks. "Show me your motion, tra la la la la, she looks like a sugar in a plum, plum, plum!" Laughter follows after the song. "Over here, Rika! Come show us your motion!"

Where on earth are they?

"Stop playing games and come out!" I yell in frustration.

Voices giggle, sounding like wind chimes. "There's a brown girl in the ring, tra la la la la la. She looks like a sugar in a plum, plum, *plum*!"

I growl at the taunting, stomping deeper into the fragrant

55

grove. Someone's playing tricks, and when I get hold of them, they're going to regret toying with me. I wait and watch for movement again. This time, there's a blur of bright blue and I whirl, going around the tree instead of toward where I saw the splash of color.

And nearly crash into the cutest boy I've ever seen.

5

TRESPASSERS AND TROUBLE WITH A CAPITAL T

"Watch it," I gasp.

"Easy there, friend," the boy says, fingers curling around my arms and keeping me from falling. Now I couldn't make myself move if I tried.

His skin gleams like polished bronze, his eyes the color of damp moss glittering in the shaft of a sunbeam. Dark lashes sweep down to his cheeks, and I swear I feel a breeze flutter against my face. A cap of wild, untidy black curls graces his head, and when he grins, my indignation falters. I blink and step back, noting his blue T-shirt as well as his bare feet.

"There's a brown girl in the ring . . . tra la la la la!"

I whip around to see a girl

and a younger boy skipping arm in arm and coming to a breathless halt behind us. Who are these kids and why are they on my grandmother's property? The first boy with the deep green eyes leans on the nearest tree trunk and reaches up to catch a low-hanging mango falling from a branch above his head.

Hold on, did that just *fall* into his palm?

"You're trespassing," I bite out. "And stealing."

"Am I?" His blunt tone matches mine. It also sounds oddly familiar. Was he the one calling my name before?

I frown, watching as he peels the mango. "How do you know who I am?"

"Everyone knows who you are," he replies, biting into the pilfered fruit without care. "Darika Lovelace, daughter of Dulcie, granddaughter of Delilah, troublemaker, menace, pest."

Each surprising insult makes my temper spark, but that last one punches me in the gut. Fisting my palms, I take a threatening step toward him, but he doesn't even look afraid. I reverse my first thought that he was cute. He's an annoying, bigheaded pain in the butt. "Who do you think you are? You don't know me."

"I've heard enough about you."

I cringe at his tone. Had my grandmother told everyone why I was sent here? She's the only one who could reveal that. But why would she tell other kids about me? My mind is racing. Maybe it was Monique. Granny had said she still visited, so maybe she's the tattletale. Are these her friends?

"Whatever," I say with a forced eye roll. "Tell me who you are or you're going to be in a lot of trouble."

Glancing over my shoulder at the other two, I lean into my scowl. The girl has rows of tightly woven braids plaited close to her scalp with colorful beads at the ends, and the other boy, who looks to be about ten or eleven, has similar shorter braids, only without beading. Sparkling eyes glow in their similar high-cheeked, russet-brown faces. They must be siblings.

"We're friends of Grandma Love," the boy and girl chime in unison.

Grandma Love? That's a new one.

"How do you know my granny?" I ask.

"Everyone knows Delilah Lovelace," my infuriating nemesis answers, flicking the palm-sized mango seed over his shoulder. He wipes sticky hands on his shorts and saunters toward me. Another yellow mango appears in his hand as if by magic. My jaw slackens as he grins and holds it out to me. "Want one?"

I reach for it automatically and then freeze. Is this a trick? My suspicious gaze lifts to the boy's.

"It's just a mango," he says. "Going once, going twice . . ."

My stomach lets out a loud growl, and I give in, snatching the fruit. I hesitate for the shortest of seconds before peeling the mottled green skin deftly and sinking my teeth into the stringy yellow center. Juice splatters everywhere, but I don't care. It's by far the most delicious thing I've ever tasted.

The boy laughs. "Good?"

"Yesh," I say, though it sounds more like a gurgle through my mouthful.

Piku pokes his head out and I offer him some of the mango,

which he takes and disappears. I see the boy's eyes widen then narrow in surprise. "Where'd you find him?" he asks.

"He found me."

"Wild iguanas aren't exactly friendly."

"He likes me."

A tail flicks against my neck followed by an irritated clicking sound. Fine, tolerates me, then.

"I'm Nox." He nods to the others. "That's Hazel and Fitzwilliam. They're twins. Though Fitz is the runt of the two."

"Hey!" Fitz protests. "I can't help it that I'm vertically challenged."

"Rika." I pause and swallow, eyeing them each in turn. "You're friends?"

Nox grins. "Most days."

"You haven't met Monique yet," Hazel says.

The sound of that name makes my hackles raise and my spirits droop. Of course she had to be friends with them, just when I thought this summer might not suck so much. Feigning a cool expression, I raise my brows. "Where's she?"

"Right behind you."

I turn in slow motion. If I'd thought Nox was something to stare at, my old frenemy is gorgeous. She'd been pretty before, but now at thirteen, she looks like she could be a model. Her skin is a rich sun-kissed shade of medium brown and her eyes are the same frosty amber I remember. Glossy black hair falls to her waist.

She prowls forward, those yellow eyes fixed on me, wearing a glower to rival mine. She looks like a wolf . . . a take-no-prisoners wolf who clearly hasn't forgotten—or forgiven—our last encounter. I cross my arms, unwilling to give an inch. "Hey, Monique."

"Darika."

The twins stare at us with wide eyes. "Should I get popcorn?" Fitz asks with glee.

"Nope," Monique says, popping the *p* at the end. "We're cool. Right, D?"

Not trusting her at all, I give a wary nod. On the surface, she seems sincere, but why does it feel like she's still holding a grudge? Her eyes are practically skewering me. "Yeah, we're good. So, are you neighbors?"

"Something like that," she says, walking over to where Nox is standing. I catch a quick, silent exchange between them, and the immediate downturn of Nox's mouth. Monique's eyebrows rise as she grins at me. "Want to see something interesting?"

"Where?"

She hooks a thumb over her shoulder past the tree line. "Over there."

"Like I'd go anywhere with you when you're probably going to leave me stranded in the middle of the woods for the bogeyman to find."

She grins, all teeth, eyes brightening maliciously at the slight wobble in my last three words. "You turn into a scaredy-cat, *Rika*?"

I bristle at the overt challenge. Oh, she's definitely holding a grudge. "Are you still mad about the bracelet?" I blurt out.

Her smile fades as she snarls, "It wasn't just a bracelet. It was a totem."

"A what?"

That mocking look is back. "No surprise that you still don't know anything. So are you going to turn around and skip back to the house like a good little girl?"

"Granny told me not to go past these trees."

"Do you always do what she says?" Stiffening at her goading, I shake off the warnings of my already overcharged brain and toss my head, rising to the dare in her gaze.

Piku's talons dig into me, as if also in warning. He obviously has more common sense than me. "Don't worry," I murmur, though the reassurance is more for me than him.

"Good. Just one thing," Monique says, and ambles up to me. "You have to swear not to tell anyone. It'll be our little secret."

Considering how many secrets I've kept from my dad, stepmom, and teachers back in Colorado, the demand shouldn't rub me the wrong way, but I cross my index and middle fingers and nod. "Fine, I swear, whatever."

A strange energy whirls through the grove as her eyes glitter with satisfaction. Hazel skips forward and Fitz rolls his eyes. "She likes to cause too much commess," he grumbles.

"What do you mean?" I blurt out, not understanding the word.

He rolls his eyes. "She likes confusion."

Nox doesn't move. He folds his arms, something grim rolling over his features. "No, Monique. She's not going. It's late and will be dark soon."

Instantly, I scowl. "You're not the boss of me." I toss my head in defiance. "And I'm not afraid of the dark."

Monique ignores Nox's warning and hums under her

breath, leaning in toward me. "What if I told you I could take you to Dulcie?"

The entire world grinds to a halt as I stare at her and my heart jerks with a flailing kind of hope before reality sinks in. She's playing me. My eyes search her face, taking note of her scornful sneer and the hint of spite in her gaze. She must have heard something about my mom from Granny or Becks. My stupid burst of hope deflates like a stuck balloon.

But then, the memory of what I painted and the weird hallucination hits me with the force of a sledgehammer. Unease trickles through me. What if my mom *is* actually in these woods? Had it actually been her calling to me before, when I'd tried to drown it out? No, because that would be ridiculous. My mom is not lost in Granny's orchard!

I hike my chin, determined not to let Monique get under my skin. "I'd say you were fibbing." I don't know that she actually is, but this is better than the crumbs I'd gotten out of Granny. Finding my mom is endgame, and a good sleuth has to follow all clues. If Monique is being truthful, then I can see for myself if Mom's in trouble. If Monique isn't, well, at least I can rule out that Mom's trapped in the woods.

"I'm not."

"Monique," Nox booms like a thundercloud.

Something's going on here that I can't place my finger on, but between Nox's obvious discomfort and Monique's taunting, I've had enough. I open my mouth to tell Nox to back off, but Monique beats me to it. "Like she said, Lennox," she says. "You're *not* the boss of me or her, and she's not afraid. Right, *Rika*?"

There's an edge in her words, but whatever it is, that's between them. I file away the fact that Nox is short for Lennox and shrug. A part of me doesn't want to tuck tail and run, even if Monique is obviously baiting me. I don't want her to win by scaring me off. This is a game of chicken, and probably nothing to do with my mom, but there's no way I'm backing down. Not with her.

Besides, we're on Granny's estate, which is gated, fenced, and safe. Even if these kids somehow snuck in, it's not like I'm going to get cooked in an oven by a witch living in a gingerbread house. La diablesse isn't real and these kids are just normal kids, not douens or lost spirits trying to lead me astray. Well, except for Monique. I snort. She's probably a jumbie on the inside.

Besides, I'm sure Becks is around somewhere. I can always call to him if I need help. With that, I make an impatient gesture for Monique to lead on. The smile on her face broadens, and I feel a sudden whoosh of breathlessness in my chest as though I've just agreed to jump off a cliff with nothing but rocks at the bottom.

Monique melts into the trees on the other side of the small grove. The twins skip past me arm in arm, singing the same children's song from before.

Nox's hand snakes out to grip my elbow as I hurry past. An odd jolt of energy bursts between us just before I yank it away. "Don't be fooled, Rika," he warns.

"By what?"

"This is dangerous. And you're not . . . like us."

"Because I'm not part of your super squad?" I shoot back,

insulted. "Tell me the truth. Is she lying about knowing where my mom is or not?"

His mouth opens and shuts quickly. Finally he says, "Your mother is one with the wood and the wood is one with her."

Stumped, I blink. Kind of like she's stuck in a tree? That must be a coincidence. And why does Nox sound like Yoda in *Star Wars*?

"What's a totem?" I ask him, curious about Monique's earlier reply.

He exhales. "It's like an . . . artifact. A talisman. Used for protection and teaching."

"Teaching what?" I ask sourly, hating the fact that my grandmother was mentoring that girl, period.

He pauses for a long beat.

My teeth grind together in frustration, but before I can nudge, he lifts a hand, stopping me. "You should go back to the house. It's not safe for you out here." He gestures to the fading light. "Not now."

"Why? Are the jumbies coming?" I widen my eyes and wiggle my fingers for dramatic effect. He flinches, and that should have been a warning in itself, but I've made up my mind. Nothing, not even the threat of a thousand monsters that go bump in the night, can keep me away. I could save my mom. "It's my call," I say. "I'm going."

He groans as if I've just made a deal with the devil himself, but then he walks past me, his face tight. The scent of fragrant cinnamon with hints of pepper fills my nostrils. "Come on, then. Just remember you asked for this."

I glance over my shoulder toward the house, though I can

no longer see the galvanized roof in the distance. I turn back only to realize I'm alone.

"Piku?" I whisper, but there's no movement from his body, though I note the light weight of him. He's probably in a mango food coma.

The echo of singsong lyrics drifts back toward me and I curl my fists, letting the remnants of mango juice stick to my fingers. For a second, I think about retracing my steps back to the house. That would be the smart, sane thing to do, wouldn't it?

Then again, when have I ever done that?

With a deep breath, I chase after Nox.

6

REAL, THIS DEVIL TREE IS

"Hey, wait up!" I shout.

Stems and twigs crash into my face, and I feel a slight sting as I run, hopping over dead branches and decaying fruit along the forest floor.

Is it my imagination or are the trees growing thicker together?

There's a strange but familiar scent in the air, fragrant and pungent. It's the kind of odor that smells sweet at first, but then climbs into your nostrils and shifts into something rotten the more you inhale it. It's the exact same one I smelled from my painting right before it sucked me in. Shivers crawl up my spine. What have I gotten myself into?

"Nox?" I yell out. "Monique?"

There's no answer from either of them, and I start to worry. I don't think I've gone that far from the house, but an unmistakable chill descends over me. The trees are thick and tall, blocking out any light, and as I peer upward in the gloom, they don't look like any fruit trees I recognize from near the house. Shadows seem to wink in and out of the gnarled bark, growing bolder with each pass. My skin itches. Why does it feel like they're watching me? One looms forward shaped like a claw, and I swallow a scream as I stumble back a few steps.

Fighting back mounting alarm, I cup my hands to my mouth. "Nox! Anyone? Becks!"

It sounds like someone answers in the distance, but I'm not sure that it isn't an echo of my own shout. I scream out again and am only met with silence. More shadows coil around me, like snakes in the dark, but that could be a trick of the dimming light. It's strange that there are no other noises—no insects, no birds, nothing—as though the entire wood is asleep. Or dead.

"Boo!"

I nearly jump out of my skin and punch out with a yell. A startled *oof* reaches my ears, followed by a groaning *thump*. Fitz is lying on the leaf-strewn ground, rocking back and forth, clutching his middle. "What'd you do that for?" he moans.

"You scared the crap out of me, jerk," I shriek, my heart still racing uncontrollably.

For a second, the ground seems to rumble beneath my feet and what appears to be a bunch of vines slither toward Fitz and help push him to his feet. What in the world? Squinting, I rub my eyes and shake my head.

"What was that?"

"What was what?" he asks, palming his belly with a grimace.

"The ground shook and the vines moved. They, um, pushed you upright."

"Did you hit your head? Vines don't move, and earthquakes happen all the time here." If it wasn't for the guilty and panicked look on his face, I'd think I was mistaken. I narrow my eyes at him.

"I know what I saw, Fitz. But whatever, don't tell me the truth."

"I'm sorry for scaring you." He sends me a hopeful look. "Don't tell Nox about the vines or the other stuff, okay?"

Aha! I was right. Strange happenings are the norm around here, apparently. While I have him here alone without the others, I jump at the chance to squeeze some information out of him. Nox's answer about Monique had been vague, and Fitz doesn't seem to think before he talks. "I'll keep your secret *if* you answer my question honestly." His eyes narrow but he gives a wary nod. "Is Monique lying about my mom?"

"No." He hesitates. "But not everything is what it seems in here."

Nose wrinkling, I glance at him. Another vague reply. Okay, do I ask him to explain more, or do I try another question on my list that I need answers to? I go for the latter. "Do you know an Ushara?"

Fitz's eyes grow huge and he clamps a warm hand that smells of earth and moss over my mouth. "Don't say *that* name loud so, girl! You dotish or what?" He looks around wildly. "That jumbie could be listening."

I blink. Did he just call me stupid? And did he call Ushara a *jumbie*? Maybe he didn't mean it literally. Maybe he meant it like how I had about Monique earlier, that she's just mean. Deep down, though, my stomach gives an uneasy swoop.

Rubbing it, I catch up to Fitz as he starts walking. "So what was that with the vines? Some kind of magic trick or something?"

He lets out a *pfft* sound, going red. "Yeah, or something."

"Anyway, why would I rat you out to Nox? Is he the self-appointed leader of your little rebel squad?"

Fitz shrugs his thin shoulders. "You could say that."

"What's the deal with him? He seems really . . ." *Cranky. Moody. Bossy. Adorable.* I frown at the last and shove that thought way, way down. "Grouchy."

"Nox is"—Fitz scratches his head and scrunches up his nose—"Nox. He has a lot of responsibility. He's a big shot around here."

"Big shot?" I ask.

"Big deal."

I laugh. "He sure acts like that. And what about Monique?" I curl my lip. "She's never liked me from the start."

Fitz grins knowingly at my sour expression. "Well, she doesn't like anyone. And she's just jealous."

"Jealous?" I ask. "Why?"

"Because she's not part of the trinity. Delilah is your grandmother, and Monique is bound to pro—" He breaks off abruptly, as if he hadn't meant to mention that last part, and strolls away.

What *had* he meant to say? Produce? Provoke?

"Fitz, she has to pro-what?" I hurry to keep up, a dozen more questions on my lips, but no way am I getting lost or left behind again. Not with the menacing shadows in these woods. This time, I stick close to Fitz's heels as he pushes through the foliage.

That is until we come to a clearing with the biggest—and I mean the most enormous—tree that I've ever seen in my entire life. Its trunk is as thick as a small house, and the thing stretches high above the rest of the thicket. Like hundreds of feet above. My mouth hangs open. Wouldn't a tree this tall be obvious from the house? Heck, from the sky?

Though what strikes me speechless is that . . . it's *my* tree.

The one from my painting. Only the leaves are dark green instead of dappled gray under moonlight, and the bark is brown instead of silver. Everything else is the same—the shape, the breadth, the complexity of its ginormous roots. Prickles break out over my suddenly ice-cold skin, my brain struggling to process the reality that this tree actually exists in this grove.

"What kind of tree is this?" I mumble dimly, staring up and up and up. A weird sensation drizzles through my veins— like a tingle of something not quite of this world. Something supernatural.

On my neck, I can feel Piku's small body trembling, and for good reason his reaction makes me nervous.

"The silk cotton tree," Fitz answers and then lowers his voice. "The devil tree."

Balking, I fight back a full-body shudder and take a hurried step in reverse. I know from my granny's folklore that there are supposedly souls trapped in this tree, tortured by a vengeful spirit some call a devil. Becks's warnings and the hallucination with my mom now reside front and center in my thoughts. I pinch my lips tight and cling to reality. No one's trapped in there, and there are no such things as devils.

It's just a tree. A seriously big plant but an ordinary one nonetheless.

I move forward.

No, Rika, don't, my inner self warns. *This isn't like your painting.*

Even Piku's sharp claws dig into my skin and he makes an urgent clicking noise. I hesitate but shake my head. He's a reptile. What does he know? Half defiant and half afraid, I close the distance to place a palm directly on the trunk and brace myself.

It has the texture of . . . bark.

Rough and completely normal. Of course it is. Because it's a flipping *tree*. Huffing a breath, I move to pull away and realize that my hand is stuck. It must have caught on some sticky sap or something. I jerk hard, wincing as if the top layer of skin has peeled away, like the skin off Nox's mango. Then the drumming in my blood begins.

Bazil. Bazil. Bazil.

I cock my head. "What's a Bazil?"

Colors flashing in my peripheral vision, I blink and suddenly the tree is gone. Instead, I'm standing in Granny's courtyard near the old well. A tall, well-dressed man wearing a hat stands beside it. I can't help thinking of how much he resembles the villain from *The Princess and the Frog* . . . and that doesn't bode well, considering Dr. Facilier, aka the Shadow Man, was an evil sorcerer.

"Not a what, dear. A who." Even his voice gives me the creeps.

"Excuse me?" I mumble, confused as to exactly how I got here. My skin buzzes as though touched by static electricity. I reach back for Piku, but am met with folds of loose fabric and no lizard.

"Bazil is a who." He points at his chest. "A me, specifically. That's my name."

"Who are you?" I scan my surroundings. "Where's the tree?"

"Oh, we're still there. I wanted to meet you, that's all, and I happen to like this old well—it whispers to me of secrets and yearnings. So many wishes you see of what people truly want. Even your *secret* wishes, sweet child." I narrow my eyes at him while my belly churns. He props a hip onto the crumbling wall of the well to peer down into its depthless center. "You want your mummy, don't you? Didn't you hear her calling to you?"

Understanding hits. "That wasn't her."

"Clever girl. You're quite right. That was me."

I don't know if this is another hallucination or not, but I follow along. "My mom's gone."

"But you saw her, yes? She's right here," the man says with a venomous, Cheshire Cat smile that makes my flesh crawl, inducing the same reaction I had when the monstrous shadow had chased me in the painting. I recoil in terror at the memory, and the man's smile widens. "Come back to my tree, little one, and visit me sometime. And bring your friend with you— iguana meat can be oh, so tender."

With that, the courtyard fades and my hand dislodges from the bark as if by magic. Piku is tangled in my hair, yanking and making angry hissing, clicking sounds. He's trying to get my attention—this little lizard's a lot smarter than I give him credit for.

"Stop, Piku. I'm fine."

Rubbing my sore palm against my shorts, I stumble backward right into a group of frolicking kids, only realizing too late what Piku was trying to warn me about. They're no bigger than two or three feet tall, are holding hands and weaving in between the thick buttress roots of the tree. Where did they come from? And when had the sky gotten so dark? I can barely see through the gloom, though a weird, ethereal glow seems to come from the tree itself.

"Ring around the rosie, pockets full of posies," they're singing. "Ashes, ashes, we all fall down!"

My knees wobble. I'm going to faint. The new arrivals appear to be years younger than me. They're all wearing floppy hats and chattering up a storm, but I can't quite put my finger on what's wrong with them. What are they even doing out here? Where are their parents?

"F-Fitz?" I stammer. "Where are you?"

"Da-ri-ka . . . Da-ri-ka . . . DA-RI-KA." The small group turns as one, and I stumble back. A shriek tears from my throat.

The intensity of their collective attention slams into me, blasting from all sides as if I'm getting pummeled by a hundred soccer balls coming in my direction at triple speed. My hands go up to protect myself even though there's nothing actually there.

Instantly dizzy, I close my eyes, my mind muddled, and draw a deep breath before opening them again, hoping beyond hope that I've imagined these kids. But once more, I can't process what I'm seeing fast enough. Images come in rapid bursts of light, like a strobe flashing through darkness, spotting my vision with strange images. *Dreadful* images.

One kid has no face besides the outline of a glowing mouth beneath the brim of his hat. His skin is ghostly pale.

Flash.

Another chortles at me, his mouth full of sharpened teeth, like a shark's.

Flash.

A third claps his tiny hands and runs around me screeching, and only at the last second do I register that his feet are turned backward. Or that *all* their feet are turned backward.

Flash, flash, flash.

Their featureless faces start to blur into indistinct shapes, and before long, I can't take anymore. None of these children are normal. Because they aren't children at all.

Douens.

No, no, no! I shake my head and try to quell the fright bubbling like lava. They don't exist! They're fairy tales. Scary bedtime stories told to misbehaving children. Because nobody has backward feet. No one except . . . jumbies. And everyone knows that jumbies only come out at night. My heart pounds against my rib cage so hard that it hurts and I feel light-headed.

75

This *can't* be real.

But I'm here, with rot in my nose and a scene of horror right in front of me. My grandmother's stories are coming alive with full force, just like at the airport. Suddenly, my gaze fastens on the grinning girl perched on the far side of the clearing, propped up between one of the huge roots of the tree, soaking up my confusion and fear with unrestrained glee. Monique.

If she'd meant to scare me, she's succeeding. No wonder Nox hadn't wanted me to go with her. But I don't have time to dwell upon either of their motives as the douens giggle and converge upon me. I open my mouth to holler for help, but a dry wheeze emerges.

"You did promise not to tell," Monique sings out.

My fingers scrabble at my tight throat, the thought of Princess Ariel after she makes that horrible deal with the sea witch curling through my brain. I have no voice! *Impossible*, I think. And yet, clearly not, because I can't utter a single word to save myself.

Piku makes a weird sound and races down my arm to leap to the ground. He stops to stare at me before dashing off. Gulping, I do what any smart, almost-thirteen-year-old would do: I follow the lizard.

Branches and twigs cut into my face as I trample like an elephant through the grove. I ignore the high-pitched catcalls from behind me, adrenaline fueling my legs. I can barely see, but the bright green of Piku's body is like a tiny beacon.

"Becks! Help!"

The dark converges over Piku and I'm on my own. It's the

kind of gloom that makes things come awake in the night. I'm lost. Sounds snap all around me. I flinch and start to pant. My heart is in my throat. I'm not scared of the dark, but there's something about this complete absence of light that's . . . ghoulish. Suddenly, something wraps around me and I scream again, punching and kicking like a wild animal to connect with what must be the muscled chest of a monster. The enormous arms gripping me tighten and I fight harder as though possessed.

"Is me, chile," Becks shouts. "I have you. What you doing past the orchard? Ent I tell you is dangerous? And in the shadows, too?"

Relief pours through me and I hug him hard, tears stinging behind my eyelids. "I'm sorry, I'm sorry. I went for a walk and I got lost. I heard . . . I saw—"

I try to explain to Becks exactly what happened and what I'd seen, but once more, nothing comes out of my mouth. Not a single word, not *one* sound beyond a pathetic, sad squeak of air. That giant dose of fear mutes me. Or maybe a vow I made to Monique to keep a secret . . .

Promises have power, especially from a Lovelace. Something else Granny used to say. I can't help trembling.

Becks and I reach the familiar edges of the grove and the top of the house comes into view. "You safe now," he tells me. "But next time, stay close to home. And doh go back in them woods."

He doesn't have to tell me twice. I pause and press a hand to my galloping heart, watching for Piku but I don't see a flash of green anywhere. Hopefully he's safe, too. "I won't. Thanks, Becks. Don't tell Granny, okay? She'll just worry. I won't do it again."

"Secrets are dangerous, Miss Darika."

Like I haven't learned *that* lesson already.

Waving a thankful goodbye to Becks, I enter to find my grandmother cooking in the kitchen. The microwave reads nine o'clock at night, but I know it's her happy place. A rounded iron pot that looks suspiciously like a cauldron bubbles on the stove.

Stop, Rika. It's a pot, not a cauldron.

I don't even try to tell her about what happened at the tree like I tried to with Becks. How would I explain what I saw? I stumbled upon a mammoth "devil" tree that I'd dreamed about and painted? Toddlers with weird feet and sharp, inhuman teeth? A few kids cutting school and pranking me with clever Halloween costumes? I fight back a sudden wave of nausea.

I know those weren't Halloween costumes.

Granny smiles at me. "I was wondering where you'd gone off to. You weren't in Dulcie's room."

Panic takes hold of me. "Did you go in?"

"No. I was waiting for you to show me what you were working on. The grand reveal of your masterpiece."

More like a master-wreck. "It's not done yet." And it's going to be scrapped first thing tomorrow. In the daylight.

Granny's eyes narrow on the soil streaking my clothes and clumping over my shoes. That, coupled with the bright paint streaks from earlier this afternoon, must make me look like some kind of unicorn mud monster. "Have you been outside?"

"Mmm, yes. I was in the orchard with Becks. I got a little dirty."

That was not technically a lie. Just a . . . slight bending of the truth. My stomach gives a painful lurch. To cover up my turmoil, I offer her a wide smile. It must work because she chases me out of the room with a tea towel. "Shoo! You're a mess. Go on and have a shower and I'll get a snack ready for you before bed. How does bread and honey sound?"

That sounds exactly like the best way to end the worst night.

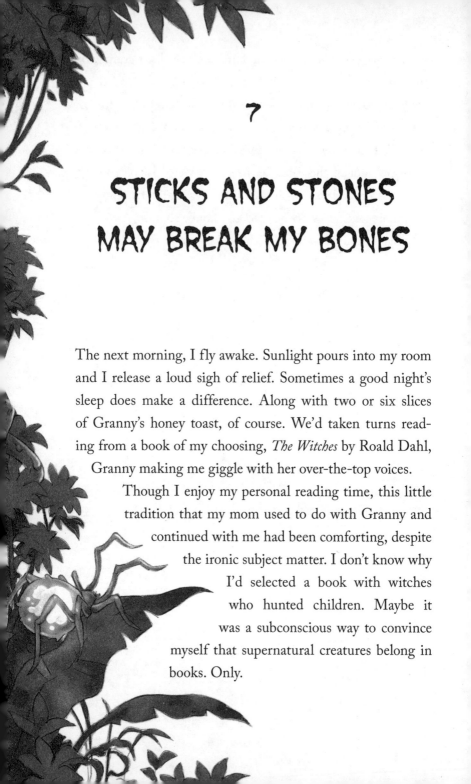

7

STICKS AND STONES
MAY BREAK MY BONES

The next morning, I fly awake. Sunlight pours into my room and I release a loud sigh of relief. Sometimes a good night's sleep does make a difference. Along with two or six slices of Granny's honey toast, of course. We'd taken turns reading from a book of my choosing, *The Witches* by Roald Dahl, Granny making me giggle with her over-the-top voices.

Though I enjoy my personal reading time, this little tradition that my mom used to do with Granny and continued with me had been comforting, despite the ironic subject matter. I don't know why I'd selected a book with witches who hunted children. Maybe it was a subconscious way to convince myself that supernatural creatures belong in books. Only.

Once I brush my teeth and comb my hair, I make my way down to the kitchen. Apart from a few barely visible scrapes on my arms and cheeks, it's like my misadventure through the woods last night never happened. Piku still hasn't shown up, so I have to suppress a twinge of worry.

Right outside the entrance to the kitchen, I hear a voice that makes my nerves go on edge. I peek through the crack of the door and scowl. *Monique.* My hackles instantly rise and I blow out a sigh. She lured me to that tree on purpose with her "We're cool, D" act and I fell for it.

Suddenly, I hear my mother's name. Dulcie. Why would Granny be talking about *my* mom with Monique? Pressing an ear to the door, I strain to listen to their murmured conversation.

"Bazil is getting stronger," Monique says in a whisper that I barely catch, but I perk up, recognizing the name. "We don't have much time, and you're getting weaker. The magic of the wood is disappearing with the fracture of the trinity. Even the Minders can sense the effects. With Papa Bois gone, there's no hope to control him."

Excuse me, *what?* This is the third time I've seen or heard something about a trinity this week. Once in the book in my mom's room that had mentioned a matriarch, a mother, and a child, then with Fitz when he'd said that Monique was jealous of me because she wasn't part of the trinity, and now. Does that mean I am? Also, what on earth is a Minder?

Granny lets out one of her dry rattle coughs, and I hear footsteps and then the tap running. "Here, drink this,"

Monique says. I blink. Why does she sound scared? "It's getting worse, isn't it?"

"No, it's the same as it always is. And Dulcie is tough," Granny says, clearing her throat. "We have a plan—we will fix this. The power of three won't break."

"If it does . . ."

"It won't. The magic might be weak, but Dulcie is not. I'm not. Darika isn't."

My frown tightens. What does any of that have to do with me? And *magic*? I struggle to hear more through such a thick wooden door. I edge closer.

"Lennox says his fa—"

I must have leaned in a smidge too far because the floorboard beneath my foot creaks. Voices fall instantly silent and I swallow a curse.

"Darika, is that you?" Granny calls out.

Darn. I would have loved to know what the King of Everything Nox had to say. I shove my hands into the pockets of my shorts and paste a neutral look on my face before walking in.

"Rika-love," Granny chirps from where she stands over the stove stirring eggs in a frying pan. "There you are. Good morning! Feeling any better today? You seemed to be very tired last night. Did something else happen you're not telling me about?"

"Good morning, Granny," I say, giving her a kiss on her soft, wrinkled cheek. "And no, of course not. It must still be the jet lag." Or, you know, being terrified half to death by a bunch of douens and a literal devil.

The small lie makes me self-conscious, and I open my

mouth to smooth it over, but Monique shoots me a warning glare that Granny can't see over her mug of hot cocoa. A plate of half-eaten food sits beside her. She certainly looks at ease. Like she belongs here. At least, more than I do.

"Monique, you remember my granddaughter, Darika?"

I instantly want to make a snarky comment that she definitely does, but she beats me to it. "How could I forget the sweet Darika? She's such a ray of sunshine and I always felt such a deep bond of friendship with her."

What a steaming heap of baloney.

"Oh, really?" I blurt, not caring how rude I sound. Did she care enough about that bond not to prank me in the forest and leave me to find my own way out? I could have been seriously hurt!

Monique's honey-colored eyes widen, a fake smile quick to follow. "Grandma Love was *so* excited for your visit. She didn't speak of anything else for weeks. Trust me, everyone living around here has heard about you coming back." She says the last part like it's a curse.

"Hush, dear," Granny says with a happy grin, oblivious to the simmering hostility between us, and glances at me. "I'm glad you two connected so well and still have fond memories. Monique lives nearby, Darika."

"Nearby," I echo.

The thought that she has any right to be here, taking my place, digs like a sharp stick. The smugness on her face tells me that she knows it too. Why does she hate me so much?

It's not like I ever did anything to her—breaking the bracelet or totem or whatever she'd called it had been an accident. I watch in slow motion as she rises to refill her cup, anger simmering in me like a pot on a hot stove. Her obvious familiarity with Granny's kitchen makes my fists clench at my sides.

"Eat, Rika," Granny says and sets a plate full of scrambled eggs, baked beans, and more hot buttered toast in front of me. "Quick, doux-doux, before it gets cold. You need some meat on those bones."

I hear Monique snicker softly under her breath. Back at home, I usually cover my body with baggy jeans and hoodies, but here, in this tropical weather, I'd melt with my usual style. Hence, the shorts and tanks that don't hide much . . . including my too-skinny legs, thin chest, and my bony arms.

I take a mouthful from the mound of fluffy eggs seasoned with fresh herbs and sigh. Granny's cooking, even something as simple as scrambled eggs, makes me feel safe. *It's in the mix,* Mom had told me years ago, *and cooking from the heart.* Food, like family, is a big part of Trinidadian culture. My culture, I guess.

"This is really tasty, Granny," I say, feeling Monique's eyes on me and suddenly wanting to dig my heels in about my place here. Granny is *my* grandmother, after all. Not hers.

"You want some more?"

I scrape up the rest of my eggs with the last bit of toast. "No, thank you. I'm full."

Monique finishes her drink and hops up, giving my Granny a hug. "Thanks for the snack. I love our time together. Best I'm not late before the teachers think I'm breaking biche—or skipping school, as you Americans say." She directs the last part of that to me. I narrow my eyes at her but she tosses her long ponytail and picks up a bag that was sitting beside her chair. "See you later, Rika-love."

"Just Rika," I tell her. "Only Granny calls me that."

She leans in, her voice low so Granny doesn't catch what she says. "Whatever. You won't be here long enough for it to matter. Go home, *Rika*. You don't belong here."

I don't know if that's a promise or a threat, but one thing is for sure—I'm here and I'm staying whether she likes it or not. So I say, "We'll see."

Fuming in silence after she leaves, I distract myself with a sip from the steaming cup of hot cocoa that magically appears in front of me, and my eyes nearly roll back in my head. Is that cinnamon? With vanilla? And maybe a hint of chili in the chocolate? No wonder Monique had gone back for seconds. I take a greedy gulp, nearly scalding my tongue in the process, and take back every bad thing I've said about being stuck here. It's worth it just for this.

"Yummy?" Granny asks, watching me over her shoulder.

"Out of this world," I say and smack my lips.

She smiles. "That used to be your mom's favorite. It's her recipe, you know."

I didn't know. "I love the chili with the vanilla. Sweet and spicy."

I guzzle more of it while she bustles around the kitchen, stacking dishes on the drying rack and wiping down counters. Curiosity gnaws at me. Besides knowing what they were talking about in whispers, I also really want to know what Monique means by *our time together*. I don't need to be replaced as a granddaughter too.

"Hey, Granny, does Monique spend a lot of time here? I mean with you?"

She doesn't look up from where she's scrubbing the stove. "Some. Why do you ask?"

"No reason," I say, blushing at the fact that I'm jealous. It's not like Granny is going to stop being my grandmother! "Honestly, I feel like she doesn't really like me much."

"Nonsense. She says she does." She shakes a curl out of her face to peer up at me. "I know you've been torn away from your friends back home and your life, but Monique is a good girl. I think you two might have a lot in common." She winks, lip twitching with sly humor. "Keep exploring that *deep* bond you share. For me, yeah?"

Not a chance. My heart sinks to my toes. I can't say no without sounding like a spoiled brat. Biting my lip, I nod. "Okay."

My brain is racing, but drinking my hot cocoa with slow measured sips seems to help. That and the fact that I'm bursting at the seams with more questions, especially after last night and the overheard conversation. How does everything tie back to Mom? I don't know that it does for sure, but I have to trust my gut. Once I have all the pieces, I'll be able to piece together this puzzle.

I clear my throat, watching her carefully. "Who's Bazil?"

Without warning, a plate crashes to the floor and shatters into an explosion of porcelain shards. Granny turns to me in slow motion, her brown face ashen. She folds her shaking hands together, ignoring the mess on the floor. "Where did you hear that name?"

I pause. Once more, words elude me. Nothing about the

grove or the tree leaves my mouth. "I heard you and Monique talking."

She doesn't say anything at first, too caught up in composing herself . . . or thinking up a way to blow me off yet again. Frown lines gather on her brow as she stoops to pick up the larger pieces of the broken dish. "Names have power," she chides, reminding me of Mom. "And that is *not* one to bandy about so casually."

I swallow my snort. Fitz had been just as cagey in the woods about Ushara. It's not like the man from my vision is actually the Shadow Man. My ribs tighten with alarm. *Could* he be? "Why?"

She eases out a breath and grabs a broom. Is she going to blow me off again? Her eyes meet mine. "The stories say he's a bad spirit that people make deals with in exchange for something they want, and when they can't meet their end of the bargains, they give up their souls."

"Has anyone ever been successful?"

She pauses. "None that I've heard of."

"And you believe that?" I scoff even though a shiver climbs my spine. Had I somehow actually *talked* to that spirit?

Granny finishes sweeping. "People believe a lot of things."

I can't help noticing how deftly she evades answering my question. "But do you?"

"Do you have to question everything, chile?" she snaps. "In my day, children listened and did as they were told."

"Mom too?"

"I don't remember your mother being as strong-minded as you are."

I grin. "I take that as a compliment."

"It's meant as one. Now, hurry up," she says, neatly changing the subject, to my complete aggravation. "We have lots of work to do this morning. We have to get to the market, and I want you to get started cleaning up another room before we paint it. Chop, chop!"

Giving the kitchen floor a final sweep with her eyes, she wipes her hand on a dish towel as I finish my drink and wash the cup. We join Becks, who is waiting with the truck outside. The open air smells like a storm has just passed through, fresh and earthy. Mom used to say that morning rain is common in the foothills of the Northern Range, and I love the way it washes everything clean. I take a deep breath, letting the air fill my lungs. The temperature, though, is climbing along with the sun. It's already hot enough to make me glad for my thin cotton shorts and sleeveless top.

Relief slides through me when I spot Piku gripping the back seat. The lizard is resilient, I'll give him that. Then again, I'd bet anything that he's used to all of this. "Glad you didn't get eaten by those creepy kids with the teeth," I whisper when Becks starts the truck.

He bristles, his tiny spines rising as if to say: *Like that would ever happen.*

It's funny how I can almost picture his words in my head. For an iguana, he's really expressive. Like right now, he's cocking his little green head and staring at me as though he wants me to pick him up. Grinning, I scoop him into my hand, then put him on my shoulder underneath my hair. I snort at the thought of him perching there like a tiny reptilian version of a parrot.

Becks announces that the ride to the bustling market in a small town called Tunapuna is quick, and I squash a giggle at the name.

"I like the rhyming," I say, lips twitching. "It's such a cute name for a place."

Becks glances back at me in the rearview mirror, eyes twinkling. "Is an Amerindian name, the original native people of the island who lived here nearly six thousand years before the arrival of the Europeans."

I smile when he pronounces *the* like *de* in his rumbly accent.

"Cool. Are you Amerindian?"

"Part," he says. "My nana's parents on one side were Carib and French. The next side was Indian and Syrian. Many a the people here are mixed race. Like you an' me."

I've always been proud to be multiracial, the child of a West Indian mother, who has mixed Indian and French Creole roots herself, and an Australian father with Scottish and Middle Eastern heritage. I like that my ancestry comes from a bunch of different places. I used to think I didn't fit in when I first started middle school because I was a brown girl in Colorado, but being different can be special. Even here in Trinidad, seeing the varying skin colors in all pretty shades of brown, from the deepest brown like Becks to a warm beige like me, makes me feel like I belong. Like I have a place here.

Becks finds a parking spot in an alley and we march into the melee of stalls. An explosion of sights, smells, and sounds pops off. Rows of stands line narrow pathways, full of fresh vegetables and fruit—bright red vine-ripened tomatoes, ropes of fat green beans, mounds of yellow plantains and purple eggplant, baskets of multicolored peppers that make my nose twitch, as well as puckered, strange-looking green vegetables I've never seen before. "Caraili," I hear someone say while inspecting one.

I watch as my grandmother greets some of the locals, noticing the air of deference as they treat her with a reverent, respectful air. Some even refuse to take her money while handing over small gifts and samples of their best offerings. I know she's well known in the community, but still, the esteem is almost over the top. As if she's royalty or something. A few glances flit to me, eyes widening with a similar level of awe that makes me uncomfortable. I'm no one to them, or so I thought.

"Why's everyone looking at me like that?" I ask Becks.

"You're a Lovelace," he says matter-of-factly, as if that answers all. It doesn't. I just feel weirder. "Stay with Miss Delilah," Becks tells me as he heads over to a stand with scary-looking blades and sharp weapons. I gape with interest as he picks up a flat-bladed, arm-length knife and swings it up and down in a slashing motion. It's called a cutlass, I know, having seen them used at Maracas Bay to cut through coconuts to get to the delicious water inside. I wonder why Becks would need one, but I have no time to dwell on that as I hurry to keep up with my surprisingly speedy grandmother.

Occasionally, Granny stops to chat with a vendor, buying produce here and there, so I take the chance to ogle my fill.

Carrots, potatoes, yams, cassava, and thick leafy garden herbs are stacked nearby. Huge slabs of salted meats hang from hooks, while shallow boxes in the next aisle are filled with ice, displaying whole fish and shellfish. I scrunch up my nose at that strong odor and hustle past, making sure Granny stays in sight. We pass stalls filled with jars of homemade jams and chutneys, and bags of picked fruit, the unique smells making my mouth water.

It's a feast for the senses . . . which is why I don't immediately notice that I've suddenly lost track of my grandmother. Swallowing my instant worry, I inhale. I'm not alone—I have Piku. Out of the corner of my eye, I glimpse a flash of flowing, bloodred skirts. Most of the shoppers around me are dressed in casual faded clothes, so the vivid color sticks out.

The woman from the airport.

Ushara.

The faint rattle of chains hits my ears, and I stumble as something like a sharp fingernail runs along the back of my arm. I flinch. My skin stings and crawls with revulsion, the menacing touch enough to make my stomach flip.

"Such a pretty girl."

I whirl around at the same moment that I feel Piku's spines jam into my nape.

A flare of panic seizes me, but I force it down. I square my shoulders. In my side view, I notice the other shoppers all walking past us, not even sparing us a glance. I might as well be a rock in the middle of a river. No one sees me; no one sees her either.

"Help!" I try to call out to a random passerby, but I am

ignored as though I'm not standing right there. What kind of sorcery *is* this? And it must be—people just don't willfully overlook children in need unless they're under some kind of spell. My mind recalls the grimoire in Mom's room. But I can't remember any of the protection chants or move to scoop up her footprint or find any pins to stick it with, which supposedly could cause a random infection.

My chest tightens with fear as a smile stretches Ushara's bloodred lips, reminding me of a vampire.

Please don't have fangs, my brain chants.

Luckily, she doesn't. White, slightly crooked, but mercifully blunt teeth appear along with a dimple in her cheek. Her eyes grasp and hold mine. Fascination, followed by a wave of almost intense admiration, creeps over my skin. Close up, she's actually so gorgeous! I've never seen anyone so beautiful. As if by magic, my fear melts away. Fear is overrated, anyway. Confusion lingers for a second in my head as her eyes seem to glow and her smile widens. She truly is lovely!

Piku is thrashing around underneath my hair like he's having some kind of emotional breakdown and I can't even figure out what he's trying to communicate, but the truth is, I don't care. I just want to befriend the woman in front of me. I'm desperate to make her *like* me.

"Stop it, Piku," I hiss under my breath.

"My name is Ushara," she coos. "You are such a pretty girl."

Something about the singsong words feels wrong; she said them earlier, but I feel a burst of happiness this time. "I'm Rika. You're pretty too." I give her a hesitant smile, and she extends a gloved hand, beckoning to me. *I should go with her,* I think. *Maybe she can help me find Granny. . . .*

Granny!

It's like a splash of ice-cold water, lifting the haze from my fuzzy brain for a split second. Shaking my head like a dog, I step back. Eyes flashing, Ushara's smile freezes, an ugly ripple surging across her face and distorting her perfect features. I blink, instincts kicking in gear, and take another step back. This time, though, she closes the distance between us, her smile reforming twice as bright. A dense perfume that smells like moldy oranges coils around me, and for a moment, I wobble in place.

Bony fingers close around my wrist. "Come, girl. I'll take you to your mother."

Yes. She'll take me to Mom. Finally. Adoration and gratitude fill me. I want to go with her. I *have* to go with her. She knows where Mom is, not like Granny, who doesn't trust me enough to tell me. "Where is she?" I mumble.

"The tree," she croons.

Of course—I saw Mom there.

Out of the corner of my eye, I see Piku dart out from the curtain of my hair, his chin flap rigid and out, dorsal crest flaring, his stance the most aggressive I've ever seen him. Ushara's eyes widen with surprise and then fury, but she doesn't back away.

"Come," she says again, reaching out a hand tipped with pointed crimson nails. "Lord Bazil sent me to bring you to your mother. He'll help you."

93

There's that name again, the one from the well and the one Granny had gotten so frazzled about in the kitchen. In spite of Piku's tiny talons digging into my flesh, I sway forward on eager feet. Piku hisses and jumps in midair, only to be swatted to the ground like a palm-sized bug. I feel a sharp prick of unease, but when cold fingers brush my skin once more, I sink into a warm daze of happiness.

"Leave her alone, Ushara!"

Blinking rapidly, I snap back to myself, staring down at the liver-spotted, skeletal hand grasping mine, and then up to Nox. What's he doing here? Cursing, the woman in red lurches away, eyes spitting hate at the boy who has appeared by my side. My wrist aches, red welts appearing where her nails had gripped. I hadn't even noticed she was hurting me!

A strange, angry gust of wind blows between us.

"Get back, jumbie!" Nox shouts again, moving so quickly that I almost miss it. But his fingers graze what looks like a velvet pouch tied to her waist, and she wails, jumping back out of reach. "You have no power here."

The wind roars again like an unsettled beast, though not a single hair on my head moves. Ushara rears away, however, as the cyclone slams into her, sending her hair and skirts flying. Nox has his palm out and I can't help noticing with a narrowed gaze that the wind seems to be coming from *him*.

First Fitz with the vines and now Nox with this gale. I want to rub at my eyes, but there's no way I'm closing them in front of Ushara.

"Rika, look out!" Nox yells when, sure enough, Ushara lunges in my direction.

94

Nearly a hair too late, I spin out of the way as bony talons catch on the loop of my jean shorts. A deep yearning to follow her again hits me just from the slight contact, but I fight the lure with everything inside of me. "No!" I snarl through my teeth.

"That's it, Rika," Nox says. "Block her out. Imagine a wall around your mind. You can do it."

Without question, I do as he says, imagining a huge blockade made of gray cement bricks that surrounds the spongy mass of my brain and protects my thoughts from her. I would laugh, but I think it's working the higher and thicker I make the wall. The longing lessens with each brick. Finally, with a shout of victory, I yank my body away from her.

Burning eyes narrow, a shimmer of her true face appearing, its withered gauntness making me gulp. She's not so lovely, like at all.

"Always a pleasure, Lennox. I'll be seeing you soon, little one," Ushara trills, her voice sounding like nails on a chalkboard instead of music, before melting away in the crowd.

Nope, I'm good.

Nox turns to me, his eyes full of concern, but I can only blink like an owl up at him, my mind suddenly on the fritz.

"Are you hurt?" he asks.

"No. Is she gone?" I mumble. "Wait, where's Piku?"

"Yes, and I see him. He's okay. You're both safe." Nox scoops the iguana's fallen body from the ground and steers me over to the side. Something in my chest clenches at the sight of Piku's scrunched-up form when I take him gingerly from Nox. I'd been so caught up in that woman's spell that I hadn't even tried to defend him. "Ushara is a very dangerous person. Are you alone? Where's Grandma Love?"

I swallow a sob. "I lost her a few minutes ago, and then I saw that woman and she came up to me saying she knew where my mom was." My breathing spikes as I think of the near-miss I'd just had. She would have kidnapped me. "She did something to me. I wanted to go with her so badly. How did she do that?"

"She's a jumbie." Nox's eyes are cold. "With bad, *bad* magic."

In shock, I come to a dead stop and stare at him, goose bumps gusting over every inch of my skin. "Like what you did with the wind?"

"Yes. And like what you did too, to block her out." He taps his temple with one finger.

"I did . . . magic?" My voice wavers.

"Yes." His face is sincere, truth blasting from those moss-green eyes.

"How?" I mumble.

"Because you're a witch, Rika."

8

WITCHES GET STITCHES

I used to think there was no such thing as magic.

Used to, being the operative words. Because apparently, witches are real.

And I'm one of them.

The thought of that makes me want to burst out laughing. I attempt, futilely, to swallow a wild eruption of giggles as Nox stares down at me with a concerned look. "You okay?"

"Define *okay,*" I say, bleating like a wild lamb. "Just processing the fact that we're all witches here and I've woken up in Banana-pants-landia. Oh, and where is Percy Jackson and Camp Half-Blood again? Down the street?"

The corner of Nox's mouth twitches at my sarcasm. "They're demigods," he says with a straight face. "Completely different creature. And I'm not a witch like you. I'm a Minder."

"A what?"

"It's a kind of protector," he replies.

That makes sense, considering the fact that he came so valiantly to my rescue a moment ago. Then again, he'd also abandoned me in the woods with Monique. I scowl. Some protector. I narrow my eyes at him. "Why are you being so nice now? Where were you the other night when I needed you?"

"I was keeping you safe, holding off—" He pauses, staring over my shoulder, eyes going wide.

"Darika Lovelace-Rose, don't you move a step!" I turn around to see Granny with Becks hot on her heels rushing toward us. She's probably been frantically searching for me. And she's using my full name, which is never good. I wince.

"Can you come over to the house later?" I ask Nox, not wanting him to get in any trouble, but also wanting answers. *Needing* answers. He nods, and I brace myself for Granny's wrath as I turn around to face her. She looks beyond upset, the relief at finding me ebbing.

Despite my mini run-in with Ushara, I'm unhurt, mostly thanks to Nox. Well, except for the fresh ring of bruises on my wrist. With my pale brown skin, the marks are noticeable. Piku is unhurt, thank goodness, though he's a motionless weight in my arms. Guilt stabs me at the thought that I hadn't shielded my only friend here from harm, when he'd obviously tried to defend me. Animals, and evidently reptiles, too, have superior senses about people.

"I've been looking all over for you!" Granny says, wheezing. "Where have you been, Rika?"

"Trying to find you after we got separated." I frown at her laboring for breath, wondering if she's going to start that awful coughing again. She looks much too sallow, sweat peppering her forehead. "Do you feel all right, Granny?"

"Yes, yes. I'm good. You just had me worried sick."

I swallow hard. If she only knew how much danger I'd been in because of my own willfulness, she'd rip into me on the spot. I release some of the pent-up emotion inside of me, and manage to produce some tears. "I'm sorry. I didn't mean to get lost. A friend helped m—" I turn around, but Nox is nowhere to be seen.

With a loud exhalation, Granny pulls me into her arms and kisses my brow. "It's fine, lovey, but next time, you have to stay close to me or Becks, okay? Let's get you home."

I let out a breath, thinking that's the last of it, but Granny, of course, with her eagle eye pounces once we're in the car and Becks steers us back on the road. "What happened to your wrist?"

My brain sputters, remembering Nox's words about Ushara—*she's an actual jumbie*—and I know from Granny's stories that that means an evil spirit. I don't want to lie.

"I ran into Ushara in the market," I confess in a blurted whisper. "The woman in red."

Granny's bellow could burst eardrums, but the blast of fear in her eyes is the only thing I can see. "What? Did she give you that bruise?"

"It's fine, Granny. I'm fine, I swear. Nox helped me get away and find you."

Those shrewd eyes narrow. "*Nox?* Do you mean Lennox?"

I nod. "Yes? He goes by Nox. Ushara wanted me to go with her to the tree, but he stopped her," I say, not wanting to get him into trouble since he hadn't stuck around after Granny found me, likely because no one with half a brain would after that nightmare.

Granny and Becks exchange a fraught glance in the front, and anger bubbles up inside me. "What does that mean? That face?"

"Nothing." Granny sighs and rubs her chin, gesturing for Becks to drive faster.

I bristle at the dismissal. "I can handle whatever it is, you know. I'm not a little kid! I'm almost thirteen! And besides, Nox told me what I am, so what does it matter?"

She swivels toward me. "What exactly did Lennox tell you?"

"Probably what you should have told me, Granny!" I mutter and slam back into my seat, crossing my hands over my chest. "You're a witch. I'm a witch. Everyone with a pulse on this island is a witch. Even Ushara." Her eyes narrow at my insolent tone, but I'm too furious to care. "What about you, Becks? You're a witch too?"

"Nah man, Miss Darika," he replies, his black eyes on the road, though I see a hint of a sparkle in them through the rearview mirror.

"Sucks to be you, then," I grumble.

"That is enough, Rika!" Granny snaps the reprimand through her teeth. "You have no idea what you are saying."

"So did Nox lie?" I demand petulantly. "Just tell me the truth!"

She stares at me as though she can see right through my bluster and bravado. Because of course she can. She's Granny. The minute I'd laid eyes on her at the market, it was as though a cloud had lifted from above me. Like something in her had joined to me—a familial, strong bond had snapped tight. Or maybe I'm making stuff up because we're supposedly witches.

"Your mother did not want any of this for you," Granny says eventually, turning back to face forward as though the conversation is over.

"And look where that got her! Lost somewhere."

"Just leave it alone, Rika."

"Why?" I press, well aware I'm treading a thin line. Granny is old-school; children should be well-behaved with polite manners and respect their elders. "When you won't tell me anything? If Mom's truly in danger and this Bazil has her, we have to rescue her." A horrid thought occurs to me. "Wait, did she make a bargain with him?" I ask in alarm. "Is that why she's gone?"

Silence.

"Tell me! Please!"

I don't even notice that we've pulled into the courtyard until Becks gets out, leaving Granny and me alone in the truck. Her jaw is clenched as she turns to me. "Let's get this straight once and for all. You're here for one reason only, Rika, and that is for *me* to keep *you* safe. You might think you can handle the truth, but you are a child. *My* granddaughter. If I have to lock you inside to keep you out of trouble, I will."

I gasp. "You can't do that."

"My house, my rules."

"You want to control me like everyone else!"

Her stern expression softens for the briefest moment. "You mean everyone who cares about you and wants the best for you?" She rubs a hand down her face. "There are bigger things at play here, and I need you safe. I have to go back into town to finish my business, but promise me you won't leave the house."

It's more of a command than a request. "Fine!"

She coughs. "I'm not joking, Darika."

"I heard you the first time, *Grandma Love*."

We stare at each other in a silent, stubborn standoff before she looks away with a loud, frustrated sigh. Eyes burning, I hop out of the car and run to my room, slamming the door so hard the walls rattle. Piku scrambles down my body with a hiss and heads for the window as if he, too, can't wait to get away from me. I throw myself onto my bed and scream into my pillow.

The tears flow, leaking out onto my sheets, brought on by frustration. Why can't she just be honest with me? I hate this! I want to see my mom again. Guilt is fast to follow as it always does when I lash out in anger. I wish I hadn't yelled at Granny. I'm upset, but I know my grandmother loves me. Probably more than anyone right now. Even my own dad.

The clunk of something hitting the window makes me sit up, distracting me from my epic pity party for one. I hop from my bed to peek outside. Maybe it's Nox, coming over after our bonding moment. But no one's there. Though it's only early afternoon, the sky has grown overcast and dark, the incoming thunderstorm making the surrounding woods look extra creepy. I frown and rub my arms.

"Piku? Are you in here?" I call out. "Where did you scamper off to?"

Relief cascades through me at the familiar clicking sound. I glance over to see his emerald head at the top of the bookcase bracketing the window. "Some storm, huh?"

There's no reply, of course, but on cue, the first fat drops break from the clouds and then it's a deluge when lightning splits the sky. I flinch at the following boom of thunder. My dad used to say that you could guess how far away a storm was by counting between the lightning flash and the sound.

Another flash rips overhead. "One Mississippi, two Mississippi, three Miss—" The peal of thunder makes my ears ring, and I swallow a yelp as a wet head emerges from underneath my windowsill. It's only a drenched Nox, dark curls plastered to his skull from the rain.

"Let me in, Rika."

I unlatch the window and shove it up, then pause. "Promise you're not a vampire?"

"Minders are way cooler than vampires," he huffs with an exaggerated eye roll that makes me giggle.

My jaw drops. "So there *are* vampires?"

He hauls himself in, dripping all over the floor, puddles pooling at his bare, dirt-splattered feet, a corner of his lip quirking upward. "Not like the ones you're thinking of with gelled hair and buckets of charm. More like a ball of fire without skin."

"Gross."

"Exactly," he agrees.

I squint at him. He looks like a wet rat instead of some

cosmic wind-wrangler. I hustle to grab a towel from my bathroom and toss it to him, stifling the question on the tip of my tongue of why he can't magically air-dry, being the master of air and all.

"Did you throw rocks at my window?" I ask.

He stops toweling. "No."

But we're both distracted by a scrabbling sound and more pebbles thrown at said window. Another soaked head pops above the sill and Fitz nearly tumbles over the edge. "Sorry, that was us. We followed Nox."

A second body follows his entrance—this time his twin with her shirt stuck to her skin. I almost expect to see Monique next, but am secretly glad when Fitz leans past me to shut the open window with no sign of her. "Where's Monique?"

"She went somewhere with Grandma Love."

My relief morphs into something else, something that feels too much like jealousy. Why would Granny take Monique with her to town and not me? I swallow past the weird lump in my throat and focus on the bedraggled kids in my room. Maybe she took Monique because of the way I'd acted. I feel a twinge of regret at the bratty way I behaved in the truck. No matter how upset I am, she's still my grandmother. I'll apologize to her later.

"Papa-yo, that storm came out of nowhere!" Fitz exclaims, rubbing his arms and shaking his head, water splattering everywhere. "It's pelting down!"

"That's not a normal storm," a somber Hazel says. "It's getting worse."

"What's getting worse?" I ask.

"Everything. The weather. The whole world."

Dismissing her overdramatic response, I frown and say, "We need more towels."

I dart into the hallway to the linen closet and come back with a pile of fluffy towels. When everyone is dried, we sit in a circle on the floor, watching the small monsoon rage outside. Rain lashes against the panes in sheets. The sky is an angry gray. Suddenly, the bedroom lights flicker and my stomach dips. I'd forgotten how easy it is to lose electricity here. Mom told me many times that when she was a girl, they'd lose power for weeks and have to use kerosene lamps and candles.

But that won't happen now, right? I mean, it's the twenty-first century. Electricity is dependable. But just then the lights blink on and off again. Someone—Fitz, probably—lets out a cry. Without warning, there's a tremendous bang from outside and every single light blacks out, shrouding us in darkness.

Nox's voice cuts through, telling everyone to stay calm. The wind howls like a wild beast outside, but inside, there's total silence. The kind of silence that makes your body clench up and your heart race. The kind of silence that makes cold fear pool in your belly like there's something awful there in the darkness with you.

I feel Piku's tiny body creep up my arm—I don't know how I know it's him, but I do. He climbs onto my shoulder and nestles into the crook of my neck. I wonder if he's afraid of the storm and the dark too.

After a few beats, the lights flicker back on, this time with an ominous pop and sizzle, but they don't go out again. For now. Relief pumps through me just as footsteps echo from the hallway. I quickly shush the others before going to my door and cracking it open.

It's Becks with a portable lamp in hand and a flashlight. He offers both to me. "In case the lights go out again. You good, Miss Darika? Not frighten?"

"I'm okay," I say. "Does this happen a lot?"

"Only with big storms. Doh worry—if it goes out, you go be safe here. Stay put, a'right? I'll check the rest a the house. Miss Delilah should be back soon."

At that, I sense a frisson of worry. Hopefully, Granny has taken shelter and isn't driving in this weather, especially since she hasn't been well physically. I wouldn't want her to get sicker being stuck in the rain. The roads here get flooded easily too, and in the mountain ranges, everything flows from top to bottom. I'm guessing that the narrow creek on the estate will be a river by now. I know Granny can handle herself, but I'm still anxious.

Piku pokes his head out from under my hair as if sensing my mood.

"Who's that little guy?" Fitz asks, peering at him.

"This is Piku," I say. "He's my friend, I guess, but sometimes, he's shy. Mostly, he's grumpy."

Nox eyes me, a thoughtfulness filtering through his gaze. "Can he understand you?"

"I get the impression that he does," I reply cautiously. "I think he tried to fight Ushara when I was under her spell earlier. If he could talk, I bet he'd have been screaming at me to run."

Nox doesn't bat an eye. "That's because he knows Ushara is dangerous."

"She's just a person," I say. "Even if she has bad magic, like you said, she's made of flesh and blood, isn't she?"

Hazel snorts. "Sure, someone *else's* flesh and blood."

A cold shiver runs through me, considering the question I'd asked Nox earlier about being a vampire. "So she's not a vampire," I say out loud.

"No," Hazel interjects. "Because that'd be a soucouyant, and trust me, you don't want to meet one of them. She's this shape-shifting old woman who strips off her skin, turns into a fireball, and sucks the blood from her victims at night. Nasty! No, Ushara is a jumbie we call the lajabless."

That's the local pronunciation for la diablesse. The female devil. I know this because, when we used to read scary stories together, Granny had explained that the name is French.

Of course she is. And of course Fitz had meant that literally in the woods. Cold realization settles through me, followed by dismay. Deep down, a part of me had already known that something supernatural was afoot, and now I can't explain any of it away because I *saw* things with my own eyes. The grimoire was one thing, but Fitz had used magic in the woods, and Nox did earlier today to guard me from Ushara. I was searching for clues to point me in Mom's direction, and now I have some—a few of the pieces are coming together. Not in the way I expected, but forming a picture nonetheless.

And the man at the well, he's the villain of this story. What kind of bargain would my mom have made? And *why*?

"Nox, who is Bazil?" I whisper, remembering Granny's warning about the power of names, but searching for more answers than she'd given me. "Is he an obeahman?"

Three pairs of eyes laser on me. "Why?"

"I talked to him," I admit. "When I was at the tree in the woods that Monique took me to, he showed me some kind of vision and said he couldn't wait to meet me. He looked like a man."

"He's not a man," Fitz spits out.

Hazel continues, "He is a devil, a real Bad John, who tricked Papa Bois and trapped him in the silk cotton tree. That's what's causing all of this."

In Trinidadian slang, a Bad John is a really dangerous person.

"You mean the earthquakes and storms?" I ask, frowning.

Nox nods. "It's gotten worse with him gone. Your mother tried to help, but she got caught in Bazil's tricks too. I don't even know if he's still alive." There's a strange note in his voice—that Papa Bois might mean something to him. The question sits on the tip of my tongue, and he smiles a little sadly. "Papa Bois is my father. Though I call him Daddy Bouchon."

Whoa. The immortal shape-shifting protector of the forest from Granny's stories is Nox's dad? "That explains a lot," I say, and I bite my lip.

"What do you mean?" Nox asks.

The shells of my ears go hot for no reason. The force of Nox's power had been out of this world, and seeing him de-fending me in the market had made me feel curiously warm inside. Fuzzy. I nearly roll my eyes at myself. *Now is not the time for a crush, Rika!*

"What you did with the wind and how you are with the others. They look up to you," I add hastily. We're in the same boat, then, if each of our parents is missing. "They're both trapped in the tree, aren't they? Your dad and my mom?"

Nox runs a hand through his wild mop of curls, made extra curly from the rain, and blows air through his teeth. "We think so."

"In the devil tree?"

They nod again, and I exhale slowly, everything falling into place. This is it—this is *why* I'm here. Not just so Granny can find tasks for my idle hands or keep me busy for a stretch of time. My mom's in serious peril, and she needs my help. And it seems like Nox does too.

I remember the slimy essence of Bazil's aura and it feels like a thousand beetles are hatching under my skin. No wonder Granny is worried about keeping me safe, if he really is a devil, but I just can't sit by and do nothing. Not when Mom's life is in danger.

That's not who I am or who I want to be. If I can save her, maybe I won't feel like everything that has happened to bring me here—my grades, the graffiti, getting kicked off the soccer team—is so bad. That I'm not unwanted or just a troublemaker. I'm here for a reason. I feel a renewed sense of determination. I can do this. I know I can.

Better to ask for forgiveness than permission.

And besides, I won't be alone—I'll have help.

Resolve filling me, I eye my new friends, firming my lips and nodding my chin. Nox shakes his head as if he can see the newfound resolve on my face. "Whatever you're thinking, it's a bad idea."

He's not wrong. It's most definitely the mother of bad ideas. I mean, we're talking about going up against an old, powerful, *bad* devil who has a taste for flesh and blood, and will likely try to kill us and eat us whole, bones and all.

We could get hurt. *I* could get hurt. Like for real, for real.

But go big or go home, right?

I squash down my fear and quell the sick roiling in my stomach. "We're going to go get my mom and Nox's dad," I vow. "Who's in?"

9

I HAVE A PLAN,
I PROMISE

"No way."

The single denial is from Nox.

I glare at him, surprised at his answer. You'd think he'd *want* to rescue his father. "Again, you are not the boss of me, Lennox. I'm doing this with or without you. If I have to let Ushara take me to that tree, I will."

"The witchen is stubborn," a tiny, growly voice says.

I blink. Who the heck said that? And what's a *witchen*?

My mind vaults back to the first question: *Who* spoke?

We all stare at each other and then at the only other living creature in the room . . . namely, a perky iguana named Piku. He cocks his head and repeats his statement, nearly making me keel over in astonishment. Neither Nox nor the others appears surprised, though they are wearing matching grins. I try, unsuccessfully, to close my mouth . . . you know . . . because lizards shouldn't stinking speak.

People don't use magic either, and yet here we are.

Thank you for the information, know-it-all brain.

I gape at Piku. "Holy banana beans, you can *talk*? Since when?"

His jowls wobble as his head cocks comically to one side like a puppy. "What is a banana bean?"

"It's a made-up expression," I say, eyes bugging. "Never mind that, though. How on earth are you talking?"

"I could always talk, but you could only understand me after you used your magic and blocked la diablesse's charm," he explains in a snarky, gravelly little voice. "You had to reduce the shields of doubt and disbelief from your mind—they were too powerful for me to crack."

Well, that makes sense. A wondrous smile stretches across my face. This is fantastic! I can talk to reptiles. Score one for Rika the super witch. *And* I have awesome mind-shield skills? Go me! I mentally high-five myself, ignoring the exasperated look from my talking sidekick.

"Wait, what's a witchen?" I ask aloud this time, and see that Piku's staring at Nox with something akin to adoration. "And stop staring at Nox like he's a ripe mango."

Piku chuffs, turning bright green, spines flaring. "A bratty baby witch."

"Rude!" I roll my eyes and gesture to the others, trying

very hard to keep my cool and pretend that my eyes aren't about to pop out of my skull like a pair of marbles at this new development. "Nox says he's a Minder. Are the twins like him or like me?"

"Like him."

I know Minders are supposed to be protectors, but there must be more to it, so I blurt, "What exactly does a Minder do?"

Nox opens his mouth to reply but pauses when Piku chitters and rolls one eye so slowly it looks like a marble in a bowl. "They mind things. You know, take care of them. They *mind*. Like minding your own business or minding the children or minding the gap."

Wow, sarcasm from a little green lizard really does hit different! I burst into breathless, slightly manic laughter.

"I get it. Don't have a meltdown, tiny mite." I exhale and glance at the others. "So you're here for me?"

Nox nods. "Every Lovelace witch has a group of four Minders. Think of us as your anchors to the supernatural world, like the four points of the base of a pyramid. You're its peak."

I hold back a snort. Monique must really, really hate that.

"So then what's the trinity?" My thoughts are whirling. Triangles and pyramids are way too much math for my poor brain to handle.

"Grandma Love, Auntie Dulcie, and you," Fitz says solemnly.

I freeze, remembering the grimoire. The matriarch, the mother, and the child.

"So they all had Minders too?" I ask a bit breathless.

"Not always. Minders receive the full force of their elemental powers when the magical balance is threatened or when the trinity needs to be bolstered. Our magic is still there, but just enough to help little things along, like a mild drought or failing crops. We exist in harmony with nature. The forest dying is only the first step."

"Which is happening now," I guess from his ominous expression. "How did the island magic choose you?"

Hazel lifts her shoulders in a shrug. "Who knows how magic works? Mine became stronger overnight when Dulcie was captured. Fitz and Nox, too. We knew something was changing for the worse." She purses her lips. "But if you're asking if we were born with these gifts, then yes. They're passed down from generation to generation to keep the supernatural balance between our world and the mortal world. When bad magic spikes, ours does too. Like if the douens cause too much bazodee or too many children go missing, we help curb them from making too much mischief." She wrinkles her nose and shakes her head. "But this thing with Papa Bois and Auntie Dulcie is next level."

It's too much information to take in. Eyes wide with wonder, I stare at their faces. They look so normal, and yet there's an otherworldliness about them too—an eerie gleam in their eyes. Their power is buzzing, I realize.

"You guys control the elements." I remember more of the conversation I'd overheard between Monique and Granny. "And you're tied to the magic of the woods."

"How do you know about that?" Nox asks sharply.

Not like I'm going to confess to eavesdropping on private conversations. A spy never reveals her sources. I rock on my heels. "I know a lot of things, including what you guys can do. I saw Fitz move the vines, and the wind at the market that blew was you, Nox."

Fitz gapes and then goes red. "It was an accident, I swear. But she deserves to know. She's part of the trinity."

"Blood doesn't lie," Hazel interjects sagely.

Nox is about to explode, but I don't care. We have a job to do, and if these Minders have to protect me, then they won't let me go into a rescue mission alone. "Let's talk about you guys and how you can help me get into that devil tree without bargaining away my soul."

There's dead silence, three pairs of eyes fastened on me in various degrees of disbelief. I huff and lift my pointer finger and then the next, punctuating each point. "Jumbies are hunting me. I'm a witch. My mom's apparently stuck in a tree by a power-hungry devil, and I have to get her out so she *and* the king of the wood aren't imprisoned for all eternity." After a beat, I add, "Staring at me like zombies is not exactly explaining how I'm supposed to do that, you know."

Fitz snorts. "Zombies aren't real."

Phew, I guess that's good to know. Not like I need the stress of brain-chomping monsters added to the mix of things that want to eat Darika. "That's not what I mean."

I glare pointedly at Nox and mimic Granny's expression when she's waiting on me to explain my behavior. It must work because Nox jolts. "You're smarter than I thought."

"You're just now realizing this?" I ask with a smirk.

"Overconfident, too."

I tilt my head. "Fake it until you make it."

Nox lets out a sigh. "You're really serious."

"Yes. My mom needs me. If I'm part of a witch trinity, I have to do this, and I'm pretty sure you *need* to do this too." I glance at them. "To save your dad. Right?"

"Yes," Nox replies in a tight voice.

"Then show me what you got."

After Nox gives a short nod, Fitz grins and holds up his hands, which glow slightly golden brown. "I have earth magic. I can move and grow things. It takes a lot of concentration. But as you could probably tell, plants love me."

The plants had come to him pretty naturally. My gaze flicks now to Hazel. "What about you?"

"Water," she replies. Before I can blink, streams of water from the puddles left on the floor in my room weave toward me in pale, silvery ribbons. Hazel's brows are creased with intensity. She glows faint blue as the fluid circles me, forming an intricate mandala in a beautiful sort of dance and then drains back to the puddle.

Whoa.

Expectantly, I glance at Nox next, and hair blows into my face. I remember the way the mango had fallen into his palm that first day, and how quickly he'd moved with Ushara and the wind buffeting me—*protecting* me—from her. I smirk. "You've been showing off since day one, haven't you?" He shrugs, but doesn't deny it.

A gust of air teases through my ponytail, and I laugh. Suddenly, the wind surrounds me so my entire body is lifted from

116

the floor to hover a few inches off the ground. "Put me down!" I squeal. "You're good at air-bending! We get it!"

With a wink, Nox sets me down gently and I resist the urge to pat myself down to make sure I'm still in one piece. I'd known deep down they were special, but seeing this—seeing their actual magic at work—is like catching a glimpse of a unicorn. Your brain tries to tell you it's just a horse, even though it's obviously much more.

"Last but not least, let me guess: Monique has power over fire?" When they nod, I purse my lips. "What's her problem, anyway? It's so obvious she wants to get rid of me."

"She doesn't," Hazel says. "Monique doesn't trust easily, that's all. She's really nice when you get to know her."

"And dragons exist," I mutter, but my nemesis is the least of my worries. "So if you have these cool powers and your goal is to mind, why haven't you guys used your magic to save Papa Bois and get my mom out of the tree?"

Fitz seeks permission from Nox before answering. "It's not that simple. We need the magic in your blood to get in. The tree's heavily warded. No one can get close on their own except for a member of the trinity."

"What about Granny?" I ask. "She has the same blood I do."

"She tried, but the tree is warded against her, too." He hesitates. "She's not strong enough. Not lately, anyway."

"What do you mean?" I ask.

"We think things went wrong when she tried to break the wards last time. She got knocked out for weeks after trying to breach the portal. Our combined gifts weren't enough to get Grandma Love through." He exhales slowly, even as my chest contracts with worry for my grandmother. Lying in a coma is a huge deal. "Monique says she gets tired a lot more now, and that cough of hers is getting worse. Trust me, we've tried everything, but the Bad John"—he lowers his voice to a whisper—"Bazil is clever."

The sound of his name makes a slithery tendril creep across my nape, but the fear that holds me in its grip about my grandmother is even worse. What if she's not sick with a cold but sick with something much worse? Like a magical virus? She'd never tell me, even if I asked. Granny would never tell anyone the truth about her health, but if she's infected with Bazil's evil tree magic, then she needs help, too.

A dark foreboding takes hold of me. There's a lot more at stake here—not just my mom's life or Granny's, but also my protectors' magic and the survival of the woods. I suspect that if this forest dies, it won't be the end of Bazil's curse. Storms and earthquakes could just be the beginning.

If I'm the key to getting into the tree—the last viable part of the trinity—what does that mean once we're inside? Bazil obviously wants me to go in or he wouldn't be sending his minion Ushara after me. He needs me, but why? Whatever the reason, I'm going to have to outthink and outsmart him. But how do you do that with a *devil*?

I might as well be a gnat going up against a giant vulture.

"Why didn't anyone tell me we were having a sleepover?" The drawl comes from the door, where Monique is lounging, propped up against the doorjamb. Her hair is plastered to her brow in wet clumps as though she went for a swim fully dressed. I ignore the instant spurt of dislike at the sneer on her pretty face.

"When did you get back?" I ask, belatedly noticing that the skies have finally cleared. "How is *my* grandmother doing?"

Her amber eyes flash at the emphasis, but she ignores me and glances at Nox. "It happened again. She's fine, but she passed out this time."

Panic hits me. "Granny did? What happened?"

"I said she's fine. She went to bed." I stand to go check for myself, but Monique blocks my way. "If you go bother her now, you'll wake her, and she needs rest. Don't be a brat, Darika."

Despite my relief that Granny is safe in her bed, I stiffen. Not for the first time, confusion, alarm, and jealousy battle inside me. Who does Monique think she is? I open my mouth to argue, but she's not even paying attention to me.

"We need to go," she says to Nox. "That flash flood was no accident. The storm was just the start. Your fath—" She breaks off with a look at me.

"She knows," Nox says.

Monique grimaces, but continues. "He won't last much longer."

One of their silent exchanges happens and he nods, but I turn back to him, tugging on his shirtsleeve. "If they're stuck in the tree, can't you just cut the thing down?"

Hazel gasps. "If it dies, we die, Rika."

"Facts," Fitz says. "That silk cottonwood, and our magic, is imprisoning the Bad John, keeping true chaos from being unleashed. We're talking disease and plagues, floods and fires . . . basically, the end of civilization. Bazil means to destroy all."

"Why?" I ask.

Fitz shrugs. "Because he believes humanity doesn't deserve the planet we live on."

I frown. What gives him the right or the power to decide that? "*Does* he get to decide that?"

Hazel nods. "If the trinity is weakened and there's no one to stop him? Yes."

"You guys told her *everything*?" Monique bites out.

"She's a Lovelace witch—she has a right to know," Fitz shoots back.

I ignore Monique's sour face. "So basically, you're saying it would be the apocalypse."

"Watch the news," Hazel says. "Forest fires, quakes, superstorms, floods, hail as big as cricket balls, snow in warm areas, disease, famine. That devil's curse has already begun."

"That's climate change, though," I say, knowing how fiercely my own dad fights against global warming at his job.

Fitz shakes his head. "Those are just the physical effects of what he can do, holding Papa Bois captive. Somehow, he is using Nox's dad's power to corrupt the earth. If the magic stays out of balance, the world eventually crumbles. We're talking mass species extinction here."

I huff. "Well, okay. My odds of success are slim to none, then."

"More like none to none," Monique snipes. "You can't win this, Rika. Because you're selfish and weak. What did Nox call you? A pest?"

My cheeks go hot with embarrassment. "Take that back!"

"Your own family sent you away. Because you're just a

120

spoiled girl who doesn't care about anything but herself. What could *you* possibly do to help protect the world?"

"Monique, enough," Nox says.

Her eyes shine gold, bitterness sparking from them. "Of course you would take her side. Guess what? Princess Pest is going to fail us."

I ball my fists. A red glow surrounds her body, halting me in my tracks. Right . . . she's the fourth elemental Minder, with fire as her power. Flames dance between her fingertips, and for a moment, I actually think she's going to hurl a fireball at me. My throat closes as sweat drips down my neck and I force myself to hold my ground. No need to give her any extra ammunition that I'm a coward. I'll go extra crispy before giving in to someone like her.

"I'm not afraid of you, Monique."

Heat radiates from her. "You sure about that?"

"Get out of my room or—" I begin and start forward, but before I can finish my rash action of confronting a maniac with a handful of fire magic, Nox gets between us, his palms raised and face grim. Her flames die out under Nox's silent command, but fire still burns in her eyes.

Monique bares her teeth. "Grandma Love's not going to like this. She'll never put her precious granddaughter in danger, not even to save her own life. If Rika's blood doesn't work, Grandma Love mightn't just fall asleep; she'd die, and then the other Minders and witches would blame us."

"What do you mean, save her life?" I demand.

For the smallest moment, I see real grief in Monique's hard eyes. "In case you hadn't noticed because you're so caught up in the wonderful life of Darika, she's sick and getting worse by the day. The magic of the other witches on the island is the only thing keeping her upright."

Fear hits me like a bucket of ice water. I don't even take on Monique's insult or become curious about a larger coven. For a moment I think back to some of the people in the market who had bowed in deference to Granny and offered her gifts. Some had been in bottles and sachets.

Had those been tinctures and potions to make her feel better? I'm grateful for their kindness, but a sense of dread slowly rises within me. How long will that magical bandage last? I have to go to the tree. I won't lose more of my family. "Then let's go rescue my mom. She'll know what to do."

Piku pokes his head out and growls. "I don't like this one bit, human."

Well, that makes two of us.

"Okay. What's the plan?" Fitz asks.

"We go in, find my mom and your dad, and get out."

His eyes widen. "That's it?"

I fake bravado. "We won't know what we're up against until we get inside. You guys are the all-powerful Minders. If we run into trouble, you can use your magic."

"This sounds like a really bad idea," Fitz says, shaking his head while his twin nods hers in agreement. Nox is holding his tongue, but I can tell from his glower that he's not happy whatsoever with my brilliant idea of me taking on that devil tree. I gnaw on my lip. Does he not think I can do it either? I mean, I just found out who and what I am, and I might not be a Minder, but I'm not weak or selfish or spoiled.

"Nah, I think it's a great idea," Monique chimes in, to my surprise. "The trinity is only as strong as its weakest link. If she wants to prove herself, I say why not."

Dumbfounded, I stare at her, wondering if she's really on my side. But as much as she might dislike me, I know she loves my grandmother.

Nox shifts from foot to foot out of the corner of my eye. "Darika—"

"I can do this, Nox." With a deep breath, I grab the bag of Skittles on my bedside table and stuff it into the pocket of my shorts. For backup. "Fine. What are we waiting for?"

10

SCARY GRANDMOTHERS ARE SCARY

Nox's expression is as intense as the thunderclouds that had blocked the sky earlier, his lips clamped shut and eyes flashing fury at a very calm Monique stalking through the undergrowth ahead of us. Every thought is obvious on her self-righteous face—she expects me to fail.

Or to run.

Or both.

Meanwhile, Nox hasn't said another word since I cut him off. I tug at his sleeve, a knot forming in my throat. "It's okay, you know," I say. "I'm not mad."

"Yeah, but Monique didn't have to be like that. And I'm sorry I called you a pest. That wasn't cool." He faces me, brow creased with concern. "You're sure you want to do this? We can find another way. Figure something else out."

I press my lips together. There's nothing to figure out—if the magic called the Minders together and expanded their powers to take on a greater enemy, then that means I'm the one from the Lovelace trinity who can help make things right. Mom is trapped, Granny is sick, and my blood might be the key to saving both of them. I *have* to try.

"There's no other way." My heart is pounding. Granny is the only one who wants me around . . . the only one left I can count on. I can't lose her now. I just can't. I shove down my fear and worry. "And it's not only them—we have to free your dad, too, or things will only get worse. More storms, more earthquakes. Like Fitz said: if Bazil gets stronger, who knows what will happen to the planet and everyone on it? Maybe he's taking all that power from our parents. If I'm part of the trinity, there's a lot more at stake here than me only thinking about myself or being too scared to act. People will get hurt."

"What about Grandma Love?" Nox asks. "You think she's going to be okay with you putting yourself in harm's way?"

Of course not. A rock would know that. But if she's resting, this might be our only chance to sneak away. I've seen her and Mom get into some huge arguments . . . and that Lovelace temper is fierce. I'm kind of hoping she *doesn't* find out because, trust me, no one wants to see my Granny rage out. I know she thinks I'm better off sitting quiet and sheltered in my bedroom, but I'm no chicken. "She'll get over it."

Maybe.

Piku nibbles at my earlobe to get my attention. "I think this is rather risky, human. Do you think waltzing up to the devil's doorstep and ringing the bell is the answer?"

My mind is still blown that he can speak, but I have to admit it's nice not having one-sided conversations anymore, even if he does sound like a mom. "You don't have to come, you know. You can stay in my room where it's safe."

"Bite your tongue. My dragon ancestors would curl in their embers."

I hide a smile. "Your dragon ancestors would be very proud, Piku. You're very brave."

"You are too. As long as you don't leap before looking."

I have to admit that winging it hasn't done me any favors lately, but we don't have time for a better plan. If what Monique says is true, Granny doesn't have much time. We walk through the orchard, the same sweet, rotten-fruit odor invading my nostrils. "Why does it smell like that?" I ground out, plugging my nose.

"The forest is dying," Nox says. "Without my father to protect the wood, Bazil's rot is infecting everything."

The lump in my throat expands until it feels as though I can't breathe when we come to the glade that houses the silk cotton tree. Once more, a magical pulse flashes over my skin like a fierce heartbeat, one that's stronger than the last time. I take in its shimmery bark, its enormous, wide limbs, and the branches that reach up and up and *up*.

Nerves skate up my spine when my gaze falls to the chunky roots, looking for the douens from last time, but they're not here. Thankfully.

My relief is short.

Where are the little troublemakers, then? Are they inside the tree, too? Waiting to ambush us?

"I've got a bad feeling about this," Piku whispers.

Yeah, welcome to the club.

I grit my teeth. "Let's get this over with."

Hazel skips toward us and holds out a penknife. Her face is somber. "You'll need a drop of blood."

My fingers are so numb that I almost drop the small knife, and Nox steadies my shaking hands to take it from me. "Here," he says. "You're going to impale yourself with that thing."

I release it gladly and go back to hugging myself. Nothing about this feels good. Not the glade, not the missing douens, not the complete, utter silence. There's no birdsong or wind rustling the leaves. Even the wood is holding its breath. "Where are the douens?" I whisper.

He frowns. "I don't know."

"Something's not right," I say, waffling on my sketchy plan. Piku's nerves are getting under my skin.

Nox stops and turns to me. "We're in this together. No matter what happens next, I have your back in there, I promise."

"Me too," Fitz pipes up, followed by his twin.

Nox stares at Monique, who rolls her eyes and flicks a wrist. "Yeah, yeah, whatever."

We stop near the expansive base of the tree where its magic buzzes. The prick of the tip of the knife on my index finger doesn't even register, and I stare dumbly at the scarlet bead of blood forming there.

"Put your finger on the barrier," Hazel says softly. "There's a wall of static energy that'll make your arm hairs stand up."

Slowly, I reach forward, the strange buzzing strengthening, tuning to the sound of my heartbeat in my chest. Panic makes me hesitate and falter.

Save Mom, save Granny, I chant in my head. At the last moment before my bloody fingertip meets the tree bark, a curly-haired tornado whips into the glade. A human tornado in the form of my very livid grandmother.

"STOP THIS INSTANT!"

We all freeze and whirl at the shriek. Delilah Lovelace stands here, fury evident in every line of her face. Each strand of hair looks like it's standing on end, her small body vibrating. I yank my hand back.

"Crapaud smoke your pipe now," Fitz mutters.

"What?" Now's hardly the time for Fitz's colloquialisms.

He blanches. "You in big trouble."

Oh.

"Granny, I can explain," I squeak.

Her earsplitting roar could level this entire wood. Even Becks flinches from where he's standing, towering behind her, his dark eyes wide. And for good reason, because I swear to God my granny has turned into a jumbie herself. Her eyes are frantic, hands windmilling like she can't control them, hair flying everywhere. Even the other Minders look scared, including Monique, which is saying a lot. Piku has disappeared down the back of my shirt.

Yikes. We're in big, *big* trouble.

"Grandma Love—" Nox begins, and her eyes flay him apart.

"Not another word, Lennox."

That icy stare drops on me like a load of bricks. Frosty, unforgiving bricks. "Darika Amrita Lovelace, get away from that tree right this minute or so help me!"

My entire body freezes when she stalks forward to drag me away from the tree's trunk. I have no choice but to follow as the two of us march back through the woods toward the house. She doesn't look ill. She looks upset. Like I'll-lock-you-in-your-room-until-the-end-of-time kind of upset.

Granny seethes as we walk, peering over her shoulder. "Go ahead, explain."

I do as bidden and tell her my slapdash plan, my rushed words punctuated by curses under her breath and plenty of frustrated steups. But it's when I come to the part where I enter the tree that she whirls and comes to a stop in the woods. "I forbid it! Have you all lost your common sense? How dare Lennox even think to share any of this with you! He had no right. What on earth was that boy thinking?"

"You should have been straight with me from the start, Granny," I say, braving her anger and planting my heels into the soft soil when she tries to march away again. "You're sick. You need my help." She comes to a halt too, though her grip on my hand remains firm, as though she doesn't want to risk letting go. I hadn't noticed before, but her brown skin appears sallow, and her eyes are duller. Panic bleats in my chest. She *is* sick and she *does* need my help, even if she'll never ask for it . . . or admit that. I soften my voice. "You should have told me about who we are. About who *I* am."

She stamps her foot. "That's not why I brought you here!"

129

The blood feels like it's draining from my body.

"Then why did you send for me?" I ask quietly. "Mom's in trouble, and no one else has been able to get inside this tree to help her. You tried and that didn't work. Now you're infected with whatever's poisoning the rest of the Northern Range. If I can help, why wouldn't you want me to?"

"It's not that simple, chile." She scrubs a weathered palm over her face and sinks to the ground, slumping over with one of those nasty, hollow-sounding coughs, her fury seeping away. "You weren't safe. I didn't want someone like Ushara coming after you in Colorado, so I asked your father to send you here. In my house, with all the protections, you're sheltered from harm. And the truth is . . . I hoped to save Dulcie and get into the tree myself with a drop of your blood."

Reason dawns. *That's* what she meant that day in the kitchen about having a plan. Only she had expected to go in my place.

I head over to where she's squatting and crouch carefully beside her. The comforting scents of her envelop me and I long to put my head in her lap like I used to when I was a kid. Instead, I put one arm around her shoulders. "Granny, you're not well. Give me a chance. I can get into the tree. My blood is the missing link. Piku says—"

"Who's Piku?"

The iguana sticks his green head out from inside my collar before I can reply, and I watch as Granny's face softens. "Dulcie used to talk to creatures too when she was a girl."

"The Lovelace witches are friends to many," Piku chirps.

Granny's gaze drills into mine. I can see her hesitation— the worry of saving her daughter and endangering her granddaughter. Her dull eyes glimmer for a moment and then deaden with defeat. "No, I can't, Rika. I can't risk losing you too. I know, of all people, what the tainted magic of *that* tree can do." She lifts a hand and rubs her chest. "It stole something from me. Something vital."

"Then it's up to me to help."

"That's not how this works, doux-doux. I'm the adult here."

Rolling to my knees in front of her, I take hold of her hands. Mom's been locked in there for *three years* . . . an eternity by any stretch, and Granny, who knows what will happen to her in a week or in a month? For the first time in a long time, I feel *found,* not lost. "I'm going to do this with Nox and the others. We also need your help. I can't do this without you, but I will if I have to."

Her mouth flattens, making my nerves quail, but I square my shoulders and lift my chin. "Granny, you were always the one to tell me if I don't stand for something, I'll fall for anything. So I'm standing. And besides, the jumbies are coming. Ushara won't give up. You can't guard me every second, not even if you keep me in your house. Please," I whisper. "I want to try."

A warm finger traces the curve of my cheek and winds into a loose strand of ink-dark hair. "I have no doubt that you can, doux-doux. But if Bazil gets his hands on you, there's no telling what he will do."

I gulp, swallowing down my dread and the icky memory of him at the well. "He won't get to me." *I hope.*

Those all-seeing brown eyes hold mine for what seems like forever before she relents, her proud shoulders sagging slightly. A single tear slides down her tanned, wrinkled cheek, and I throw myself into her embrace, hugging tight. Strong arms wrap around me and squeeze back just as hard.

"Fear is healthy, Rika. Fear keeps us ready to act," she says, and then pulls herself to her feet, bringing me up with her for a hug. "I should have known you'd be this stubborn. You're a Lovelace. If we do this, we do it my way. Do you understand, chile? Which means I am going with you. You don't make a move unless I say it's safe, understood?"

"Yes, Granny."

I nod, too nervous to celebrate, as we make our way back to the others. Nox's hair is sticking up as if he's been yanking on it in frustration. Monique hasn't moved from where she stood, cool eyes tracking us the minute we step back into the woods. Fitz lets out a cheer with a fist pump, he and Hazel wearing matching looks of relief. Becks is still here too.

Retracing my steps, I squint at the smear of dried blood on my finger where a translucent scabby bead has formed. I look to Granny and she gives me a solemn nod. I flick the scab off and slam my hand against the bark of the tree before she can change her mind.

For a charged moment, nothing happens, but in the next heartbeat, it's as if my breath stills and time freezes. Magic flares wildly around me, and then the spot where my palm grips the rough bark starts to glow a kind of dark orange that's much too familiar. The circle ripples outward in front of our very eyes until a portal forms, big enough to walk through.

"I'll go first to make sure it's safe," Nox says, his low voice breaking through my slack-jawed awe. "Monique comes after me." He glances over his shoulder to where Granny is standing next to Fitz, her lips stretched tight. "Grandma Love, send Rika in, then you, and then the twins, okay?"

Nox's commands hum with power—and once more, I'm struck by the fact that he's more than just a leader. Not to mention the fact that Granny is calmly taking direction from a boy decades younger than her. No, not a boy . . . a *Minder*.

He smiles at me. "It will be okay, Rika. We've got this."

Throat dry, I nod. He disappears into the glowing doorway. I try to see if I can spot anything on the other side, but the surface is somewhat reflective, only showing my own nervous face. If you'd told me a week ago that I was a witch who had to enter a magical gateway into a devil tree to save my mother, who's also a witch, I would have laughed in your face. But here I am.

Hazel takes my hand. "Hold your breath as though you're jumping into a pool. I've never been through a portal, but I've read in our grimoires that it's easiest that way."

Grimoires, like the one I'd found in Mom's room? The finger that touched the ink in the book prickles.

Thankful for the advice, I inhale, hold, and step hesitantly forward, feeling magic wash over me the moment I graze the barrier. Pushing past, I huff a relieved breath when I see Nox and Fitz, and then suddenly, I can't move. My hand is stuck. Or *Granny* is. Her distorted face is terrified, her fingers digging into mine where our linked palms are frozen in the shimmering surface as though trapped in ice.

I tug, but my hand doesn't move. "Granny? What's wrong?"

"I can't get through," she says, her voice sounding as though it's far away. Her features, too, are indistinct. "Something is blocking me. Come back."

I move to step back through, but the portal doesn't let me. "I can't." Frantically, I scrabble at the barrier that feels like cool, solid Jell-O. "Nox, what's happening? Why can't she get through? Why can't I go back out?"

He shakes his head and looks to Monique, who shrugs with her usual scorn. I narrow my eyes at her, wondering why she doesn't seem all that surprised, but who knows with her? She'll probably leave me behind the first chance she gets.

"I don't know," Nox says. "That shouldn't happen. Can Fitz or Hazel get in?"

A blurry Granny motions for Hazel to step through, and she does with no problem. So that means whatever the block is, it's only preventing *Granny* from entering. This can't be an accident. Someone—Bazil is my guess—doesn't want her here.

"Rika," she cries, eyes panicked, her fingers squeezing mine.

"Granny!" I shriek. "Don't let go!"

Nox and I both watch as she fumbles with something at her wrist and presses it into Fitz's hands, followed by something that appears to be a tiny jar the size of a nail polish bottle.

When Fitz joins us, Granny and I stand there for an interminable moment linked only by our palms. I open my mouth to tell her not to worry, that I'm sorry for being stubborn, and that I love her, but suddenly the portal goes opaque and my grip rips away from hers. The doorway seals shut, closing her off from view. "Granny, wait!"

But my grandmother's gone, and I'm trapped on the other side of a silk cotton tree that eats souls for breakfast.

For one gut-wrenching second, I wonder if that's the last time she'll see me alive.

11

IN WHICH I SUCK AT NEGOTIATION

I stare at the place where my hand had been joined with my granny's—which is now a smooth wall of tea-colored bark. There's no sign of her and no sign of the woods beyond. Instead, it's quiet and dim, the bright light of day dribbling through a pale brown filter. My mind is hammering, my fingers numb with the loss of her touch, a numbness that sinks into the rest of me. I shiver hard and rub my bare, goose-pimpled arms.

"Here, take this," Nox says, and unzips his hoodie.

I'm freezing in this striped tank top, so I accept the offer and slide the warm cotton zip-up on. Nox's warm scent of peppery cinnamon lingers on the fabric.

Fitz sidles over to me with

a sympathetic gaze and thrusts a few things into my palm—a braided hemp bracelet with several beads made of abalone and moonstone, a second bracelet made with jet and gold, and a small weird-shaped gourd. "They're from Grandma Love," he says softly. "She said to wear the bracelets on each wrist, that the protection magic would shield you from harm, and that you would know when to use the pot. She'll be okay, Rika. She's strong. She would want you to be strong, too."

She would. My granny wouldn't let this sudden setback break her, so I won't either. Sniffing, I hold up the small clay pot and remove the lid. The smell is oaky and slightly sweet. On the inside of the cover is a tiny brush. Holding it up to the shadowy light, I peer into the pot. There's some kind of iridescent paint within, but I have no idea how such a small amount is going to help us. The bracelets remind me of the one I'd snapped, the one that belonged to Monique. She obviously has the same thought too, based on the sour expression on her face.

I bite my lip and pocket the items. I'll put them on later when Monique's not shooting me a death stare.

Current mood: about to die a gruesome death and potentially be devoured by monsters.

But hey, on the bright side, at least I'm not here alone. No, I'm with four Minders who have powerful elemental magic. One of whom might just want to shove me off a magical cliff the first chance she gets, but still. And I'm stuck in an evil tree that collects souls for fun. Instead of losing my cool like I want to, I start to laugh.

"This is nothing to laugh at, human," Piku points out drily.

"Oh, come on. This is so full of suckage, it's kind of funny."

"No, it's not."

He's not wrong. That there seems to be only one way out of this place suddenly reminds me of the Upside Down in *Stranger Things*, and surprise, it's dark and spooky, full of who-knows-what. Let's just hope there are no monsters here—I don't need to see humanoid creatures with flower heads made of teeth. I've had enough jump scares to last me a lifetime.

My finger throbs from where the knife had poked the skin and I rub the tiny injury against my jean shorts. I turn to face Nox. "So what now?"

"There's only one way forward," he says, pointing at a gloomy corridor on the other side of the entry space. Of course it's a tunnel that looks like a gaping maw. *Calm down, imagination!*

Nox and Monique go first and I'm followed by Fitz and Hazel. No one speaks, and the silence grows deeper with every step until the quiet is pounding in my brain.

Whomp. Whomp. Whomp.

Like hard, clodding footsteps hot on our heels, the thuds coming closer together.

"Do you hear that?" Fitz asks from behind me, making me jolt.

My eyes widen. "You hear it, too?"

"Something's coming!" Hazel shouts. "I've got this. Run!"

Taking off in a dash down a single passageway, I peek over my shoulder to see a huge wave of water crashing back down the way we'd come, and the sides of the walls turning to mud. I'm glad I'm not on the receiving end of Hazel's magic. But one thing's for sure—the way back is gone for good now. Nothing remains of the tunnel we entered except for the biggest mudslide I've ever seen.

"Move, human," Piku urges, his tiny claws pinching.

The corridor is narrow, but I keep Nox's silhouette in sight as I pump my legs hard behind him. My lungs are burning, and my body is aching from the strain. Without daily soccer practice, my fitness levels have gone way down and I'm screaming for breath by the time we tumble into a humongous cavern. I turn to see Hazel coming up behind us. She's soaked and covered in dirt, but safely so.

"Welcome, friends!" a deep and very familiar voice booms.

An imposing figure sits on a huge chair at the end of a long table. I recognize the woman standing beside him in her old-fashioned gown and hat, and I fight a shudder. Ushara had tried to lure me here that day at the market, but I would have been alone and on my own. I gape at Bazil, who no longer resembles the man I saw next to the well. One, he's twice the size of any normal man, and two, he wears a spiked crown on his head.

I'm also certain this chamber was empty just a minute ago, and now it's furnished and carpeted like the throne room of some fancy medieval castle.

Magic . . . or devilry.

Feeling more and more like Alice dumped in the buttcrack of Wonderland, I try to stay cool. Nothing is as it seems here, I remind myself. And neither is the monster who'd so charmingly welcomed us into his lair. He's probably as nasty as the Queen of Hearts. Or worse.

"Bazil," Nox says, sneering, one long arm reaching out to grip me and keep my body positioned behind his. The other Minders band together at our backs.

"Lennox," Bazil drawls. "It's been an age, hasn't it?"

"Not long enough. Where's my father and Auntie Dulcie?"

The monster tuts, waving a finger. His voice is soft and melodious, reminding me of Ushara and the way she had enchanted me in the market. The sound makes my blood curdle. Once more, my finger throbs and I press the oozing tip to my jeans. Bazil's nostrils flare as if he can scent the trace of blood and he pushes to his feet.

"Come now, don't be shy, children. Let the granddaughter of Delilah Lovelace step forward. You have entered here because of her, have you not?"

"Stay where you are, Bazil," Nox warns. "I know your tricks."

"Yes, yes, I'm oh so tricky. But I just want a look, I promise."

The nearer the devil gets, the harder my heart pounds, and by the time he's a few steps away, my heartbeat feels like a galloping horse trampling over my chest. He's monstrous in size and appearance. Nox and the others guard me closely, but when Bazil narrows the distance to peer through the gap between Nox and Fitz, my breath fizzles.

I was wrong to think of him as a man, because he is definitely not. He might have resembled Dr. Facilier before at the old well, but now he's far from human. His huge muscled olive-green body resembles decaying bark. His eyes are green, but not the rich green of the woods . . . a putrid kind of green like sludge from a polluted river or the mold on a slice of rotting cheese.

"Hello, child."

I find my voice, though it wobbles slightly. "I'm not a child."

"It speaks!"

A glower forms before I can think the better of it. "I'm not an *it*, either."

"Lively, too," he says in an approving tone. "I'm glad you came, little Darika Lovelace. I will enjoy watching you try to escape my realm." His lips part in a mockery of a smile and his eyes drift to my shoulder. "I see you brought me a little snack."

Piku shrieks and dives, his terror clear. I don't blame him. I wouldn't want to be gobbled by this guy either.

"Where's my mom?" I ask.

The fiend grins, the sight of razor-sharp fangs making me tremble. "She's at the top of the tower, waiting for you to rescue her. Are you her knight in shining armor, Darika, or just a helpless princess?" He laughs when I refuse to answer, only raising my brows. "I'll tell you what. I'll make it easy for you. Get through the nine levels of my maze and save your mother. If you make it to the end, you can go free."

Even I know that that seems like a trick . . . and too good to be true. His maze is probably impossible, and we'll end up stuck in here forever. "That doesn't seem like much of a deal," I shoot back, totally faking swagger. "You're trapped in here, too. How do I know you'll keep your end of the bargain? And how do I even know that my mom's here? You could be lying."

Bazil's face lights with pleasure. "Smart girl. Well, let's see, shall we?"

He waves an arm and one of the walls shimmers with a burst of magic. A small yelp flies from me at the sight of my mother sleeping on the small cot I'd seen before. Her chest rises and falls. I frown—this could be a trick too.

"Mom?" I say.

My mother lurches up at the sound of my voice, her face twisting toward us and eyes going wide, as if we're somehow visible to her as well.

Her face contorts. "Rika, no, you have no—"

And before she can finish what is obviously a frightened warning—*no idea what I'm doing, no business being here, no hope of victory?*—the wall goes blank and back to normal.

"So now you know, Mummy Dearest is alive and well," Bazil pronounces. He studies me for a long moment, seeing the twist of my mouth and the mistrust in my eyes. "And yes, I could be lying, but Lennox here knows that your mother is indeed here, don't you, dear boy? Her magic is delicious, just like her daughter's."

"We go with her," Nox replies referring to this nine-level challenge.

"Naughty, naughty Minder, you know that's against the rules," the devil says. "The contender of my maze goes in alone." Nox's fists clench as Bazil cants his head, still staring at me. "But I'll tell you what: since I'm in such a generous mood, I'll allow it just this once." He wrinkles his brow. "Considering that she's an infant in the ways of magic. If she lasts longer with your help, it will be more entertaining, at least."

I bite my tongue and curb my sarcastic response. I'm glad he thinks me helpless. Underestimating me will be his gravest mistake. I square my shoulders and meet his soulless muck-green eyes. "So all I have to do is solve your dumb maze and we go free, including my mother and Papa Bois."

His mouth twists, a strange quizzical expression descending over his face. For a moment, his entire appearance morphs into another—one that resembles a bearded man with intelligent eyes—but the mirage is gone as fast as it appears. I blink. That was kind of weird. Then again, he's a devil, so who knows what trickery he's capable of? For all I know, Papa Bois's soul has already been devoured, and my mom's is next.

Bazil smirks, shaking with mocking laughter. "Yes, resist and overcome the trials in my maze, and you all win. Simple enough for a baby witch, yes?"

Ignoring his taunts, I drop my hands to my pocket to palm the bracelets and pot tucked in there. I hope it will help with whatever Bazil has up his sleeve. Obviously, I can't trust him, but I need something more to go on. I remember the vow I'd made in the grove with Monique, when I couldn't speak a word about the strange things I'd seen, and the magic that had shivered across my skin to seal my lips. Would such magic work here?

Shoulders back, I say, "Swear that you won't interfere in the trials once they begin and that we will all be safely released when we reach the end."

"Such confidence for such a paltry human," he murmurs. "I see Delilah in you. Where is she, by the way? I would have sworn she would be glued to your side."

Wait—hadn't Granny's blockage been *his* doing? "She couldn't enter."

Surprise flickers through his gaze as Bazil folds his arms across his chest. "Pity. I would have loved to see an old friend. Delilah was once a force to be reckoned with."

"Still is," I say, despite the bothersome fact that something else had stopped my grandmother from entering the tree. It doesn't make any sense, but I can't worry about that right now. "Stop stalling. Your word, Bad John." Fitz gives me an approving wink that bolsters my bravado.

"Lord Bazil to you, child," Ushara growls.

"Ouch," he says, pressing a fist to his heart. "You wound me. I have a name, you know."

I roll my eyes and glance at Nox before taking the most grandiose bow. "Your word, Lord Drama Devil?"

Nox grins as Fitz bites back a cackle, but Bazil's dark green lips curl down, irritation at my cheekiness flashing in his eyes. "Very well. I give you my word I won't interfere. But if you lose, you have to give me a thimbleful of your blood."

"Rika, no," Hazel hisses. "He'll use it to control you forever."

I get the warning, really I do, but we won't lose. I *can't* lose. Not with my mom's life on the line. I shoot Hazel a we've-got-this expression and then nod at Bazil. "Deal."

"Good luck, witchen," he drawls, and I scowl. I'm really starting to hate that word, or at least the way he says it . . . as though I'm a toddler with zero skills. I grunt. Who am I kidding? I've never done magic before. A grin pulls wide over his face as if he can see right through me. "It's six o'clock in the evening now. You have until sunrise. Twelve hours should be enough, don't you think?"

"Wait, what?" I squeak.

"You did not specify a time limit in your terms," he says with smug glee. "So I'm giving you one."

I grimace, resisting the urge to push past Nox and clock him right in the jaw, all-powerful being or not. "I didn't know I could, you cheater!"

Bazil's laughter is full of satisfaction. "What did you expect from a devil?"

12

WHOEVER SAID QUESTS ARE FUN STRAIGHT UP LIED

"You just had to go and antagonize him, didn't you?" Monique grumbles for the dozenth time as we stumble through a tunnel that smells like dirty socks.

"I didn't see you helping," I retort. "And give me a break for only just learning last week that monsters and magic exist."

She turns away. "This was a mistake."

I blink, the bleakness in her tone trickling through. She sounds . . . regretful, but it's not like she has anything to feel guilty about. "I'm the only shot we have."

"Yes, well, that's great," she snaps in a hard voice. "Since we now have a time limit, genius."

I bite my lip. Yes, that blunder is squarely on me. Honestly, though, *most* of my plans are stitched together with an armful of bluster, a few facts, and a whole lot of luck. Not that we're having much of the last at all. A wry smile curls my lips—hey, at least we're in the tree. That's farther than anyone else got, so that counts, right?

"I'm sorry I messed up the time thing," I say.

"Whatever."

Nox growls. "Chill, Monique. It's not her fault. It's ours—we should have been better prepared for naming the terms. Anyway, the first time you saw Bazil, don't forget that you cried and might have peed yourself a little."

"That was Fitz."

"Ay!" Fitz shouts from behind us. "It was definitely not me."

Monique sniffs, but doesn't speak anymore. Truth is, I was close to peeing my pants too. I scrub a palm over the back of my neck, sensing a thousand cobwebs skating over my skin again. I don't even want to think about the size of the spiders that are in these tunnels, but we don't have much choice.

"Piku, you okay?" He'd tucked himself in the hood of the sweatshirt I borrowed from Nox when we faced Bazil and hasn't reemerged since. A part of me wishes I'd left my iguana buddy with Granny. Poor thing.

"Fine, human. Don't worry about me. I have the heart of a dragon, you know."

I stifle my giggle and trudge onward. "I know."

Three tunnels of varying sizes appeared at the end of the room where that two-timing devil grinned like he was gorging on cake. One of the tunnels had been much too small and would have required a lot of crawling and wriggling. Another smelled like rotten broccoli. Just the first whiff made my eyes water. And the third and final tunnel had been as black as pitch and made every single hair on my body stand at attention. Luckily, we had Monique. Which meant we had fire and light, even if it reeked of sweaty gym socks.

So tunnel number three it is, not that any of us are happy about it.

"Why is this tunnel so long?" Fitz whines, his voice echoing through the shaft.

Hazel sniffs. "Because it's meant to discourage you from trying to beat the maze, dummy."

"I'm hungry."

"You're always hungry," she says.

On cue, my stomach lets out an obnoxious rumble. I haven't eaten since this morning, which seems like an eternity ago. As it turns out, confronting a shady monster and being trapped in his maze of uncertainties can really take the energy out of a girl.

I'm starving. In fact, I'm so hungry that I start to imagine I'm smelling the most divine food ever put on this planet. Something like crisp roasted chicken in thick gravy teases my nose, followed by the mouthwatering scent of fresh-baked rolls.

"Um, guys?"

Fitz groans. "Weys, what is that smell?"

"You smell it too?" I ask him warily, knowing how tricky things can be and not trusting myself. Or my rapidly palpitating nostrils.

"*Yes.*"

The tunnel finally ends and we tumble into another room. A massive table straining under the weight of hundreds of mouthwatering dishes meets our eyes. Platters upon platters stack the enormous surface. Brown sugar–baked ham with cloves and pineapple slices, delicious yellow pastelles wrapped in banana leaves, simmering yellow curry with thick chunks of meat and vegetables, mounds of fragrant rice, golden plantains, and fruit galore.

After we all emerge, the tunnel collapses behind us. I jump. Even though I'm distracted by the sight and smell of the food, I force myself to be smart and scan the area. Two walls, the caved-in tunnel behind us, and what appears to be a stone-shaped door at the end with no handle. I last approximately five seconds being smart before turning back to the table. My stomach gurgles. When did I get so *hungry*?

I'm actually drooling. Fitz rushes the table and starts cramming food into his mouth, and I hustle to do the same like a ravenous zombie with one goal: to feed.

"Is this a trap?" Piku growls.

Horrified, I stall midstride. "Hang on, Fitz, stop!" I shout, barely able to form actual words in my salivating mouth when all I want to do is dive teeth-first into the nearest dish, which happens to be my favorite—macaroni pie. I almost faint at the rich scent and the hot, bubbling, creamy, cheesy goodness. "What if it's a trick? Like in the Greek underworld and we get stuck here forever?" Bazil and Hades probably have a lot in common.

Fitz gapes at the rest of us, eyes full of horror. "I already ate some." He wipes his mouth on his sleeve and then forms a watery smile. "I'll just be the guinea pig, then. If I explode or start melting, don't eat the food."

Nothing happens for a few seconds and Fitz nervously swallows the rest of whatever's left in his mouth. Suddenly, out of the blue, a crack of light emerges under the stone door without a handle. There's no more movement. Curiouser and curiouser. It has to be a clue or something.

"Eat some more, Fitz," Nox says suddenly.

I glower at Nox. "Don't make him do that."

"He's already eaten and seems fine. Besides, I have a theory," he explains, and gestures for Fitz to continue. We watch as he gobbles down a meat pie, and after a few more seconds, the door cracks open a tiny bit more.

"We have to eat to open the door," I deduce.

"Looks that way," Nox says.

Grimacing, I stare at the mountain of food and the sliver beneath the door. There's no way one person can eat enough to get it open all the way. We're going to have to do this together. If I were alone, I'd never make it out of this room. Or it would take days, not hours. That's how Bazil traps so many souls in the tree.

"Hope everyone's hungry," Nox says. "Let's eat."

Hazel shrugs and heads over to the table, helping herself to a huge slice of corn bread. My mouth waters, but I'm not convinced. I've read Percy Jackson. Challenge quests always mess with you. "What if we're really eating dirt and thinking it's delicious when it's dirt?"

"Then dirt never tasted so good," Fitz says through a mouthful of pholourie and chutney, a dish that's fried split pea

149

and flour dough balls with a spicy dipping sauce. Saliva pools under my tongue.

I watch as Monique bites into a chicken drumstick, and feel myself start to sway on my feet. I'm so hungry I feel dizzy.

"Do you think it's safe?" I ask Nox. "What if it kills us?"

Monique is the one who answers. "Bazil doesn't get anything if you get stuck here for all eternity. He gets a kick out of watching us. He won't disrupt you this early, trust me."

"It's the first trial," Nox says thoughtfully. "We need to eat to get out of here before time runs out."

What a choice: eat and fail, or don't eat and fail.

Stop thinking about failure, you ninny. That means he'll steal your soul.

Nox holds out a handful of warm, fluffy paratha roti to me. That's it. That's all it takes for my willpower to disappear. I snatch the buttery flatbread like it's going to grow legs and run away, and swallow it whole. As we dig in and fill our bellies, the stone door rises a half-inch at a time.

But it's working!

We eat until my belly feels like it's going to explode. The feast reminds me of Thanksgiving dinner back home—first courses, second courses, third courses, dozens of desserts. Keeping an eye on the door, I gorge myself until my eyes start to close from sheer exhaustion.

I'm so tired. Maybe I'll close my eyes for five minutes.

Wait. *Wait.* There's something I have to do. I frown, tapping at my brow as if I can make the knowledge appear. Well, whatever it is, I'm sure it can wait.

A huge, boisterous belch makes me nearly fall out of my

chair. Fitz burps again and I cross my fingers that no more wind comes out of him. "Gross, dude!" I say.

Giggling at his expression, I shake my head. Then my eyes find Nox, who is covered in pastry crumbs and slumped in his own chair, while Hazel and Monique softly snore in a plush sofa near the blazing fireplace. My frown deepens. Where did that sofa come from? A soft lullaby begins to play, and my entire body slouches with a blissful groan.

"Oy, don't go to sleep!" Piku nips at my fingers, making me wince and bolt upright. "Rika, wake up. You don't have time to waste, remember?"

Oh. My. Skittle. Fairy.

"It is a trap!" I yell at the top of my lungs, making Nox startle awake and Fitz topple off his seat. Hazel murmurs and goes back to her nap. "The food, the hearth, everything. Wake up!"

"Ten more minutes," Monique whines.

"No. Don't go to sleep. We got the door open, but there's still a clock, you guys. Come on, wake up! Bazil's just trying to stop us from getting to the first level!"

"What happened? I want to conk out," Fitz murmurs around a bite of stodgy fruit-filled black cake and clutches the bloated stomach that's peeking from beneath his shirt.

"Food coma," I say, guessing he means he's going to pass out. "Sneakiest trick in the bad-guy handbook."

"I can't move," he moans from the floor. He pokes his snoring twin. "Hazel, get up, and then help me get up."

Nox's brown cheeks are dusky with embarrassment. He got tricked too, but this time we're all at fault here. I offer him a smile. "We needed to eat the food, Nox. You said it yourself: we had to open the door."

He doesn't smile back. "I should have known there'd be a trick. Bazil doesn't do things for free. There's always a cost."

"Live and learn, Granny always says. The door is open, and we're fed and no worse for wear, so let's go." I give Piku a pat. "Thank goodness for you."

"Dragon power," he says with no small amount of pride.

I dig into my pocket for my old flip phone. There's no service—no surprise there—but the clock still works. It's just past dinnertime, which means we have less than ten hours before sunrise by my count. I yawn, my body too weak to carry on.

"Here," a sluggish Hazel says, shoving a glass into my hand that she fills with her magic. "Drink this. Water will help you feel less tired. Move around and jiggle your body if you can."

She fills a large cup for everyone, and we do as she says. If we'd fallen asleep, it could have been much worse. After doing a dozen jumping jacks to get my blood flowing, I head for the door that's almost three-quarters of the way open—enough for us to crawl through on our hands and knees.

"Over there, come on!"

A groaning Fitz is followed by his twin. Only Monique looks normal, though her eyes are red-rimmed from her cat-nap. She tries to act above it all, but she fell for the same ploy we did. Rolling my eyes, I clamber through the doorway and gasp. I mean . . . we're kind of inside a tree and what I'm looking at is fantastical.

A huge warren of vine-ridden walls and groomed hedges

extends out as far as the eye can see, also climbing upward in places like several multidimensional levels. I've never seen a maze like this before. It reminds me of *Minecraft*.

"That's the next part of the maze?" Fitz bursts out. "That thing is massive."

"It's bigger than a baseball field," I agree. And totally not all vertical like I expected for a tree. Then again, this is a *magic* realm.

"Baseball?"

I glance at him, remembering that cricket is the most popular sport played here in Trinidad. It's a similar bat-and-ball game as baseball, with runs counted, only there are two wickets that players run between instead of four bases. Granny had taught it to me in the front yard of her house. "Cricket oval, then."

He nods, shading his eyes and whistling. "Weys, papa. Bigger than that, even."

"There's something in the middle," Hazel announces, pointing over the neatly cut hedges to what looks like a tiny ring of pillars from this distance. The shimmering stone stands out in the sea of green. "Maybe that's where we have to get to."

This place is Bazil's domain. With our luck, those hedges will probably have teeth and try to scarf us down.

"Come on," Nox says, taking the lead. He's obviously still salty about the food, but beating himself up isn't going to help anyone and we have an entire maze to solve before the sun comes up.

I have a trick up my sleeve, too. I wasn't humblebragging about being good at gaming. Before I got into art, I was addicted to role-playing games. Dad got me into RPGs . . . but then he met my stepmom and my baby stepbrothers came along. After that, he didn't seem to have time for me or our shared passion anymore.

Gaming became . . . lonely. But then for my tenth birthday, Dad got me a sketchbook and a tablet fully loaded with drawing tutorials and applications, and I felt connected with him again. I bite back homesickness. I miss him. I miss my dad and my stepmom, Cassie. Even my annoying little brothers, Theo and Max. I guess I'm risking my life for all of them, too. Because if Bazil truly is the harbinger of the apocalypse, then no one will be safe. *Anywhere.* My overstuffed stomach rolls a little.

"Any ideas?" Nox asks. "I'm not great at mazes."

Banishing my worry, I focus on the task at hand. "Can we use magic? Like use your wind to levitate us to the other side?"

"The walls would just grow," he says. "We can't cheat; we have to go through and outsmart it."

Mazes have patterns, and most are easily solved if you know how to read them, but you can quickly get frustrated. Especially when faced with a dead end or sent right back to where you came from. At the start, I place a palm on one wall, feeling a slight hum beneath my fingertips. It's surprisingly warm and alive. I suppose things are never what they seem in here. I'm going to have to trust my gut to escape.

"Follow me," I say. "I have an idea."

"Do you know what you're doing?" Piku asks.

"Maybe."

Monique lets out a loud sigh. "Great, we're going to be walking in circles forever."

I shoot back, "Do you have a better idea?"

"Yes. Figure it out while we're inside."

Thanks to me, we'd done that to get in the tree and ended up in a maze with a countdown.

"Sometimes it pays to pause for a full minute and think about things." The words are out of my mouth before I can stop them. I sound like Dad. I remember when he said that to me after the school called him in for the vandalism. I'd scowled and turned away, lost in my own bitterness, but I guess some of it sank in. "My dad said that," I add quietly.

"He sounds really smart," Hazel says, bumping my shoulder with hers.

I bite my lip. "He is."

"So tell us your idea," Nox says.

"The key is not to let your palm up," I say with more confidence. "Ever. Keep it on the wall, and we should get to where we need to be."

He gives me a puzzled glance. "That's all?"

"People think that there's maybe a number pattern, like turn right every second passageway, but sometimes, there's no rhyme or reason to these things. But Mom showed me this strategy once in Granny's house."

"Okay, worth a shot." He glances at the others. "Stay alert. We don't know who or what to expect. This is Bazil's playground. There're going to be traps everywhere."

"Like booby traps?" Hazel says.

Fitz, the toddler that he is, starts to giggle. "You said *booby*."

She shoves him. "What are you, five?" But I can't help grinning at him. Laughter—the one thing a girl can depend on in mortal peril.

Humor fading faster than normal, we enter the maze in single file, right palms to the wall. After a few dozen twists and turns, everything starts to feel the same. I'm doubting Mom's advice now, especially since that next turn is disappointingly similar to the turn we took fifteen minutes ago. It takes us into an identical clearing with a matching rock formation at the center, down to the bright green vines with tiny yellow flowers tracing the stonework.

My vision starts to waver and hope leaks from me like sand through my fingers. I'm not sure what Nox was worried about earlier either—the passageways have been empty except for us. Maybe Bazil intends to beat us with sheer boredom.

"This is a waste of time," Monique whines. "Water in the desert could freeze faster."

"You're welcome to try something else," I reply with a deep breath, getting a big whiff of air that smells like the lavender perfume my stepmom loves. Weird.

"Maybe I will."

Nox makes an exasperated sound. "No, we stick together. We're making progress."

"It seems the same to me as when we started," Fitz points out meekly.

"Yes," I say, inhaling again with a frown and then a slow grin. "But the *scent* isn't the same."

Fitz takes a big sniff, his eyes brightening. It definitely has a lavender aroma now when it had been more lemony before. Nox lets out a whoop. "You're right. The flowers are the real clues. They smell different each time we enter a new section of the maze. We're not actually walking in circles."

I twist to shoot him a thumbs-up. "See? Guess you're not as bad at mazes as you thought you were."

"You're the one who figured that out." He raises his free arm to fist-bump me and then stops. His eyes widen at something over my shoulder and I almost don't want to know what. But when Fitz lets out an audible gulp, I pivot on my toes.

A horde of douens are blocking our way with crazed looks on their little creepy faces, slobbering at us like we're the dessert from the room full of delicious food.

And they look *famished.*

13

DOUENS AREN'T CUDDLY LIKE EWOKS

Piku clicks his jaw and hisses. "They're getting closer!"

"There's like a hundred of them!" Fitz squeals.

More like forty, but with their little bodies swarming from every direction, it might as well be way more. I didn't think they were cute the first time I saw them dancing outside the tree, but this bunch ogles us, ravenous. One of them in front of me actually licks his chops like I'm a big ole slice of chocolate cake. "Um, should we be afraid?"

"They're usually docile," Nox says. "Mischievous, not feral."

I frown. "These guys don't exactly scream docile."

Nope, because we're going to crash and burn in the first trial and get attacked by a bunch of sharp-fanged, hairless hobbits with backward heels and knees. Why couldn't they have been like Ewoks in *Star Wars*? Now those were cuddly *and* adorable, even if they were mischievous.

Nox frowns. "Not if they're doing Bazil's dirty work." He eyes me and then the other Minders. "You know what to do. Rika, don't take your hand off that wall, whatever you do. We don't know if the labyrinth will change and try to throw us off course."

I watch as Nox and the elementals square off against the horde coming from each of the adjacent passages. He sends a blast of wind into their midst as they shriek with rage and converge on the Minders. I focus on keeping my hand lodged on the wall, though my fingers are already shaking from sheer pressure.

You have one job, Rika. Don't blow it.

Easy to say. Harder to do. Because now my palm is starting to sweat like my forehead after an overtime soccer game on a sweltering summer day.

Heat blasts into my face as Monique throws fireballs into the melee, making a handful of the monsters of mayhem holler as their clothes catch fire. Meanwhile, on the other side, Hazel is using her water magic to form a wave to block any more douens from entering the clearing. A few of them resemble muddy soccer clothes. To my right, Fitz yelps out a curse just as he sends a rope of vines to wind around four of the douens currently attached to his leg.

He howls in pain. "The nasty little turds are biting!"

My first thought is rabies. And then, *could* you get rabies

159

from a jumbie? Maybe there's such a thing as magical jumbie rabies?

Besides hyperventilating, there's nothing I can do to help my protectors, except for watch and leave my hand glued to the wall. I should be helping, not just observing, but what kind of magic can I do? Mind block them to death? The shield magic I'd used with Ushara in the market won't work, and I don't have any other skills besides painting. That makes me think of the tiny pot in my pocket that Granny gave me, but I groan in the same breath. I can't retrieve it *and* paint with one hand.

Feeling more and more useless, I inch my way forward as my hand remains pressed against the wall—the least I can do is continue to advance until the next turn so we're ready to make a run for it, if we have to. I glance up at what goes for the sky in Bazil's devil tree realm, even though rationally I know there's no actual sky here. It's a strange burnt-orange color that dapples the maze with sinister tones. Could be worse . . . it could be pitch-black. I swallow a lump in my throat at the thought of braving this maze at night.

My fingers pulse against the wall and thumping starts up in my ears again.

Whomp. Whomp. Whomp.

Bazil's near. And he's laughing at me . . . at the fact that I'm clearly way out of my depth. As he'd predicted. I grind my teeth, wanting to prove him wrong.

"What should I do?" I ask Piku.

"Throw rocks at them?"

That's . . . actually a really good idea!

I think back to what I know about douens, excitement

starting to course in my belly. According to Granny's stories, they were thought to be the lost souls of children who died before being baptized or christened. Despite how they've manifested right now—like goblins out of a horror movie—they're still little kids. And what little kid doesn't like candy?

"You're brilliant, Piku!"

"Yes, human, I know."

Shoving my hand into my pocket, I grab my bag of emergency Skittles.

"Rika, what are you doing?" a windblown Nox asks, strain evident in his voice.

"Hang on, I have an idea."

Please work, please work, please work.

Thank goodness there's a lot left since it's a sharing-size bag . . . not that I ever share with anyone, but desperate times call for desperate measures. I shake the bag, the sugary treats sounding like a magical bell in the clearing. "Hey, you creepy beasties, over here! Auntie Rika has a present for you!"

Every single douen halts at once, and then I'm the object of their laser-like focus, not that they have any eyes to speak of. Just gaping, diabolically glowing mouths . . . open and greedy and drooling. A chorus of whooping and hollering fills the space. Fitz covers his ears, and Hazel winces. My knees start to shake. There's no way I'll survive if they come at me all at once, even with the Minders on my side.

This was a mistake.

Panicking, I empty some candy into one hand and fling the handful as hard as I can to the opposite side of the clearing. The colorful rainbow pieces go soaring, and the douens' cheers grow louder. The sounds of the sugared pellets hitting the ground is eclipsed by the thunder of small feet moving like a herd of elephants in the same direction.

"It's working, Rika!" Fitz shouts, still clutching his ears.

Brimming with excitement, I toss another handful even farther, channeling all the energy I can muster in my throwing arm. Go, me! I have two more handfuls, which I deploy with glee, until the clearing is completely empty.

"There," I say with a proud grin, dusting the remnants of sweet shells off my palms. "That should keep them happy and off our heels for a bit. Hopefully, they'll hunt for every last one of those, because trust me, they're worth it. You have no idea the sacrifice I just made. Skittles are life. . . ." I turn and trail off at the dismayed look on Nox's face. My cheeks warm. "I mean, they're not life *life*, they're just candy, but they're pretty delicious."

"No, Rika, not that—" He rolls his lip and goes silent, but not before I see the frustrated flash of disappointment in his eyes that he tries to hide.

Why would he be *disappointed*? We won, didn't we? I look down. I'm fine. I haven't been bitten or anything. My eyes immediately go to Fitz, who is checking himself over, but he doesn't seem to be wounded either. Hazel is standing beside Monique, who's sporting a smug sneer.

"Well done, smarty-pants," my nemesis drawls, staring pointedly at my hands.

Following her gaze, I raise them to see if there's still sugar clinging to them, but they're fairly clean. I don't know what that tone is about. It was *my* idea and *my* Skittles that got rid of the douens! And then understanding hits me.

Son of a turd bucket.

I'm staring at *both* my hands . . . which means one of them is not where it should be. In other words, against the maze wall. Ugh. I had one job—one!—and I failed. My head falls as humiliation rushes through me. "I'm sorry, I wasn't thinking. I just wanted to help."

"I know, and you did. That candy was a brilliant idea," Nox says.

"I thought so too," Piku says loyally.

Monique tuts. "Yeah, but now we're in no man's land."

I spin around in alarm. Of course she's right. I couldn't even say where I'd stood last and what the next turn should be.

"She gets it, Monique," Hazel snaps, and I see Monique's eyes widen at the scolding from her usually mild-mannered friend. "Rika tried to help. Everyone makes mistakes. Your blood isn't on the line here."

I try to rally at the support, but it's no use—I can't tell the walls apart. "No, but I messed up. I shouldn't have taken my hand off the wall. Now we have no idea where to go."

"It's not your fault," Fitz says.

"It *is*. I should have shared my idea instead of wanting to be the hero. I guess I didn't want to feel so useless while you guys were, you know, doing all the work."

Nox walks to my side, every trace of his earlier frustration gone. "You're not useless, Rika. And from now on, we do this together, okay? Hazel's right: we all make mistakes. When I first got my magic, I thought I could handle a jumbie invasion on my own and caused a windstorm that nearly took out Arima, a well-populated town to the east of Port-of-Spain. Grandma Love helped me learn to control my magic." He gives my shoulder a reassuring squeeze. "We're a team. We will figure out how to beat this maze."

My heart warms at that. Exhaling, I lift my chin.

"We don't have much time until the douens come back," Hazel says in a low voice. "Anyone have any suggestions?"

"I do," Monique volunteers.

I stare at her with suspicion. Technically, as a Minder, she *should* want to safeguard her magic and save the king of the wood, but maybe her dislike of me goes deeper than duty to protect the trinity or her love for my grandmother. She wants *me* to lose more than anything, and that makes her dangerous.

"Someone said before that there are different smells," she says, and I scowl—Monique knows very well it was my idea. "If that's true and the scent here is lavender, we know lemon is the wrong direction. So we can use that to get to the next section."

I let out a surprised breath. That . . . makes a lot of sense.

"Good thinking," I tell her grudgingly. Even if the distrust is mutual between us, I'm a big believer of giving credit where it's due. Girls have enough problems without ganging up on each other.

She shoots me a weird look that's half gratitude, half puzzlement. "Thanks."

"Wait, what if the smells are a trick too?" Fitz asks. "Leading us to a dead end?"

Nox frowns. "They could be, but then we can always go back and try another path. Monique is on to something. Stick together. I wouldn't put it past the maze to shift to split us up."

He's not wrong. We each throw our noses into the air and take a deep whiff. I bite back a snicker at the concentration on Fitz's face. He's like a miniature bloodhound, sniffing a track around the perimeter. Even Nox's nostrils are flared wide, air whooshing in and out as he inhales deeply with every step. "Found lemon," Nox says. "So . . . not that way."

"Try here," Hazel calls out. Faint lavender leads us down another passageway. Unfortunately, that one leads to a dead end. We retrace our steps.

Fitz points to a right-hand turn leading into another section of the maze. "Over there smells different—like vanilla."

We hustle over to where he's standing, and sure enough, I breathe in freshly baked sugar cookies. So all we have to do is follow our noses to the next scent. Maybe that one will be brownies. We fall into formation again, with Nox leading and me at the center, the guard of Minders on either side.

I swallow my worry as everyone keeps sniffing the air and we hurry through this new section. There's nothing in here but graveled stone and more bright green vines with the same clusters of yellow flowers, though I can't help sensing that we're being watched or followed. Neither option is reassuring.

I nearly crash into Nox, who has stopped. "What's the pro—"

But my question breaks off abruptly as I cringe and almost dry heave. The most hideous odor comes from the next turn. Instead of getting delicious, chocolatey brownies, I breathe in a whole lot of sewer scum with a dash of fish guts on the side. Barf! The other side smells like spring water again. Spring water, it is.

Dead end!

Groaning, we head back to the rank path. It's even more pungent than before, making my eyes water. Gross. I guess Bazil, aka the devil drama llama, wasn't going to make this easy or pleasant. Hazel ducks her face inside her shirt, and Monique lets out a miserable moan. Even Piku disappears down my shirt pocket, and I'm pretty sure he encounters yucky things all the time as a lizard.

"Oh, geed! Hope you can hold your breath while you run," Fitz mutters, going a bit green.

Gross indeed. I don't even bother to remind him that our entire current plan of action on solving this part of the maze is based on *sniffing* our way through it. After retreating a couple steps to inhale one last whiff of unpolluted air, I take off.

With any luck, this reeking section will be quick. But the farther we go, the longer it seems, and the worse it gets.

This maze literally stinks.

14

TIME TO LEVEL UP

My lungs are burning, my eyes are stinging. The others aren't faring much better either. Fitz is howling like he's on the brink of death-by-stench, and Nox just made a gagging noise. We'll be lucky if we don't vomit all over each other. When is this rotten part going to end?

Just when I think I can't take another second, we tumble past a pretty stone archway. I breathe in a tiny sip of air and nearly faint at the pure heaven of laundry-scented oxygen. Seriously, I'm transported to a memory of Granny folding freshly washed, air-dried sheets! I'd give my right nostril—maybe *both* my nostrils, at this point—to be back in my nice, comfy bed.

But Mom, Granny, and the magic . . . and the fate of the world . . .

Right, no pressure or anything.

Gulping in a huge lungful of clean air, I take stock of the new area. The thick moss-covered walls of the maze form a wide semicircle, with tall, upright stones in a ring at the center. It reminds me of a rock formation in England called Stonehenge that I learned about in history class. Funnily enough, there are myths about magic in that place, too. Maybe it's a portal to another realm just like the silk cotton tree is. That wouldn't surprise me. I'll bet there are all kinds of portals to different realms in places where a person would least expect it. The universe must be endless.

"What's this?" I ask, moving past the girls to Nox.

"A test, I think."

Great. Well, I knew the trials weren't going to be easy, not after our shaky start. The air shimmers between the huge stone pillars. I stick out a finger and push against a translucent barrier that springs back like some kind of elastic substance.

We got through the last part of the maze using our sense of smell. In any game, moving on to the next level means fighting a boss or completing a specific objective. So this is the boss. I rack my brain—what did we miss? I stare up at the five slender stones that are set in a circle. This is just another puzzle, but every challenge has its own set of clues and a key to solving it.

I try to shove through the pliable barrier and only end up flat on my rear. Monique laughs, and I scowl at her as Hazel helps me up. "If it makes you feel any better," Hazel tells me, "I was just about to try that."

I rub my sore behind. "Ten out of ten don't recommend. Unless you like bouncing off a sideways trampoline."

"This is the only way out, right?" Fitz murmurs, staring over our shoulders and wincing at the thought of returning to the last putrid section. I shudder. That's so *not* happening. I'd rather kick rocks. Good thing there's no shortage of them in here.

"Yes." Nox palms the back of his neck with one hand, frowning up at the stones, and I follow his stare.

Focus, Rika. You can do this.

There are five stones, and five of us.

"Okay, everyone, take a stone," I suggest. "See what you can spot, if there are any clues or signs that we can use to figure out how to get past this."

The others do as I say, even Monique, who surprises me. I stare at the cool oblong shape of my pillar, noting the beautiful quartz-like shading of its creamy exterior. I scrutinize the edges, frustration starting to bubble in my stomach. It is . . . just a pretty rock.

Pretty and devoid of clues!

Piku scrambles from my pocket and leaps onto the surface of the stone, his tiny claws digging in as he scrambles upward. "Piku, what are you doing?" I bellow. "You don't know what kind of magic is hidden in those things. Get down!"

But the stubborn reptile ignores me, scaling up almost to the top. He stops right at the center of the uppermost edge, and I squint at a drawing lightly etched into the rock face. "Wait, what is that?" I ask.

169

"A stick with a yellow orchid-like flower," Piku says after licking his eyeball, head tilting and peering down.

Light bulbs pop in my brain like fireworks on the Fourth of July. "That's a vanilla bean! *Vanilla*, like the smell of cookies." The only reason I recognize it is because Dad had bought them once at the grocery for a cake recipe and we had joked that they should be called vanilla twigs, not beans, based on the picture. I turn excitedly to the others, but am faced with an alarmed Hazel, whose brown complexion loses color as she glances over my shoulder. "What's wrong?"

"The douens," she cries. "They're coming!"

Fear erupts. If we don't figure this out, then we're going to be cornered by a bunch of insatiable jumbies with no way out. And I don't have any more Skittles. We have one chance to get this right before we're swarmed.

"Hang on," Hazel says urgently. "Does anyone remember the order of the scents from the last part of the maze?"

Monique narrows her eyes. "I think so. Why?"

"There are symbols carved into each of these rocks. I think if we get the order right, it could open up the next section." She cuts off with a squeak and cocks her head, listening to the pitter-patter of feet. *Many* feet. "The next level."

Nox purses his lips and nods excitedly. "Worth a try. Okay, first was lemon, then lavender, right?"

"What's next?" Fitz asks. "All I can remember is fish guts and rotten eggs."

"Me, too," I say. Maybe that scent was meant to confuse us. I wrinkle my nose, the lingering odor nasty.

"Hurry!" Hazel urges.

The ground starts to rumble and I shoot a glance to Fitz. "Please tell me that's your earth magic."

"Not me," he replies, eyes popping wide.

We don't have any more time to think back. I rush past Fitz to where Nox is standing. His rock glows a pale yellow color, and without pausing, I brace my open palm against the lemon icon. The barrier lights up into an almost glowing neon and stays lit. What's next? Lavender.

"Over here," Monique yells.

I rush to where she stands, with Nox on my heels. Her rock glimmers in a soft lilac color, and even though I didn't recognize the sprig of lavender, it looks purple enough for me. I slam my hand against the rock, which quickly shines even brighter. If I wasn't so scared of being eaten, the vivid hue would be cool, like the inside of a gaming arcade.

"This one!" Fitz shouts. I race over to him and crash my fist into the stone without even checking out the corresponding symbol.

The reverberation from the impact flings me to the ground, and suddenly the other colors fade, making the circle turn dark. What the heck just happened? The ground rumbles even harder, pieces of the rock shearing off, a huge crack zigzagging up the center of the rock.

"That wasn't right," I gasp. "We must have messed up the order. What was this one?"

We peer up at the top of the stone, but the symbol there isn't clear. The mini-quake had made the top of the gray stone slough off. It's down to the law of chance now. Which one's the right choice, if we can't see the matching symbol? *No, no, no*. We can't afford to make any mistakes, especially if the rocks crack apart.

"Quick!" Hazel screams from the other side, her voice strained as if she's using her water magic to block the passage. "They're almost through. I can't hold them back much longer!"

Huffing a breath, I hustle back to the first stone—lemon yellow—and press my palm against it. The same neon color flares forth as I race to the second, lavender. Purple brightens the circle. I skip past the third gray pillar that had broken the pattern and waver between the last two. One is a pale blue and the other is the vanilla bean Piku had discovered.

Think, Rika!

But I *can't*. My brain feels completely fried, fear beating an ugly drumbeat in my ears and drowning out everything else.

"Vanilla," Fitz prompts. "That's next, remember?"

I lift my arm and hesitate. If I make a mistake, this will cost us. My gaze pans between the bluish stone and the cream-colored one. We don't have time for any more mistakes.

"What are you waiting for?" Monique snaps. "Do it."

Halting, I shake my head. No, this doesn't feel right. There was something else before the vanilla turn. I'd been tickled at how ridiculous we'd all looked sniffing like bloodhounds, but there had to have been another scent. The stench of sewage must've only been a distraction.

I step in front of the blue stone and exhale.

"That's the wrong one!" Monique shouts the words just as I thump my palm onto the surface. The rock glows blue, the scent of fresh spring water filling my nostrils. It had led to a dead end twice, but my gut had said it still counts for this piece of the puzzle. Five stones, five smells.

"Now the vanilla," I say, and tap on the first pillar Piku had climbed. It, too, lights up. Hazel rushes in, breathless, just as we reach the last—it's still an ominous gray color with that crack stretching up its middle. I send up a fervent wish that it isn't broken. This one has to be laundry.

Please work, please work.

With a shaky breath, I put my palm to it. The responding lights gleam so brightly that I have to squint. I see the others doing the same, and even through my nearly shut lids, I can feel the heat as the colors merge into a whirling kaleidoscope. Something's working! Air whooshes around my head, lights flashing like we're on some kind of amusement park ride, and then suddenly, there's darkness and silence.

Tentatively, I crack open one eye.

Oh, thank goodness. The maze has transported us into a new section!

Fitz claps me on the back so hard that I grunt at the pressure. "You did it!"

"Not me. Hazel guessed the puzzle," I mumble, relief rushing through me. "Plus, Piku was the one who saw the symbol. Everything after that was pure luck."

"Don't underestimate yourself, Rika." The quiet praise is from Nox. "You got the order right."

"Team effort," I say with a blush, and then busy myself scanning the new area. Seven levels left out of the nine, which seems like a lot, but we're making progress. We just have to be fast and not run out of time.

Now to assess the next level of this banana-pants maze . . . Yeah, it looks *hard*.

Like requires a ton of physical effort hard.

The stones had spit us out into some kind of rolling countryside and we're standing in front of a huge obstacle course. There's a thin walkway stretching across some kind of pit after several pieces of rope hanging at intervals from trees, a massive mud pit, a climbing structure, and like actual flames shooting up in the distance.

"We have to get across *that*?" Hazel squeaks.

Even Monique blanches, her golden-brown skin going pallid. I have to admit, I'm not thrilled either, especially when I get a good view of the sharpened stakes at the bottom of the enormous pit. If we fall, that's certain death. Plus, I hate heights.

I hide my dismay. The Minders might have a chance since they're not your average humans. Unlike me. No amount of magic will stop a stake from tearing through delicate human skin. I shudder and wrap a hand around my middle. I'm athletic enough from soccer, but I'm not a flying superhero. Though the Minders might be.

"Can you airlift us over?" I ask Nox hopefully.

"I can try." But even as he concentrates to call the winds, he can barely pick himself off the ground. "Magic must be diluted for this trial," he says with a gasp. "I think we each have to complete the task."

"We can do this," Fitz says confidently. "Just follow me."

We all watch as he runs to the first rope, reaching up for the second and swinging himself across to the other side of the gulch before dancing across the plank like a trained acrobat. He gestures for us to come along.

"It's a breeze, Hazel," he says to his twin as she leaps for the first rope.

When my turn comes, I suck in a few calming breaths that do nothing except to make me more terrified. Adrenaline courses through my veins, my heart nearly bursting through my rib cage. The ropes I can handle—they're just like the rope swings over the lake back home.

I do that part with ease and then balk. The plank over the stakes is so narrow, barely the width of a gymnast's balance beam. I'm not a clumsy person, but I'm not exactly graceful either. And being nervous about how high it is and getting impaled doesn't help.

"You've got this, Rika," Hazel calls out. Yeah, even with all her nerves, she'd made it seem as easy as Fitz had.

"Don't look down." That piece of advice is from Monique, who is already waiting on the other side too. She had zoomed past Hazel to get across the thin beam right after soaring through the ropes. I envy her bravery.

"One foot in front of the other," Nox encourages from behind me. "I'm right here. I'll be behind you the whole way."

I'm not usually the kind of girl who needs a boy to help her, but I'd be lying if I said I don't mind Nox having my back. Not that he could do anything to help me if I tumble into oblivion . . . but his presence is still comforting.

Placing my right foot on the plank, I test it with my weight. It doesn't move. With a little more confidence, I step out with my left, keeping my weight dead center. I repeat the action six more times until I'm in the middle of the plank and halfway across. I try not to glance at my feet—*thanks for the idea, Monique*—but almost can't help myself. With effort, I keep my gaze straight ahead.

Nearly there.

Suddenly, the ground rumbles, making me squat and straddle the beam with my hands and legs. "Fitz, cut it out!" I shriek. "This isn't funny."

"That's not me!" His eyes widen at something—or someone—behind us.

I glance over my shoulder. Ushara is across from us, grinning, hands outstretched, and doing some kind of chant that makes the ground quake. Soil starts to crumble down the banks on either side. "Don't fall, little girl," she sings out.

"Ignore her," Nox says from behind me. "The bridge will hold, trust me."

I start to pant with fear. "It doesn't feel stable."

All I can do is hang on as the reverberations continue, nearly dislodging the plank from one end of the gorge. I have to move! It's not ideal, but I drag myself along like a spider monkey, clinging for dear life. Those sharp stakes look way closer and way *pointier* than before. I gulp.

"Almost there, Rika," Piku says in my ear.

I'm surprised he's still with me. I would have left by now and taken my chances on my own. The fact that he hasn't abandoned ship gives me some courage.

"One step at a time, Rika," Nox murmurs. He's right behind me as promised. I push myself up, despite my unsteady knees, and crawl the last few steps to the others. Just as I claw my way to solid ground, a huge boom tears through the disintegrating earth and the plank goes tumbling down into the spiked ravine, taking Nox along with it. Ushara cackles madly.

"Nox!" I scream, scrambling to the collapsed edge of the ravine. Fitz and the others drop beside me, their faces frantic.

Is he . . . *gone*? I don't even want to check the bottom, fearing a gruesome sight of Nox. But he's nowhere to be seen. I rock back to my haunches, stomach souring and fearing the worst. When one soil-crusted, brown arm launches itself over the edge, followed by an equally dirt-covered face and body, I'm beyond relieved. He's alive!

Together with the others, we drag Nox up and over until we collapse into a heap. Maybe he'd had enough wind magic to propel himself to the side. Or maybe it was pure luck. Either way, that was too close for comfort. Nox could have died. We both could have.

"I thought you said the plank was stable!" I say and punch him.

He rubs his chest with a wan smile. "It was until there at the end. You did great."

I huff a breath and fold my goose-pimpled arms. Suddenly, these trials feel too monumental. Because there's more than a good chance we could get hurt in here, and unlike online games, there are no magical health items and no respawning in real life.

There are no second chances, no restarts or resets.

If we lose . . . the game's literally over.

15

KID-SHAPED WAFFLES AREN'T ON THE MENU

There's no way we're escaping this place. Like our chances are completely zilch.

I'd had the desolate thought before, after Ushara made Nox fall, that we could die, but there'd been a tiny part of me that had been hopeful that we could do this . . . that we could still beat the stupid maze because we're in it together. We've got each other's backs.

Until this particular trial.

Because it's definitely impossible.

The earth had rumbled where we'd collapsed at the end of the pit of stakes, making me feel like it was going to buckle beneath us, before shifting into a dark, weird space with a metal door at the end leading to the next level. It was disorienting, but I'm getting used to the tree's transformations. Sort of. I squash down newfound nausea in my belly. Okay, maybe not.

"This place is full of suckage," Piku mutters from his spot in my hoodie, making me snort. He's starting to sound like me instead of an iguana-sized Baby Yoda.

But he's right. It really is sucky.

Because behind door number one, the next trial looks like a giant waffle iron. Make that a dozen waffle irons all squeezing in at different intervals, waiting to make children-shaped waffles. No lie . . . it's a passage of moving parts.

I gulp at the many interlocking pieces, pumping up and down and then sideways, like a sandwich press, and can instantly imagine my bones flattening. I suppress a shiver and catch Fitz doing the same. For all his bluster with the previous challenge, he's balking now. No one wants to be squished and none of the Minders can use their full elemental powers to prevent said squishing. Nox had already tested his and he's definitely not at maximum strength.

Technically, he could fly himself across, but it might take a miracle to survive intact. The timing would have to be perfect. Fire and water won't do anything, so Monique and Hazel are out of luck. Fitz can't earthquake his way out of the trial without bringing down the walls on us. And me, well, everyone knows that I'm the least capable with my puny shield-magic skills.

So basically, no cheat codes on this one.

Not even Piku, who can probably fit through anything.

We watch as Nox tosses a fist-sized rock into the mechanism. It misses the first set of hydraulic plates, bounces through the second, and we hold a collective breath as it just squeaks past the third. Maybe this is doable. I mean, if a rock can do it, bouncing at the right intervals, perhaps we have a chance too. But that idea is shot down when Hazel lets out a whimper as the rock is pulverized to dust between the last set of smashing metal plates. I gasp. That could easily be a human skull. *Our* poor, fragile human skulls.

"We can't do this," Nox says. "It's too dangerous."

I let out a shaky breath. "We don't have much choice. The only way out is through, remember?" I point at the ominous passageway that looks like the inside of a train engine with well-oiled steel parts. "To that door at the other end. And we can't go back unless we want to become barbecue."

We turn in unison, and sure enough, the maze has made a wall of flames at the end of the last section that's pretty much impenetrable. Monique shrugs—easy enough for her, since fire is her element—but that doesn't mean she won't have to brave a horde of angry douens *and* get to the start of the maze to make it back out. At this point, it's better to go forward than in reverse.

"One wrong step, though, and we're as flat as pancakes," Fitz says, his brown face a sallow color. I snort—good to know we're on the same wavelength with the food analogies. Waffles, pancakes, all the same batter.

Blowing air through my teeth, I squint at the problem facing us and consider the options. Like the previous puzzles, there has to be a key. We just need to figure out what that is. The metal parts move together seamlessly. The rock Nox had thrown had made it through three of the clamps, but that's because its momentum had slowed.

"Have any of you ever played *Super Mario World*?" I ask with a narrowed glance at the lethal pistons.

"The video game?" Monique scoffs with a scowl. "This isn't a joke, Darika."

I brush off her surly comment. Everyone is on edge. And meeting her energy won't help us get past the next trial.

"Is it like hopscotch?" Hazel pipes up.

I stifle a giggle. I forget that the Minders don't seem to care about social media or gaming like most other kids our age. Then again, who needs role-playing games when you can do actual magic?

"No, not exactly. There are a bunch of levels, and when you get to the end, you have to go through flames, then lava, and then flaming whips to get to the final castle to fight the boss. If you hesitate, you're toast."

She frowns as if trying to follow. "Okay?"

"So our game strategy is like that, except we're the characters trying to get to that door over there. Timing is key."

Hazel bites her lip and then gives a timid nod. "I guess that's one way of seeing it."

I don't share that I'm back to thinking of us as video game characters, considering I've just come face-to-face with the fact that we are live kids in a live gaming scenario with no second chances. But that's the only way my mind can assess the situation. I study the trap, watching each piece of it in motion like an efficient machine. The more I stare at it, the more doubtful

I get. Everyone has the same scared, disheartened expressions on their faces. The clock is ticking, too. I check the time on my phone and it's close to eleven. We'd lost hours in the first trial, barely making it out of our food comas.

I sigh and gnash my teeth in frustration.

"Don't give up, Rika," Piku whispers, his teeth nibbling my ear in a gesture I imagine is supposed to be comforting.

I crane my neck to peer at him. "Hey, you called me Rika and not *human*."

He licks his eyeball. "Yes, well, don't make me regret it."

"I don't suppose you have any ideas, do you?" I ask him. "From your long dragon memory?"

Piku makes a clicking noise. "This monstrosity is beyond my scope of experience, but every mystery has an answer, even the hardest ones."

Groaning, I resume staring at the moving pieces, my optimism fading by the second. My pulse drums in my ears, almost in time with the beastly mechanism. I huff a breath as my fingers start tapping against my leg—one, two . . . pause . . . three. One, two, three . . . pause . . . four. And repeat. It's like a beat that goes in time with each clang.

One that reminds me of a song . . . I used to have a pink music box heart that played a lullaby my mom always sang. *Rock-a-bye baby, on the treetop, when the wind blows, the cradle will rock. When the bough breaks, the cradle will fall. And down will come baby, cradle and all.*

Not ominous or anything.

I try to ignore the irritating beat and focus on the puzzle when I gasp. Wait a minute . . . it's a rhythm!

"There's a pattern!" I exclaim, blinking and counting it out once more just to be sure. "Listen closely and follow my fingers. You'll get it."

We concentrate as I tap out the tempo, and then I see the others' heads start to bob.

"Brilliant!" Fitz yells after shadowing me for a couple measures.

Excitement makes us rally. "So, we just have to count the beats to move past each clamp, and then we're home free."

"There's enough room that we can do it in two groups," Nox says, his eyes shooting a proud glance that causes me to grin. "I'll go first. Hazel, let's pair up." A still-apprehensive Hazel nods and then firms her lips. "Rika, you follow with Fitz and Monique once we're through, okay?"

I know why he wants to go first: to make sure those beats we've been counting out stay the same, to ensure we're safe. I wish there'd been room for the entire group to go through as one, but of course nothing can ever be that simple in this maze of mayhem and madness. A part of me worries about being separated from Nox and being stuck with Monique, whom I still don't trust, but at least I have Fitz. He won't shove me between two metal clamps when I'm not paying attention.

"Okay," Nox calls out, and I nearly leap out of my skin. "On my count."

I mimic the taps of his fingers with mine, counting evenly, my heart climbing into my throat with each beat. And then he and Hazel dart past the first, then the second. I lose sight of them for a pulse-stopping moment as two plates crash together.

Did they get squashed? The breath whooshes out of me

when I see them again, right before the place where the rock got smashed. My instant panic makes me lose my count, but I know Nox won't. A natural leader like him—son of Papa Bois and the future king of the forest—likely doesn't know how to fail.

I kind of wish I'd gone with him instead.

"We're through," his voice echoes from down the passageway. "Start when you're ready."

Squaring my shoulders, I try to get my racing heartbeat to calm, though that's a futile effort. "Just give me a second," I mutter to Fitz and Monique, hoping to catch my breath.

She shoots me a mean glare. "Oh, come on already!"

Piku hisses and flares his dewlap, making her eyes widen. "Relax, Minder. If you don't want to wait, you're more than welcome to go ahead alone."

Fitz cackles at the shock on Monique's face. Schooled by a reptile. I almost kiss my little scaly green hero, but I know he'll hate that. Monique, to no one's surprise, doesn't go on alone. Instead, she firms her lips and rolls her eyes as if this is beneath her. But it's the trace of fear in her gaze that stops me from saying anything petty. For all her bravado, Monique is just a scared kid like the rest of us.

On a whim, I reach out and take her hand, giving it a reassuring squeeze. She stares at me for a second, confusion blanking out the panic in her eyes. What resembles shame flashes there as well, but it's gone quickly when she snatches her palm away, cheeks going red.

Oh well, I guess I should have expected that.

Swallowing hard, I take a deep breath, and then another. If I don't go soon, I might never. I grab Fitz's hand with clammy fingers, and he takes hold of Monique's. "Okay, I'm ready."

I'm nowhere near ready, but it's now or never.

We stand in front of the machine, my heart thudding in my ears, and I count out the beats again. "Ready, steady . . . go!"

When the rhythm restarts, we edge past the first set of clamps, the banging sound of the metal smashing together behind us. The three of us are clumped together before the second set of compressors. I hadn't realized that they were larger than the first set. Longer, too. Doesn't matter—we have to stick to the plan . . . and most of all, the rhythm.

"Go!"

We dash through to the third, my heart beating so fast, my head feeling unsteady. The musical pattern restarts as we face the next set of clamps. I blink, my rapid pulse throwing off my tempo. Does it seem like the beat is faster? Or is that my imagination?

I'm sweating so much, the fingers of my free hand leave wet spots against my trembling leg. I eye the clamps. The next one is even longer than the first two. We will have to run to get through it alive.

"Go!"

Hustling to the final set of plates, the breath in my lungs is reduced to wheezing pants. Those last clamps seemed to close much faster than the ones before. White spots start to gather in my vision and my skin feels hot as though I'm on fire. It's not me, though. Monique is glowing, her entire body radiating waves of heat. She's terrified, I realize, and not actually trying to melt us.

"Nearly there," I whisper, the words scratching against my raw, burning throat. "Okay, now."

But the beat seems weird, discordant. My brain is so fuzzy that I can barely focus. We have to go—there's only one more clamp before safety—but something doesn't feel right. At the last moment before we move, I stumble and pull back, nearly colliding with Fitz behind me.

"What's wrong?" he huffs.

"I lost it," I say. "I can't feel the beat. It's too fast."

"Calm, Rika," Piku whispers. "Start from the beginning. You're safe in this spot."

But there's nothing except death by smelting if Monique gets any hotter. I don't point out that little nugget to Piku. And I have a bad feeling that the maze is once more trying to outsmart us. It has to be the reason I can't focus.

"You've got this!" Nox calls out from the other side. Down the long shaft of the widening compressors, I see his face, stoic, as though we aren't trapped behind two clanking metal plates that are designed to crush our bones to powder. "I'll count with you."

"The slabs got longer," I yell.

He nods. "You'll have to sprint, then."

Forcing my fears aside, I imagine me and my soccer ball and the goalposts on the other side of the clamps. We're in the last seconds of play with a tied game. I can do this. Focusing on Nox's face, I draw in a breath and release it. I clear everything out—all the noise, the heat, my fears, the hazy fog in my brain. And I count once more, shadowing his voice. One, two . . . pause, three. One, two, three . . . pause, four.

A crashing sound from behind makes me lose the rhythm as I peer over my shoulder. "What was *that*?"

"The passageway is closing!" Fitz shouts.

Of course it is.

Everything in this awful maze goes from bad to terrible in a blink. "I'm really starting to hate this place," I mutter.

"Starting to?" Fitz shoots back with a watery grin.

I grunt and refocus my efforts, ignoring the rumbling beneath my feet and the sound of metal parts grinding together, and find the beat again. An earsplitting crunch nearly makes me whirl around in a blind panic, but I stay the course.

I nearly drag the other two with me as we full-out gallop through the opening. Time stretches and it feels like we're sprinting forever, muscles burning and lungs aching, until the end comes in sight. Relief whooshes through me when someone crashes into me and I tumble straight into Nox. "Fitz, what the heck, dude?" I say and turn. But it's not Fitz, it's Monique.

"He shoved me," she gasps.

My eyes lift, watching the plates slide shut in agonizing slow motion, with Fitz barely past the middle. Holy death zone, those last two clamps have rows of teeth—like a monster-sized bear trap. He's not going to make it! I hadn't even realized we lost hold of each other, I'd been so focused on myself.

"Move, Fitz!" Chest squeezing, I jerk toward him, but Nox's arms restrain me as if he fears I'll run back between the shark-toothed slabs. "No!" I scream. "Let me go!"

"I've got this, Rika," Nox says, and sweeps in front of me.

Fitz's scream is loud, and I instantly fear the worst. But something propels him forward, I realize, peeking around Nox's shoulder. A sharp gust of wind almost shoves him off his feet. I feel Nox's body vibrate as more power bends from him. Sweat breaks out on his forehead, and his face goes purple with effort.

I wish I could help. For emotional support, I grab Nox's shoulder. Something sparks between us like a bolt of lightning, and I gasp. With one more huge burst of air, Fitz launches from the passage. I collapse against Nox, becoming suddenly and weirdly weak.

"Weys," Fitz wheezes as Hazel rushes over to tackle him in a hug. "I thought I was Fitz-food. Thanks for the assist, Nox."

"That wasn't all me," he says, a faint frown on his brow as he peers down to me. Fitz's gaze follows to where I'm standing, his eyes going wide.

I blink, not understanding. "Don't look at me, I don't have wind magic."

"No, but there at the end, something happened," Nox says quietly. "When you touched my shoulder, I got a boost. I couldn't even fly myself out of the pit in the last trial. Not being at full strength is like sipping instead of gulping. I know I couldn't have done that last bit without you."

Oh.

So does that mean my magic works? Though I'm not really

sure what kind of supernatural power I have, but that has to be good if it can boost a Minder's abilities, right? I stare at my hands, willing them to glow or do anything remotely interesting, but nothing happens. My excitement deflates. I guess I still can't do cool tricks, but at least I'm not a total dud.

"Thanks, Rika," Fitz says with a wobbly grin, pulling me into a hug. "You saved my butt."

I pat his back, blushing at the praise. "Well, we can't exactly do this without you. We're a team."

"Yeah, we are."

He holds out a palm, and I slip mine on top. Nox joins next, and then Hazel. Monique purses her lips, but then her hard gaze softens as she extends her palm to cover Hazel's. Piku jumps on the hand pile, and we all laugh. For one euphoric, perfectly awesome moment, we celebrate our slim victory against this section of the maze.

The joy won't last, but it's good to celebrate wins, no matter how small.

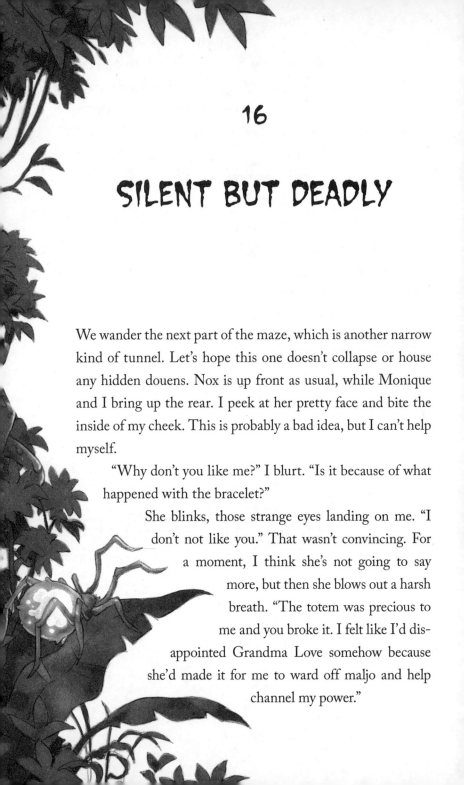

16

SILENT BUT DEADLY

We wander the next part of the maze, which is another narrow kind of tunnel. Let's hope this one doesn't collapse or house any hidden douens. Nox is up front as usual, while Monique and I bring up the rear. I peek at her pretty face and bite the inside of my cheek. This is probably a bad idea, but I can't help myself.

"Why don't you like me?" I blurt. "Is it because of what happened with the bracelet?"

She blinks, those strange eyes landing on me. "I don't not like you." That wasn't convincing. For a moment, I think she's not going to say more, but then she blows out a harsh breath. "The totem was precious to me and you broke it. I felt like I'd disappointed Grandma Love somehow because she'd made it for me to ward off maljo and help channel my power."

"It was an accident," I say.

Her expression darkens. "Doesn't matter. After that, she asked another witch to help me control my magic. I lost her trust because of you. Because you always—"

"Because I always what?"

She flattens her lips. "Nothing."

Guilt swamps me, though it hadn't all been my fault. Monique had fought back too. "I didn't even know what it was for, that any of it was magic."

"That's not the point," she snaps, eyes flashing. "You're a girl who has everything, and you just don't see it."

"You don't know me," I shoot back.

"There are people who care about you. Who'll do anything for you. People like your mom and Grandma Love. And now she's sick. . . ." Her eyes turn suspiciously red and glassy. Monique shakes her head and pushes past me. "Never mind. Forget it."

I falter. I get that she's upset, but Granny's important to me too. Pushing Monique from my head, I trudge forward, following the others.

At the end of the path, the next room appears to be like the first massive ballroom we were in, only it's empty now. I wonder if it's somehow the same one as we gingerly enter, half expecting Ushara to jump out from behind a corner. Every step we take on the polished marble gives off an eerie echo. The hairs on the back of my neck rise at the recurring sounds, making it seem like there are hundreds of us in the hall, and I spin around to see if we're being followed.

We're not. It's just the five of us.

"I'm starving," Fitz exclaims. The echo of his voice comes back a half-dozen times and we all clamp our hands over our ears. Right, that's not creepy whatsoever. The echoes fade and Fitz gives a wicked grin. "Fitz is the bessssss!" he yells at the top of his lungs.

I brace for the onslaught of repeated Fitz voices and am not disappointed. "FITZ IS THE BESSSSSS!"

"Stop," I tell him, only to have my own scolding echoed back to me.

Nox lifts a hand and we stop as a group. He doesn't look too worried—as usual, that composed face of his doesn't give much away—but he still gives us a warning in a voice so soft that I strain to hear him. "Let's try to keep it down. The last thing we want to do is attract attention. In this place, echoes might not be echoes."

What on earth does *that* mean? That they're not echoes? You know, a noise replication made by sound waves hitting a hard surface? I frown, scanning the huge, cavernous space with wary eyes. The room might be empty, but now I know more than ever that nothing in this maze is as it seems.

And based on what Nox just alluded to, we might not be alone. I lift my eyes to the vaulted ceilings, but most of it is in shadow. I wonder how many of these shadows are alive, and then banish that thought with a shudder. No sense in inventing monsters when we have enough of those to contend with in the flesh.

"Aren't you hungry?" Fitz asks me and rubs his stomach, trying to keep his voice as low as Nox's, though the volley of whispers sounds even creepier than before. "Nearly dying always gives me an appetite."

I shake my head, dubious. "You've nearly died before?"

"Oh, at least once a day," he replies with a jaunty grin. "One time, I stole one of the douens' hats as a prank, and a pack of them followed me in droves for days, eating my food until I was on the brink of starvation. Concerned for my health, I gave the silly hat back, of course. And then, one other time, I fell down the well at Grandma Love's."

"You fell down the wishing well?" I forget to speak softly and my words reverberate against the walls or are tossed back by invisible goblins. I cringe as both Monique and Nox shoot me exasperated glances over their shoulders. "Sorry," I mouth and then turn back to Fitz. "What was down there?"

"Coins and lost wishes," he says.

My eyes widen. "Lost wishes? What do those look like?"

For a moment, Fitz's eyes glow a greenish brown and I remember that he's not a regular kid, which I tend to forget, with all his funny quips and laid-back nature. "Like pale gray bubbles that have lost their color. They're lost when people make them but don't truly believe in them. Part of what makes magic work is trusting in it. You have to know anything's possible."

My heart shrivels as I remember the last wish I made on that old well. It had come true, even though I hadn't believed it would at the time. That wish would have been one of those gray bubbles—empty of hope and wonder. But I'd wished for Mom to be here, and somehow she is. That first day, I knew deep down that there was no way a stupid coin thrown into a well could bring my mom back, and yet I'd made it anyway.

The truth is, I've never believed magic was real . . . and until I'd seen evidence of it with my own eyes in the last handful of days, I couldn't be convinced otherwise. But now I know I come from a line of witches. And I have magic of my own, even if I can't use it to attack or defend, unless I'm preventing someone from getting in my mind or boosting someone else. Hardly awesome. Call me Backup Charger Rika.

I glance at Fitz. "What do *not* lost wishes look like, then?"

"Like your favorite candy." He grins. "Imagine bubbles in a kaleidoscope of every color imaginable with sunlight shimmering through them. That's what true wishes look like."

I can't help smiling at Fitz and the picture he paints. That's exactly how I would imagine real wishes to be—brightly colored, gleaming, and whimsical.

"How did you get out of the well?" I ask. "Did Granny help you?"

He shakes his head. "She told me that if I got myself down there, I'd have to get myself out."

"That sounds like Delilah," Piku interjects from his place in my hood.

With a grin, I nod. My grandmother would say that, for sure. She's a big believer in getting yourself out of trouble, especially if you found a way into it. I peer at Fitz curiously. "So how did you get out?"

"I was cold, and wet, and hungry, but I managed to use my earth magic to coax a ladder out of the stones in the side of the well, like the smallest staircase in the world going around the inside. I scaled the brick very, very carefully."

"That's cool," I say, impressed. "How did you fall in, anyway?"

Embarrassed, Fitz's russet-brown face going ruddy as he scrunches up his nose. "I made a wish that I wanted back."

"What was it?" The question is from Piku.

"I'll take that to the grave," Fitz says, sticking his nose in the air and miming zipping his lips shut. That's fair. Wishes are kind of personal. And everyone knows that if you tell anyone about a wish, it won't come true.

His twin skips up beside us, her face full of mischief. "He wanted to be taller."

"That was a secret, Hazel!"

I want to laugh at Fitz's annoyance, but when a dozen echoes of *Hazel* boom around the room, we all nearly jump out of our own skin. Not because of the noise, but because some of them don't sound like Fitz's voice. In fact, some sound downright menacing. My amusement fades quickly.

With a dark frown, Nox holds up a hand again and then places a finger to his lips. We huddle. For some reason, this section has been taking forever to get beyond, even though we've been walking at a brisk pace. I can't see the door where we came in, but I can't see the other side either. An endless sea of pale marble, barricaded on each side by marble walls, lies before us.

And we're definitely not alone.

We probably never were.

"Who's there?" Nox calls out.

We wait for an answer that never comes.

That can't be good.

Instead, we're greeted by cackling hoots from above. I glance up with alarm. Those shadows I'd noticed before and hoped weren't hiding something horrible? Well, color me unsurprised. They're full of magical monstrosities, breaking apart into overstuffed, ball-shaped furry animals with webbed wings.

Without warning, a few of the ugly puffballs dive-bomb us, and we drop to our bellies on the floor. Monique lets out a horrified screech, hands covering her hair. A trail of oily, dark purple mist floats in some of the beasts' wake.

"What the heck are those?" Hazel shrieks.

"Bats, I think," Nox guesses.

Monique makes a gagging sound, peering out from under her elbow. "Never mind what they are. . . . What is *that* coming out of their butts?"

I'm suddenly reminded of the little snake I saw in my mom's old room. I wonder if the bats' defense mechanism is the same. Maybe they're more scared of us.

"Hazel, any idea what that spray is?"

"Don't ask me. Fitz is the poison guy."

Fitz gives a tentative sniff of the air, eyes squinting up at the dark streams that dissipate without much of a trace. Maybe because vines and plants are his thing? "I'm smelling bitter tomatoes. Maybe deadly nightshade. I'm pretty sure it's some kind of airborne venom."

"Venom?" I squeak, throwing out my theory about them being afraid.

Great. Now we have to deal with killer bats with either venom breath or venom farts. Fitz and I creep to our knees when the ugly little beasts fly back up to their roost, and then we fall flat to the ground again as they attack again. Guess we can't stand up.

"Here, follow me," Nox says, lying flat on his stomach. "Stay away from the mist. Doesn't seem like the vapor lasts, but I'd rather not find out what it does."

Imitating Nox, we army-crawl across the floor, hoping our new beasties don't trail us. We're not that lucky. They do. With this slow pace keeping us to the ground, we'll never escape. I wriggle my phone from my pocket. It's nearly midnight, which gives us about six hours to sunrise, and we have four levels to go if we get past this bat-tastic one. We have to stick with the pace, but with these farting puffballs slowing us down, it might be a problem. My elbows and knees are screaming in pain already.

"We need to get rid of them," I whisper. "Does anyone have any ideas?"

Monique clears her throat. "I could burn them."

"Worth a try," Nox says.

It's a long shot, considering there are a few dozen of them and none of the Minders' magic is in top form, but I don't say anything. Because right now, their limited power is the only thing we have. Monique hops to her feet and begins to glow a dull red. Flames dance at the edge of her fingertips, which, I won't lie, is pretty cool.

When a handful of the bats zoom from the swarm toward her, she zaps them with a weak river of flame. A few swerve out of the way, but the fire catches the leader. A piercing shrill noise like a balloon deflating fills the room as the bat drops writhing to the ground several feet away and then explodes.

The charred smell is nauseating, but that's not the worst thing.

No, what's worse is the fact that what remains of the creature turns into a purple puddle of goo and starts to *melt* into the ground. Literally, there's a hole in the marble floor. We exchange grossed-out glances. So not only is the creature full of poison, but on the inside, it's made of acid.

Though queasy, Nox resumes the slow belly crawl. "Let's keep moving while we think through our options."

Options that are most definitely dwindling by the second.

"Wait, what's that over there?" Piku asks, scrambling down from his perch on my neck to the floor. He scampers off to the right. I don't see anything but light-colored walls heading up to the darkened ceiling until something like gossamer flickers into focus. There's definitely something there . . . something nearly invisible. Piku has almost reached the wall, his head cocked up. He reaches out a tentative claw, and my stomach clenches.

"Don't touch it, Piku!"

But it's too late.

A piece of spindly gauze curls around the baby iguana, trapping him in place. He struggles wildly, his tail thrashing, but that only makes him more hopelessly tangled. The entire weblike mass ripples, and Hazel lets out a terrified scream, her eyes nearly popping out from her head as she looks up in revulsion.

Skeletal legs descend, followed by a bulbous, near transparent body. This really is a ceiling of nightmares—first bats, and now spiders the size of small dogs. I want to run, but I can't abandon my friend. Ignoring the threat of the bats, I leap to my feet and race toward Piku, skidding to a stop while keeping an eye on the arachnoid creeping downward.

Bile rises in my throat. Some spiders can be cute, but this one is hairy and *ugly*.

"Don't move."

I glance back, noticing that the others have joined me, and the warning is from Nox. Strangely enough, the bats hover some distance away, almost as if they're afraid of the webbing. "Monique, can you burn this?"

She nods, a stream of thin fire hitting right above Piku. I brace for explosion, like with the bat before, but the web shrivels with the heat, releasing my lizard companion. Above us, the spider chitters at the loss of its prey and we quickly scramble out of reach. I hold my breath and hug Piku close, wondering if the monster spider will come after us again, but it doesn't, only staring balefully from its web.

"Thanks, Rika," my stricken iguana bleats.

"You would have done the same for me," I say. "And thank Nox and Monique. It was his idea, and she fried you free."

Whatever those sticky strands are, they'd been hidden before, or at least, they were harder to see against the pale white color of the walls. Now that I've noticed them, though, I can't unsee them. They look like a rectangle of pale gray interwoven webs . . . almost like soccer nets. Soccer *traps*! Was this trap truly made for me?

A glimmer of a really bad idea pops into my brain.

"Hey, Nox, can you use your magic to make those bats come toward me?"

Fitz tugs on my arm. "Rika, what are you doing? Why do you want those things anywhere near you?"

"Just testing a theory." I meet Nox's eyes and nod. "In front of me if you can, about knee-level." I see the understanding glimmer in his gaze and the beginnings of a grin curl his lips.

I hop to my feet and am immediately dive-bombed by one of the bats soaring above us. Nox shoves the bat into position in front of me with air, and I suck in a huge breath right before I yank back my leg and pretend I'm kicking a penalty goal. My foot connects with the bat's somewhat squishy body—*so gross*—and pings it right into the waiting "net."

Within seconds, the spider drops and starts to spin its web around the trapped bat, not in any hurry to let more prey escape. I squash down my revulsion as two more of its eight-legged siblings join in. One down . . . a few dozen to go. "If you kick them quick enough, they don't have time to release their butt gas."

"Anyone up for some devil tree football?" Nox asks.

"Let me try!" Fitz says, his smile wide with excitement. He pounds his first bat ball into the upper right corner of the sticky web goal, and I offer him a giddy thumbs-up. I have to admit that kicking the thing was really satisfying in a sick, revolting way.

We exchange places as Nox sets up two more winged creatures and I dispatch them with World Cup–worthy goals.

Hazel squeals with disgust as she kicks hers, and Monique hits hers so hard it nearly rattles one of the spiders.

"Nice job," I tell them both, offering each a fist bump.

To conserve Nox's weakened magic, Fitz and I tag-team, jumping up and down to attract the bats while the other kicks them into the walls. I try not to notice that more of the spiders have appeared, so there are at least six of them greedily spinning cocoons around the trapped bats. My guilt comes and goes—the fart-bats *were* trying to kill us. I'm so busy celebrating that I'm not paying attention when a nearby bat lets out a stream of its deadly mist right at my face.

Suddenly, Monique, of all people, crashes into me, making us both land in a heap of tangled limbs on the ground. The mist passes harmlessly overhead. I stare at her in surprise. "Thanks."

She bites her lip. "We're a team, right?"

Could Monique finally be warming up to me? A huge smile makes my cheeks hurt. She stands, rolls her eyes, and gives an exaggerated huff. "Don't get excited. We're not besties or anything. We need you alive and well to save Grandma Love, Dulcie, and Papa Bois. Besides, we've already come this far. It would be a shame for you to die now."

I smile wider. "Sure thing, Monique!"

"Oh, for heaven's sake, we're not going to hold hands and plait each other's hair just because I pushed you out of the way."

"I'll have you know I'm an excellent hair braider."

She scowls, trying to hide the barest twitch of her lips. "Whatever, weirdo."

RIDDLE ME THIS, BATMAN

We have to be getting close to the end . . . or to the top, or wherever this cursed maze goes. Pretty sure it defies gravity and architectural logic. Then again, it is a magical realm. Anything is possible. After the ballroom—I shudder to think about the bat buffet we'd left behind for the spiders following our impromptu penalty shoot-out—we decided to stop for a rest. What's strange is that the maze was mostly trying to kill us, but the moment I groaned about needing a break and being hangry, a weird moss-covered grove had taken shape.

I mean, figuring out that the silk cottonwood tree is likely sentient, alive, but feeding us—or fattening us up for slaughter—takes the stakes to a whole other level. A part of me wonders whether I could just tell the tree to take me to my mom.

Asking can't hurt. I mutter the words and hear a faint rustle of laughter through the swishing of the branches. It sounds like Bazil and I stick my tongue out, hoping that if he can hear me, he can see me too.

Jerk!

A sharp buzzing sound fills my ears, and suddenly my vision clouds.

Oh no, not again!

When my sight goes back to normal, I'm no longer in the grove, and no one's with me. Well, no one except for the devil I summoned by being cheeky. Go, me! Bazil is standing with one hip propped against the wishing well—our special meeting spot, it seems. I should have known he wouldn't let such an insult pass. Clenching my jaw, I groan on the inside, cursing my sassiness.

"What do you want?" I ask him grumpily.

"You're the one who summoned me."

"I'm pretty sure that making faces at someone isn't an invitation to jump inside their head."

"I like this old well," he says conversationally, staring into its depths. "There's a hopefulness to it."

"Fitz said he fell down there once."

The devil man laughs. "He made a vain wish."

"What's vain about wanting to look different? Everybody wants to change something about themselves. Even you, I'll bet."

Bazil regards me with his murky, sludge-colored eyes, a surprisingly human expression of empathy crossing them. He's wearing the face of a regular man again, and it's unnerving because I know exactly what lies underneath. He's a monster in disguise, even if he can mimic humanity. "How are you liking my maze, child?"

"Piece of cake," I boast, shrugging.

Lips part over white shark's teeth. "That easy? I should up my game, then. Maybe give you something to challenge that bored brain of yours."

"Why do you want to get out and destroy the world so badly?" I ask him, countering his question with one of my own, even though the threat of the maze becoming *more* difficult makes my insides quail. "What did we ever do to you?"

He looks genuinely flummoxed by the question. "You infected me."

I know he doesn't mean me. Does he mean people in general? Even so, it's a strange answer. He's a devil. How would people have infected *him*?

"What do you mean? Are you sick?"

"You could say that."

"Can you take medicine?" As soon as the words are out, I want to kick myself. *Idiot*. Of course there's no medicine for a supernatural creature.

An ugly guffawing noise fills my ears. His laughter, I realize. "You're the first one to ever ask me that. It's much too late, I fear, little human."

Bazil's mouth twists, his different faces oscillating beneath his skin: a greenish reptilian face followed by one that looks like weathered tree bark. Once more, something jerks to life inside me. Something like recognition. But how would I know him? He's no one to me, though the truth is, he reminds me of someone. I just can't put my finger on who.

"Your friends are calling you," Bazil says.

"Never lose hope," I say to him, but my vision is already blackening and distorting at the edges. I blink and I'm back in the grove, startled as Fitz snaps his fingers in front of my face. Was that whole meeting with the Bad John just in my head? Besides Fitz, no one else seems to sense that I'd gone on some kind of wild mind trip. Not even Piku, whose weight I can still feel on my shoulder. Piku must have known, right?

I give my head a hard shake and focus on Fitz. "Stop snapping. What?"

"Weys, I've been calling you for the last two minutes! Get a load of this!"

A mouthwatering, tropical scent distracts me as I belatedly take in what Fitz is screaming about. A selection of thickly laden fruit trees. Mangoes, I recognize, my taste buds salivating. There's also a tree covered in knobby red pear–shaped fruit, and another with a greenish speckled yellow oval-shaped bounty.

Fitz and Hazel whoop as they race for the trees, nimbly pulling themselves up into the lower branches and picking the ripest fruit they can find. Even Piku scampers down my body and disappears with a series of happy chirps. Monique saunters at a slower pace, but is quick to peel one of the oval fruit and sink her teeth into the pink-orange flesh.

I make to follow them, but Nox is already handing me a juicy mango. Practically yowling my thanks, I pounce on it like a feral animal and gobble the thing down. When I finish, I toss the seed to the side and hunt for more.

Nox grins and wipes his mouth on the back of his sleeve. "Try this one."

He holds out one of the dark red fruit.

"What is it?" I ask.

"A pomerac. It's tart, and not as soft as a mango, but it's really good. You should try one. I'm surprised you haven't before. Grandma Love has some of these in her orchard."

I accept the fruit. The first bite is almost bitter, making my tongue curl up and my taste buds sit up and take notice, but the firm white flesh inside is surprisingly refreshing. I'm reminded of an apple mixed with a pear, with more of a tangy edge.

After I finish, my mood lightens. A small snack can seriously cure crankiness. With a contented sigh, I glance over at Nox, who is polishing off another mango. I have to admit, the more I get to know him, the more I'm curious about him. It's weird to think that he's the son of Papa Bois . . . and the future king of the wood.

"So should I call you Prince Nox or what?" I ask him, trying to make a joke that falls flat. I cringe on the inside.

He stops eating. "No, or I'll be forced to retaliate and call you Princess Rika."

I snort. "I'm not an actual princess, but you're like the future ruler of the forest. All the land is going to be yours someday."

Wiping his mouth, he tosses the seed away. "I just want to find my dad. Just like you want to find your mom."

"How long has he been gone?" I ask, his sadness spilling over to where I'm sitting.

"A long time."

I squeeze his hand. He doesn't let go. "I'm sorry. We'll find them, Nox. I promise. No matter what Bazil has in store for us, we can do this."

For the first time since I've met him, I see uncertainty on his face. There's a lot on the line for both of us. His dad, my mom. Granny's sickness. The dying magic and the fate of the Minders. The rest of the natural world. If Bazil isn't stopped, we're pretty much guaranteed a future full of storms, starvation, plague, war, and death. The apocalypse for real.

"Do you think they're okay?" I wonder aloud.

Nox squeezes my fingers back. "They have to be."

My stomach sours as I think about Bazil, and then I think about my mom and Papa Bois. I've seen signs of Mom, but not of the supposed forest king who is also trapped in this tree. Where *is* he being held, then? I hold those thoughts close to my chest, not wanting to upset Nox. His dad has to be here somewhere. Nox wouldn't be searching for him if he wasn't.

After we've stuffed our faces full, and Hazel has conjured some cool spring water to quench our thirst, we group together on the soft, mossy ground in a loose circle. We probably don't have time to waste sitting around, but some rest won't hurt. Our bodies need to settle and replenish. Mistakes are made when you're tired or overstuffed. And we can't afford to make too many missteps. Not in a place like this that thrives on blunders.

"Bazil said there were nine levels. So far, we've had the

scent maze, fake Stonehenge, the obstacle course, the smash-a-kid-to-pulp gauntlet, and the bats versus spiders challenge. Not counting the trick feast at the start, that's five. Assuming he didn't lie, there should be four more to go. What do you think they are?" I ask no one in particular.

Hazel purses her lips. "Who knows? Hopefully no more bone-crunching machines. Or foul-smelling pits of death."

"Could there be more mental tests?" I say, remembering Bazil's words at the well.

Nox nods, and I bite my lip, worry leaching through me. My grades haven't been the best. It's not like I've paid much attention in school over the last year. "Do you think we'll be able to work together?"

He shrugs. "Maybe."

With four of the nine tests left, there's more than a good chance they'll go into physical territory again, and while I've been lucky for the first five, that luck can change in a blink. I'm grateful for my athleticism even though it's been a while since I've exercised—soccer was the only thing that got me through the obstacle course and the gauntlet.

The Stonehenge rock test used a few of the senses—smell, sight, touch—and also depended on memory. So that was a bit of a mental test as well. The maze at the start tested patience and endurance, and even though I'd failed, we'd found another way through together. And while the obstacle course was mostly physical, the gauntlet also required musical appreciation to keep track of the beats. I suppose fighting off mutated bats and spiders is another test of physical strength.

I shudder. I'm grateful I'm not alone.

Nox stretches out his legs, and I see Fitz practicing his magic. Envy fills me at the sight of his golden-brown earthy glow and the vines that dance over his feet. Besides being basically a magical battery charger for Nox, my own magic has remained dormant. I stare at my hands, willing my magic to make them glow, but nothing happens. I wonder what color I'd be. Brown like Fitz, red like Monique, white like Nox, or blue like Hazel. My hands drop. Maybe my magic is colorless.

"Hey, Nox, do you know what kind of magic my mom has? Or Granny?"

He shrugs. "It's hard to explain. It's not elemental like ours. It's spirit."

"Spirit?"

"From the heart, from inside you. Like a bright spark of creation energy."

Oh.

After what seems like a way too short amount of time, Nox stands and dusts his hands on his shorts. With a sigh, he offers a palm down to me and pulls me to my feet. "We should keep going."

"Yeah, good idea."

We leave the mossy grove with some regret, knowing that our brief reprieve is over. The ground starts to shift beneath our feet. It's unnerving when the maze shifts like a fun house full of mirrors and perception is distorted from one mirror to the next. I've never liked fun houses.

Closing my eyes, I exhale and count to five.

When I open them, the grove has disappeared and we're facing a huge set of wood doors with intricate carvings on them.

I know it's too much to hope that my mom is on the other side, but I cross my fingers and hope anyway when Nox pushes them open. I'm kind of glad we haven't needed my blood for anything else. My index finger still aches from the prick.

The next room is somehow suspended in space. I glance down—my feet are on a solid surface, but feel like they're floating. No one's around save for a woman a few steps away. At first, I think it's Ushara, but it's not. Mostly because this lady is *ancient*. Ushara at least looks like she's my mom's age.

This crone is way older than Granny, with thin, stringy brown hair and wrinkled skin. I can't quite see her eyes beneath the brownish leather cowl covering her brow, but I imagine they are as weird as the rest of her. She doesn't speak or move, but she's blocking what appears to be a shimmering oval opening behind her. Our exit, I'm guessing.

"Come hither, if you dare, and test your wits against my fare," the crone intones, and I instantly want to cover my ears at the creepy whisper that makes my flesh crawl. "Answer me these riddles three, and you will find the pathway free."

I blow out a breath with a scowl. Riddles.

Lucky me.

Well, at least I have help. The lady didn't say anything about having to work out her riddles on our own, and five brains are always better than one. We shuffle closer. I sense Piku's distress in my hood, but for whatever reason, he stays hidden in the cotton folds.

"If you fail, a price of a soul you must pay, should you wish to continue on your way." *My soul?* I groan. Just when I thought I'd avoided that. Her mouth stretches into a gap-toothed smile. "Now you must pick three of three, to test your mettle against me."

Nope, nope, nope.

"Are you any good at riddles?" I whisper. "Because I suck at them."

Monique's mouth twists. "Me too."

Nox cracks his knuckles. "Okay, then that leaves me, Fitz, and Hazel. You up for it?"

When Hazel gives a hesitant nod, Nox steps forward in front of the lady. A strange chime echoes in the air. Then Fitz goes, followed by another chime. But when Hazel tries to step in line next to them, she can't.

"What's wrong?" Nox asks.

"I can't go," Hazel says with a frown. "I think Rika has to do it because she's the main champion."

I blanch, feeling my breath throttle in my lungs. Of course one of the three riddle solvers would be me. I inhale a resigned breath and step forward into Hazel's place. Another chime sounds.

"You good?" Nox asks.

I tamp down my panic. "Yeah."

"The Minder Prince has first honors," the lady says. I grimace. Why didn't she speak in rhymes that time? I glance expectantly at our host, expecting her to speak to me next, but she leans forward instead, gnarled fingers twitching like they want to burrow into my flesh. "The witchen is guilty of trickery. The game is forfeit."

My jaw hangs loose. I didn't do a stinking thing! "What are you talking about? I haven't tricked anyone!"

"Three are required to begin the trial; you have four yet bear denial."

So we're back to rhyming?

Wait . . . is *this* one of her riddles? Do I need to answer it? I'm so confused. I meet Nox's concerned gaze; his dark green eyes widen with sudden understanding. They dip to my shoulder, to where the tip of Piku's spines are just visible.

"It's just an iguana," I mumble, not adding that said iguana can talk and is probably smarter than all of us combined.

"Three are required to begin the trial; you have four yet bear denial," she repeats.

"The maze has accepted the challenger," Nox says in a cool voice. "*With* her familiar. If it had not, there would have been no chime. The game must continue."

I gape at him. That's a sound argument. Everyone knows a familiar is a witch's companion. We glance back at the woman, whose displeasure is obvious in the fingers practically tearing holes into her cloak. She dips her head in reluctant agreement, but I still get the sense she's glaring at me from beneath her strange-shaped cowl. I squirm and return my gaze to Nox, who seems calm as ever.

Suddenly, the darkness around us lights up and words appear one by one in midair.

The first riddle!

WHAT IS LIGHTER THAN A FEATHER, BUT EVEN THE WORLD'S STRONGEST PERSON CAN'T HOLD IT FOR MORE THAN TEN MINUTES?

I must be the most clueless person alive because my mind goes blank. I read the words again for good measure, glad that

I didn't get that question because I can't even begin to think of an answer. Paper might be lighter than a feather. Anyone can hold a piece of paper for way longer than ten minutes. So that doesn't work. What about cotton candy? That's pretty light, but I can hold that for hours. My brain hurts already.

Nox clears his throat. "The answer is your breath."

Whoa. That's so clever. I send Nox an admiring look.

"You are correct," the woman croaks. "You may step back. The Minder of Earth may proceed."

I blink. Wait, what? Why do I have to go last? Everyone knows the last questions are always the hardest. Maybe it's my imagination, but the woman's satisfaction at the order of things is clear. No doubt she's going to make it as difficult as she can.

Great. Piku nibbles gently at my ear, and I take comfort in the fact that he's with me. Nox is right—the maze allowed for a familiar, after all, and even if it was an unintended mistake, it's an advantage in my favor.

WHAT DO THE NUMBERS 11, 69, AND 88 ALL HAVE IN COMMON?

I stare anxiously at Fitz, who has a perplexed look on his face. Glancing over my shoulder, I see Hazel's eyes light up as if she knows the answer, but I'll bet anything she's barred from speaking. Turning back to the riddle, I squint in concentration. Those numbers don't really have anything in common other than being double digits.

They can't be divided by the same number. Eleven is a prime number, which can only be divided by one and itself, so it's a multiple of one and eleven. While eighty-eight can be divided by eleven to get a whole number (eight), sixty-nine can't. They're not all even or odd numbers, as eleven and sixty-nine are both odds, while eighty-eight is even.

This is impossible!

Poor Fitz.

I can see his face growing redder the more frustrated he gets. Out of the corner of my eye, I see Hazel jumping up and down, one hand pointed up and then pointing down. Even though we can't hear her, it's some kind of hint. I try valiantly to decode her movements. One up? One down? What does *that* mean?

But Fitz doesn't see her, instead hanging his head in a defeated slump. "I give up."

"No, don't!" I blurt.

But it's too late. The woman cackles, and suddenly the floor beneath Fitz opens up and he disappears. Like vanishes completely. "Fitz!"

Nox, Hazel, and Monique are shouting too, but because of the enchantments, I can only see their mouths and bodies moving frantically. "What did you do to Fitz?" I demand of the cackling woman.

"Bound to the vow of his life's sacrifice, the sweetest morsel thus is the price."

"What? Are you going to eat him?" I screech, instantly thinking of the witch in Hansel and Gretel who cooks children in her oven.

But she refuses to answer me, even as thick tears pour down my face. I don't even want to make eye contact with

Hazel, knowing she will be devastated and we're only in here because of me, but I turn anyway. Hazel is crumpled in Nox's arms, her small body shaking with uncontrollable sobs. Oh my gosh, is Fitz truly gone? Knees buckling, I collapse to the ground, eyes nearly blinded by tears, staring up at Fitz's unanswered riddle from the floor.

And I cry harder . . . because the answer is there and now so obvious.

11, 69, and 88.

They all look the same *upside down.*

It's just the kind of riddle that Fitz would have appreciated. The letters fade, the wall going blank once more. The woman's lips gape into a grin as she peers down at me—I can almost feel her eyes glittering in glee . . . or greed. Her hunger blasts into me. She *wants* me to fail. "Do you forfeit, witchen?"

The word is on the tip of my tongue: *Yes.*

Piku leaps onto my cheek, his sharp claws pricking at my tear-dampened skin. "Get up. I know you can do this. I'm here, and while I cannot give you the answer, I can help. Pull yourself together, human, and be the crafty girl I know you are."

"Oh, I'm back to *human* now," I mutter.

He hisses. "You'll go back to Rika when you start acting like Rika."

"Fine," I snap, shoving my trembling body upward. I stare at the crone. "I don't forfeit."

But I'm not ready when the final riddle appears.

I AM GREATER THAN GOD, AND MORE EVIL

THAN THE DEVIL. THE POOR HAVE ME, THE RICH NEED ME, AND IF YOU EAT ME, YOU WILL DIE. WHAT AM I?

I read the words over a dozen times with no success and send a panicked stare to the others.

"You can do this," Nox mouths.

Can I, though?

"Got any ideas?" I ask Piku. Does he even read? He might be a magical reptile, but he's still an animal. Not wanting to embarrass him, I read it back to myself aloud, slowly.

What about poison? That can kill you. But that's not greater than a god or a devil, and it makes no sense to the rich and the poor needing it. What do the poor have that the rich need? Love? Happiness? I glance back at the others, but their faces are glum. As expected, this one's harder than hard. Panic starts to gather in my chest, making my neck overheat.

"You've got this, Rika," Piku says. I glance down at his earnest green face. I wonder if he knows the answer. I'll bet he does, but he won't give it to me, just in case the woman figures out some loophole to disqualify me, even if we did have the ring of approval. "You know the answer," he says.

Do I?

"I don't know it!" I bite out in a frustrated whine. Nothing's coming to mind. If we had more time, I could probably figure it out, but even though there's no time limit, time *is* running out to find my mom. We've got to keep moving. Staring at the words, I rack my brain and still come up empty.

I slump to a crouch. "I've got nothing, Piku."

To my surprise, the iguana chuffs with laughter. Well, it's

more of a maniacal cackle than a laugh, and it's kind of off-putting. "Why are you so happy? I'm about to go the same way as Fitz." He keeps making that annoyingly amused chitter, and I'm starting to get mad. "Seriously, didn't you hear me, lizard, I said I have *nothing*."

Blood rushes in my ears and my eyes sting. There is complete silence in the room as if the entire maze is holding its breath. Piku's triumphant gaze blazes into mine.

Oh. Oh. *Oh.*

I glance up to the letters and huff a delirious breath. "The answer to the riddle is *nothing*."

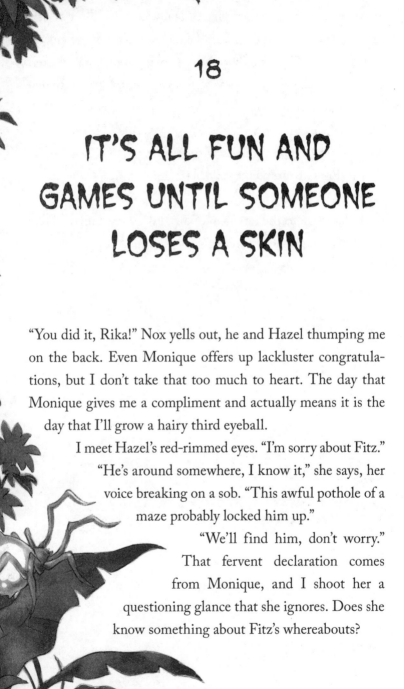

18

IT'S ALL FUN AND GAMES UNTIL SOMEONE LOSES A SKIN

"You did it, Rika!" Nox yells out, he and Hazel thumping me on the back. Even Monique offers up lackluster congratulations, but I don't take that too much to heart. The day that Monique gives me a compliment and actually means it is the day that I'll grow a hairy third eyeball.

I meet Hazel's red-rimmed eyes. "I'm sorry about Fitz."

"He's around somewhere, I know it," she says, her voice breaking on a sob. "This awful pothole of a maze probably locked him up."

"We'll find him, don't worry."

That fervent declaration comes from Monique, and I shoot her a questioning glance that she ignores. Does she know something about Fitz's whereabouts?

"Let's get out of here," Nox says.

We turn toward the portal, but it's blocked by the woman, who is no longer hunched over and sitting, but standing and barring the way.

Nox frowns. "We won the challenge fair and square."

"Two riddles, not three."

Scowling, I glare at her. It's a technicality. "And our friend paid for his forfeit in flesh and blood, didn't he?" I snap. "But if it's an answer you're looking for, the numbers all look the same upside down. There. Satisfied?"

The air fairly crackles with fury . . . and no small amount of warmth. At first I think it's Monique, but there's no red glow on her skin suggesting she's using her power. No, the obnoxious heat is coming from the crone.

"You smell delicious, young witch," she singsongs, abandoning her scripted rhymes. "I admit, your blood smells so divine, not the scrawny Minder's, though I will delight in drinking him dry."

Why does her threat make Fitz sound like a human juice box?

"Where's my brother, you evil hag?" Hazel screams, her entire body glowing blue as she gathers her magic.

"No, Hazel, wait!" Monique shouts. "It won't work."

But streams of water gush from her, only to hiss and evaporate when the woman throws back her cowl, which looks disturbingly like human skin up close, and transforms into a giant, monstrous fireball.

Hazel's and Nox's eyes widen. "Soucouyant!"

Vaguely, I remember the word from when Hazel was in my room during the storm. That seems like a lifetime ago, despite only being a few hours. Wait, hadn't she said that a soucouyant was a type of vampire? No wonder she wants to guzzle Fitz. I shake my head and back up a couple steps. Bloodred eyes and a maw rimmed in scarlet fangs rest where the woman's head should be. Yep, definitely some kind of grotesque bloodsucker.

"Stay behind me, Rika!" Monique yells, and I frown, wondering why she's all about protecting me. Not that she can do much to fight fire with fire, but for some reason, the creature stays a safe distance from her. Maybe they use different kinds of heat. Needless to say, I don't turn down the Fire Minder.

Nox blows strongish winds at the creature, but his magic only makes her blaze burn hotter. "It's not working. We need to get her skin. That's the only way to defeat her."

"Her skin?" I shout in confusion, and then a thought hits me. That weird leathery cloak must be her skin. *Gross.* I scan the area, but don't see any sign of an outer shell. "There's nothing there."

"It'll be in a mortar," Nox says as he dodges a swipe.

"What's that?"

"Like a stone container," he replies.

Apart from us, the room is empty. She must have stashed it somewhere. Or maybe her skin is invisible.

"No luck, Nox!" I yell out.

"Here, take this!" Monique shouts, shoving a small paper sack in my hand as we both dance out of the way. The soucouyant snarls with hunger and rage, her eyes spearing me from where I am using Monique as a human shield. I feel weird about it, but she has practical magic, and I don't. And again, for reasons I can't figure out, the ancient flaming vampire avoids contact with her.

Squeezing the palm-sized bag between my fingers, I unfold the edges of the paper and wonder at the sight of uncooked rice. That's a strange thing to carry around. I go to fold the sack back up when Monique makes a frustrated steups sound. "Throw it, dummy!"

"The bag?"

Her eye roll is epic. "No, throw the rice *in* the bag at her. She'll have to count every grain. Don't you know anything?"

Well, I didn't know *that*.

Not wasting another moment, I fling the contents of the sack toward the fireball. A few seconds pass as I hold my breath, and then the soucouyant lets out an aggravated scream. Within seconds, her fire dims as she drops to her knees and starts counting each and every grain. There have to be thousands of them. Her eyes lift malevolently to mine, but she doesn't stop in her work. I can't stop staring in morbid fascination.

"Rika!" I startle out of my thrall to meet Nox's eye. "We have to move. The portal is closing."

Sure enough, it's *way* smaller than it'd been earlier. I follow him to the shimmery portal and then pause. Monique crouches down and crawls through before Nox indicates for me to do the same. "Wait, where's Hazel?"

"I'm not going with you," she says. "I'll stay here and make sure she counts every single one of those."

"Won't she hurt you?"

Hazel shakes her head. "She's compelled to count them all

221

before the sunrise comes. In the meantime, I'll search for her skin. It must be here somewhere."

I narrow my eyes. Dawn has to be close. I hate the fact that we have to leave Hazel behind, especially after what happened with Fitz, but the clock is ticking. She must see my hesitation because she forces a grim smile to her lips.

"Don't worry about me, Rika. I'm in this for a little payback too. And if I find that skin, I can make her tell me where Fitz is."

I watch as the Water Minder blasts a stream of water at the soucouyant's tallied pile, scattering the grains she'd already counted. A ferocious screech rattles through the space, but there's nothing for the creature to do but start over. The hard yet gratified look on Hazel's normally pleasant face takes me by surprise.

"Remind me never to get on your bad side," I say, remembering that for all her gentleness and sweet demeanor, she's still a Minder . . . and a dangerous one at that.

"Find your mom, Rika, and Papa Bois," she says. "Trust in yourself."

I choke up. "Thanks, Hazel."

Nox gives his friend a crooked smile. "Have fun."

"I can go all night, bamsee-head," I hear Hazel say as I enter the doorway with Nox on my heels. I snort at the Trini insult—she just called an ancient, wicked soucouyant a . . . butthead. "Tell me where my brother is and we'll talk."

"She's fierce," I tell him.

"The quiet ones always are."

"You're not worried for her?" I ask just as the portal narrows and closes behind us, cutting off the sight of the Minder and the vampire.

"Hazel knows how to take care of herself," Monique says, but she softens her sharp words with an unexpected smile that makes her pretty face even prettier somehow. "And if Fitz is anywhere in the tree, she'll find him, don't worry."

"You think he's okay?" I ask.

Nox nods. "We would have felt otherwise. The four of us are . . . connected. There's no telling what Bazil will do to him, though, so the sooner she finds him, the better."

Satisfied, I glance around, spotting a narrow staircase that climbs up and up and up. The three of us crane our necks, taking stock of the never-ending steps. I am exhausted just seeing it.

"How many steps do you think there are?"

Monique groans. "Hundreds."

She starts the long trek up, but I can't bring myself to move, even when Nox comes to stand beside me. "Only three levels left, right?" I ask, glancing at my phone. The battery is low, but I note the time. It's nearly two in the morning. No wonder sleepiness is taking over—it's way past my bedtime. Not that I'll admit that to a soul.

"We have to hope so," he says, but I can hear the slight thread of despair in his voice.

For all his usual calm, Nox looks troubled too. While I believe that Hazel and Fitz are capable warriors, I'm sure he's worried about his friends. He wouldn't be the leader he is if he weren't. The fact that we are down three from six, if I count Granny at the start, doesn't help with the odds of beating these trials.

Granny . . .

She must be worried sick. That reminds me: I reach into my pocket and pull out her beaded bracelets. When Fitz had first given them to me, I hadn't bothered to put even one on. I do now and feel a weird zing as if something has snapped tight inside of me. Granny had told Fitz that they would protect me, so maybe that's what I sensed—the protection charms taking root. In hindsight, I probably should have been wearing these five levels ago. I sigh, stroking a braided cord on my left wrist.

I'm okay, Granny.

When we'd been outside of the trec, I'd convinced her I could do this. We've come too far to give up now. Thinking about my grandmother fills me with some renewed motivation, and I lift my foot onto the first step. *One . . . two . . . three.* By the time I reach two hundred, I'm gasping for breath and it doesn't seem like we've made any headway in the endless climb. And my fatigue is weighing on me like a bucket of bricks. When I see bones propped up in a corner of one stair, I almost gag.

"What is that?" I gasp, staring at the skeleton.

"Someone who probably died here because they failed to complete the levels," Monique says from above me, and my stomach roils. It's been hours since we've eaten the fruit and my belly feels sour. I can't take it. I need to sit for a minute. Maybe a bit farther up.

"Or it could be a scare tactic," Piku remarks.

Twenty steps up, Nox pauses next to me as I lean over to catch my breath. "Keep going," I tell him, embarrassed by my sweaty, panting state. I sound as loud as a freight train. "I'll catch up."

"No, that's okay. I need a rest too."

He sits on the step and pats the spot next to him. I flop down into a graceless heap, my legs wobbling like jelly. Monique has already disappeared above us, but maybe she's scouting. She doesn't look sweaty or tired or bothered whatsoever. I squash down my resentment and focus on calming my galloping heartbeat.

"What do you think this staircase tests besides endurance?" I ask Nox. "Could this be another level?"

"Maybe the Bad John is testing our willpower," he replies. "Most people would have given up by now."

"That's not an option for either of us." I roll my shoulders and scowl at the thought of the devil holding our parents hostage. "So Bazil is the OG spirit of this tree?"

Nox leans back on his elbows. "Yes."

I think of the skeleton we'd passed and shudder, wondering what that poor soul did to end up as nothing but bones and how long they'd been there. "So do you think my mom and your dad made a bargain?"

He shakes his head. "Not a chance. But I think, somehow, Bazil captured my father in a plot to escape this prison, and he's using Daddy Bouchon's power to cause chaos that can only be thwarted by one of the trinity."

"My mom." I breathe out. With Granny being sick, Mom was likely the only one who could stop Bazil. So he stopped her first. "And now they're both stuck." Sighing, I reach over and squeeze his shoulder. "We'll beat this maze and save them, Nox. No one is giving up, not when we've come this far."

Piku pops his head out, his eyes panning between Nox and me. "I thought I heard the sound of crickets. If you're staying here for a few minutes, I'll just check for snacks."

I shoot him a playful frown. "Maybe after your snack, I should make you carry me up two hundred stairs while I take a nap."

"You want some crickets too?" he asks, licking his eyeball.

"Uhh, no thanks!"

We both watch as he scampers up a window ledge, his long tongue darting out to trap the unsuspecting insects. I'm not hungry enough to eat bugs, but I could do with some water. Too bad our Water Minder is busy tormenting a vampire flame ball. I swallow some gritty saliva down my parched throat.

"I don't suppose you have any water, do you?"

"No," Nox says. "But I do have these."

He reaches into his pocket and hands me four colored balls. Skittles! I narrow my eyes at him. "Where did you get these? Wait, some greedy munchkin didn't vomit these up, did they?"

He laughs. "No, I saved them from the maze. When you threw them, a few got caught in my wind stream." A flush colors his cheeks. "I kept them."

Now that I know they haven't been in the digestive system of some random douen, I cram the bunch into my mouth and nearly sigh in complete delight as my taste buds come to life and water fills my mouth. I swear by my statement: Skittles are life.

A bit of regret comes because I didn't offer him one, but that's gone now. I'd like to think a nicer me would have shared, though I probably wouldn't have. I give him a shy smile though. "Thanks."

Nox drags a hand through his curly hair, clearly uncomfortable. "I should be the one thanking you. I haven't said how grateful I am, Rika, that you're doing this. I know it's been hard, but we couldn't have gotten this far without you." He falters over his words. "I wouldn't have been able to find my dad."

"Do you think he's here?" I venture. "I mean, I haven't seen anybody else besides Bazil, his minions, and my mom."

Nox sighs. "He has to be. He's the reason your mom is even here. She braved the tree to rescue him."

I hear a note of guilt in his voice, as if he thinks it's his dad's fault somehow that my mom is in trouble. But what I do know about my mom, my granny, and myself is that we Lovelaces have a stubborn streak. Nobody forces us to do anything. If my mom felt she could have helped Papa Bois, nothing would have stopped her.

I study the tall, skinny boy sitting next to me, take in the tight dark curls and his smooth brown face. I wonder if he's Papa Bois's look-alike, whether there's any resemblance.

"What's he like?"

"Daddy Bouchon?" I remember Nox saying out in the glade that he called him that. When I nod, he continues. "He's kind, smart, and funny. Stern, too. He doesn't like when we mistreat the environment, obviously. But that comes with the territory, being father of the forest and all. He's great with animals. Part of his magic allows him to transform into them sometimes. He likes being a deer the most."

"Can you shape-shift too?"

"Not yet."

"What's your mom like?"

Nox smiles. "Everyone calls her Mama D'Leau. She's the protector and healer of the rivers. She has the most beautiful voice."

"So protection is kind of in your blood," I say, smiling softly back. "Where's she?"

His face grows thoughtful. "She left. My dad changed in the last few years, becoming angrier and more detached, almost as if he was growing apart from the woods. He would hulk out at the hikers who littered or made fires and didn't put them out. He'd have bursts of rage, disappearing for periods of time, but he always came back." He sniffs. "Then Bazil trapped him."

"How?"

Nox shrugs. "No idea. One night he was just gone. Other witch doctors say he went mad."

"What do you think caused it?"

"Magic is strange. Like anything powerful, it can fail. Maybe he was caught in a moment of weakness."

I reach for Nox's hand and squeeze. We're so similar, it's uncanny . . . both caught between our parents and our futures, and both trying to figure out our places in the world. "I'm sorry."

"That's life."

We sit in silence for a few minutes. "Nox, what do you know about Bazil besides him being the self-crowned king of this silk cottonwood tree?"

"What do you mean?"

How do I explain that I sometimes let Bazil dream-walk into my head? I don't think that's going to go over well. "I spoke to him once, after I painted a picture of this tree in Granny's house. He said that people infected him." I rush out the rest of the words. "It got me thinking. . . . Not everyone starts out being bad, right? I mean, I didn't plan on getting in trouble for painting over public property. I just wanted someone to see me, to hear me. I'm not a bad person, so maybe Bazil isn't either. Maybe he just wants to be heard?"

Nox's moss-green eyes meet mine. "Bazil is the worst of the jumbies, Rika."

"I know that he's bad now, but what if he wasn't always?"

"You can't compare having a tough time at school and being upset with your family to a creature that's out to destroy the entire world, and imprisoned two of our parents in the process." He stares at me, his eyes cutting deep. "What brought this on?"

"I don't know." I peer at the ground. "I get flashes that he's sad."

"Is he in your head again, Rika?"

Blushing, I bite my lip. "Sometimes?"

Nox makes an exasperated noise. "You need to use your shield. Remember the way I taught you with Ushara? Do the same. Don't let him in. He's only going to try to confuse and manipulate you. He's beyond dangerous, Rika. You can't trust him." He turns to face me, his face resolute. "I'm going to try to take magic from you, okay? Try to stop me."

What?

"Nox, no. I'm tired."

But there's suddenly a huge blanket thrown over my brain as though something—some outside presence—has momentarily clouded my senses. It's weird and invasive. Nox's eyes glow emerald and I know that he's mounting some kind of magical attack.

"Push against me, Rika." He tugs, and I feel myself weaken. Not in actual, physical energy, but in spirit, as though some force is pulling directly from my heart. My skin vibrates with shock. I'd accused him of being a vampire once, and this experiment isn't convincing me otherwise.

I build the wall as he told me, feeling the pull lessen as my wall thickens and heightens. I envision my shield as being impenetrable, and Nox gives me an approving look when I don't feel him anymore. "That's good. If Bazil comes to you, block him out."

I'm about to yell at him to never do that again—because Nox being anywhere in my brain is weird—but footsteps echo from above us, and we both look up as a red-faced Monique stumbles into view. "We have to go. Douens are coming!"

"They're seriously like cockroaches," I mutter. No matter what we do to escape them, they're always showing up.

"From below?" Nox asks Monique, reaching down to help me stand.

She shakes her head, something clouding in her gaze as

she stares at us before it's gone. I'm at a loss trying to work out what goes on in that girl's head. "Up top. They're way up, but I saw a door before. Maybe that's a hiding place or a way out? It's not far."

"Yes, good idea," Nox says. "Let's go."

I spot Piku still enjoying his cricket buffet. "Piku, come on!"

He scrambles up my leg and perches in my hood. We run behind Monique for a few minutes, breaths loud in the silence. I don't hear anything that sounds like footsteps coming from above, but maybe the douens are not that close yet. My heartbeat is hammering too loudly in my head for me to be sure anyway. Monique comes to a sudden halt and I see the small metal door she's talking about. It's not that large, but we can definitely fit through.

"Come on, come on," she says, taking my hand. "They're nearly here."

Nox leans past the railing to stare upward. "I don't hear anything. Are you sure you saw them, Monique? You know this maze can make us think something's there when it's not."

But Monique is already yanking me with her through the opening, and the last thing I see before the door seals shut behind us is Nox's astonished and utterly betrayed face.

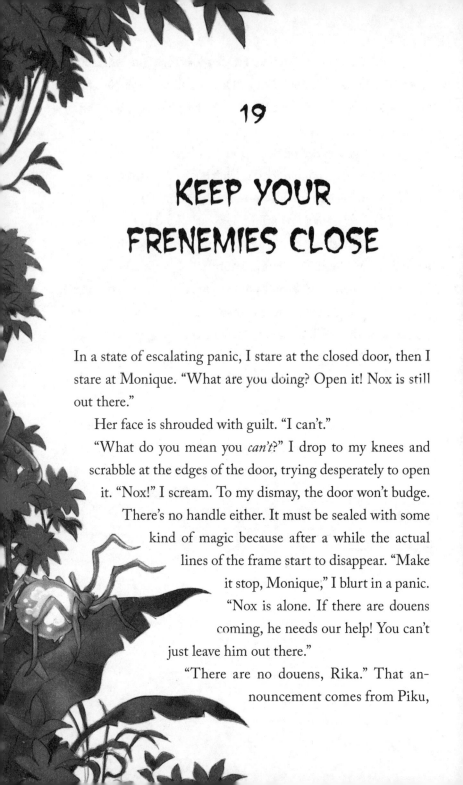

19

KEEP YOUR
FRENEMIES CLOSE

In a state of escalating panic, I stare at the closed door, then I stare at Monique. "What are you doing? Open it! Nox is still out there."

Her face is shrouded with guilt. "I can't."

"What do you mean you *can't*?" I drop to my knees and scrabble at the edges of the door, trying desperately to open it. "Nox!" I scream. To my dismay, the door won't budge. There's no handle either. It must be sealed with some kind of magic because after a while the actual lines of the frame start to disappear. "Make it stop, Monique," I blurt in a panic.

"Nox is alone. If there are douens coming, he needs our help! You can't just leave him out there."

"There are no douens, Rika." That announcement comes from Piku, who is clicking his jaw in disgust, perched on my shoulder and flaring his dewlap. "This no-good Fire Minder misled us."

"You lied?" I glare at Monique. I should have guessed that Monique was going to throw me under the bus, but I didn't think she would do that to Nox. They've been friends for a long, long time. Does she truly hate me *that* much? We were a team . . . we were working together. And she was warming up to me. Unless it was all an act.

"Lennox will be fine. The douens don't want him."

Right, they want *me*. I scowl, fingers balling into fists at my sides.

Piku cocks his head. "Are you sure of that?"

A hint of worry crosses her face, but then she tosses her long hair and shrugs. "He can take care of himself, just like Fitz and Hazel."

"Why are you doing this, Monique?" I ask. "I mean, I know you've always disliked me, but Nox is your family."

Her face twists with a combination of bleak sadness and regret. "You don't understand. She's the only one who truly loves me, and I can't risk her. Not even for you." A single tear slides down one cheek before Monique swipes it away like she's angry for showing any emotion.

"Who are you talking about?" I ask.

A blush blooms on her cheeks. "No one. Never mind."

That's the second time she's said *never mind* to me. I'm baffled. Had Monique been planning to sabotage us the whole time? Even when she saved me from the bat's butt mist? It doesn't make sense. I glance back at the door that's nearly gone. "We're so close, Monique. Let's get Nox and finish this. Open the door, please."

"I can't because it's not my magic."

I swallow, my stomach tumbling, my eyes narrowing on her. "What do you mean, it's not your magic? What did you do?"

She waves a hand, her face hardening. "I didn't do anything that wasn't already going to happen. You're never going to beat the maze, don't you understand that? This is a distraction, a diversion. A game."

"My family is not a game," I say quietly, watching her and seeing the struggle in her features. I have to figure out a way to get her to help me or to get away from her and find Nox on my own. Easier said than done . . . this girl could turn me into s'mores in a hot second. "We're talking about my mom, Monique. And Nox's dad. You're a Minder; your job is to protect, isn't it?"

I said the wrong thing, and I want to steups in vexation—it really is quite satisfying when you're frustrated—but I roll my lips instead, seeing the moment my words sink in.

"My job is to lose the one person who cares about me?" she says.

Does she mean Nox? I mean, Nox is kind of awesome, but I wouldn't risk the world for a guy. If she likes him that way, she's welcome to him. I feel a weird twinge inside, admitting that as though it doesn't quite ring true. I recall Nox's smile of approval when I got the last riddle correct, and my heart warms. Fine, I might have a tiny, tiny crush, but even I know the rules. Everyone in my middle school knows about girl code: your friends' crushes are off-limits.

Not that Monique and I are even remotely besties or anything, but still . . .

"You don't have to worry about Nox. He's just trying to get to his dad, same as me."

"You think this is about a *boy*?" She lets out a hopeless laugh. "Of course you would."

"Then who?"

I'm distracted by the flash of red in my peripheral vision and recognition is fast to follow. *Ushara*. Her again. She's like a dog with a bone. The rush of anger at seeing her is quickly replaced by alarm.

Is this another trial?

La diablesse saunters toward us, her scarlet skirts swishing like they're alive. Fear climbs into my throat as I remember how close she'd nearly gotten to me last time and charmed me with feelings of adoration. On instinct, I draw my shield close, remembering Nox's lessons on how to build the walls in my head to keep her out. My shield won't do anything on the offensive, but at the very least, it'll stop her from getting into my mind.

"Piku," I whisper. "I can't beat her alone. What do we do?"

"Minder," he says to Monique. "Do your duty. Defend the trinity."

With Monique's fire magic, we might have a slim chance to get out of this. My frightened gaze pans to the Fire Minder who looks, once again, like she's fighting some kind of internal battle. Shame and defiance war on her face as the jumbie approaches.

"Well done, Monique."

The words feel like someone has punched me three times in the gut: *Well. Done. Monique.* This takes betrayal to a whole new level of jerkdom.

"You planned this?" I whisper.

Even Piku lets out a disbelieving hiss when I back away, reeling in shock. Monique had fully intended to hand me over to the enemy. No wonder she couldn't open the door to let Nox in—the magic sealing it shut must have been la diablesse's. I can't even comprehend the depth of her deception here and what such a betrayal would mean to the other Minders.

"I'm so sorry," she whispers, eyes sliding to me. "I had to. Grandma Love is sick, Darika."

"I know she's sick. She's my granny. That doesn't mean you had to sell me out. We're trying to fix it."

Sadness burns in Monique's guilt-ridden gaze, her voice cracking in misery. "Not quickly enough. Day by day, she's wasting away, and Ushara said she would help her if I did this."

"She's tricking you!"

Monique shakes her head. "She promised to give back the bit of Grandma Love's soul that the tree stole. The promise is binding."

"And you believed her?" I scoff.

She squares her shoulders and gives her head a shake just as Ushara reaches us. "I have your word, Bazil's word, that she'll be whole again?"

"As agreed, your precious Grandma Love will be spared."

"Monique, you know that this will not win you any favor," Piku says. "Delilah values family and loyalty above all. She will never forgive you for putting Darika in danger like this."

A ragged sound rips from her throat as a defiant, tear-filled gaze turns to us. "Why? Because she's one of the trinity and can do no wrong?" She spears me with a bitter gaze. "You didn't even want to be on the island. Grandma Love has me, she doesn't need you. I tried to keep her safe. That's why I blocked her from entering."

Ushara is watching our exchange with no small amount of glee. She's enjoying this, I realize, even as it feels like someone is stomping on my chest. Monique's words are as painful as kicks to my rib cage.

"*You* blocked Granny?" I ask incredulously. "Why?"

"I told you. To keep her safe. She was too sick to come in here, couldn't you see that? *I* was going to help her fix everything." Her voice breaks on a sob. "You should have just gone back home."

I think of the way Monique had looked at me in the kitchen after the trickery in the woods, when she'd told me that I didn't belong here.

"Monique, what are you talking about? Granny doesn't love me more than you."

"Doesn't she?"

My goodness, Monique was jealous. I'd had the exact same thought . . . that Granny loved her more than me. I shake my head. "I never imagined that you would feel threatened by *me*," I admit. "That's how I felt about you, Monique. That you made a better granddaughter than I ever could. She adores you."

She stares at me. "What?"

I swallow and stick my irrational jealousy where it belongs. "There's room for both of us, Monique. That's how love works." Even as I say the words, I recognize how true they are.

I see her hesitation, but before she can act on it, Ushara is between us. "The bargain has been made, the soul healed as agreed."

"Wait," Monique says, eyes darting to me, suddenly uncertain. "What's going to happen to her?"

"She's no longer your concern, *Minder*." Ushara spits the last.

"Hang on a second!"

Monique's hands begin to glow red, but she's a beat too late. I know the maze is going to transform before the ground starts its telltale rumbling. Maybe I have a chance to escape Ushara if I can convince Monique we're in this together, but I'm distracted as red-painted nails reach out to hook into my hair, yanking me back. A wide grin cracks Ushara's face as I'm swarmed by fondness for la diablesse. I'm so glad she's here. I'm dimly aware of Piku scratching at me, but I ignore him.

Monique is screaming something, but her voice seems so far away. We're shifting on huge checkerboard squares. A crevice appears, widening until Monique is a glowing little red ember on the opposite side, and I can't imagine what on earth I was so worried about. I'm safe and I'm with a wonderful lady who only wants to help me.

I hear Nox's voice in my head: *Resist her, Rika.*

"Rika!" a panicked voice screeches in my ear. "Don't give in."

"Nox?"

But Nox isn't here.

Where *is* here?

"Where are we?" I mutter thickly, as though my thoughts are jumbled and drowning in maple syrup. *Bricks.* I have to build them.

A cloying perfume fills my nose and I realize I'm being held next to someone. I glance up to see a gaunt, skeletal face that shimmers in the next heartbeat into a breathtakingly gorgeous face that anyone would die to have.

A blur of green flies off my shoulder, only to be followed by a scream and then a thump. For a moment, the grip on my hair releases as a limp Piku gets scooped up by a clawed hand. My brain clears. A wall . . . I have to create a wall. A shield. To help my friend!

"Bricks," I mumble.

Unable to do much else, I focus on the construction of my mental barricade, one building block at a time. In any scary situation, small steps are the answer. I push my escalating alarm and dread to the side. Those won't help me now; only single-minded focus will. When you're cornered, the best thing you can do is not panic. Fear is healthy. Panic in the face of it is deadly.

Granny's words come to me: *Fear keeps us ready to act.*

And so I *act.* I build. With each block, I feel the drowning sensation lessen. When I'm certain that Ushara is completely blocked out, I whirl away, leaving a clump of my dark strands in her bony fingers. The creepy attic we're in is dank, low-ceilinged, and has no exits that I can see. It's also shaped like a weird ring. Maybe there's an exit on the other side. I'd take the ballroom with the bats and spiders over this place, which smells like a janitor's closet.

"What are you doing, chile? Come back. I'll take you to where you want to go."

"Don't lie. You're trying to trick me."

She flinches as if being called a liar hurts. Her crimson dress is in tatters, I notice, much like her emaciated face. Now that my shield is firmly in place, the illusions of both her beauty and charm are wiped away. And instead of perfume, she reeks of decaying flesh.

An ugly snarl curls her lips as she brings my hair to her cheek. "I'll drag you by your neck if I have to, witchen."

"I'm not going anywhere with you! Where's Piku?"

"Your green pet?" She pats a pocket on her ratty gown, and I'm relieved to hear cursing and hissing from the inside, which means he's still alive. For now. "That little reptile is a menace."

"If you hurt him, you'll pay."

Ushara leers. "Don't worry, the king wants him alive. Tastes better fighting, or so I've heard."

I blanch at her meaning. Bazil intends to eat him.

Don't worry, Piku. I'll get you out. You're not going to be anyone's meal.

I back away from her and run down a long passageway, only to come upon her again. This place is a loop that has no end. I wasn't far off when I thought it seemed shaped like a crop circle. For the hundredth time, I curse this rotten maze and its creepy traps. "Where are my friends?"

"Friends?" She cackles. "Like the one who delivered you to me?"

Strangely enough, I don't feel any anger toward Monique. Well, not as much as I did earlier. I'm ashamed of how I behaved because I was jealous of her, too. What she did wasn't right, but those actions were hers. I can only control me. "She messed up, but she tried to fix it. I am going to try to forgive her."

La diablesse's eyes narrow. "What? She lied to you."

"We all make mistakes," I say with a shrug. "And your biggest one was to underestimate me. I *am* a witch. And I am a Lovelace."

"You going to fight me, little girl? You and what army?"

I bring my palms to my sides. "Just me."

A pointed tendril of *something*—dark magic, maybe—reaches out toward me and recoils. La diablesse snarls and a dozen more shooting tentacles come my way. I brace, but as before, they slither back. Her eyes fall to the glowing moonstones and abalone shells on the bracelet on my left wrist and she mutters a curse. It must protect against harm. Just like the jet gemstone beads on my right are supposed to ward off the evil eye. People in Trinidad give them to babies. Mom told me Granny had made one for me as an infant, but it would obviously be much too small now.

Thanks, Granny!

There's no time to celebrate my good luck, however, as a wicked claw swipes out and I feel a stinging on my arm before a line of fresh blood wells up. By the time I can dart out of reach—hard in this narrow space—another jab catches me on the soft, fleshy underside of my other arm, followed by another bloody welt. Ushara's grin is mocking as though she's a cat playing with a mouse. I'm the mouse, in case there was any question.

But mice are small, and they're fast.

Smart, too.

Never underestimate something because of its size . . . or age.

She can't use magic, which means she has to come at me physically. I don't have much of an advantage, but it's enough. I run for a few minutes, the evil creature hot on my heels, when I realize how much energy I'm wasting. Obviously, running around in a literal loop is getting me nowhere fast.

Focusing my efforts, I whirl around to face her head-on. I anticipate her next two strikes and crouch to roll out of the way. I gasp as the jet bead and gold bracelet on my right wrist breaks and falls to the ground. But I have no time to worry as Ushara kicks it out of the way and comes at me again. Every lunge she makes toward me, I manage to leap aside at the last moment. Her frustration is clear, but even I know that I can't avoid her for long. I have no offensive magic and I have no weapons.

Feinting left, I dive to the right, feeling her talons rake across my back, tearing through layers of cotton. *Ouch*, that's going to leave a mark . . . or four. Ushara brings her clawed fingertips to her mouth and licks them with a forked tongue. "Delicious."

What is with the obsession with making me a snack in here?

Focus, Rika!

While her milky eyes are rolling back in her head, I scan the place. Still no exits that I can see. No hiding places either. Is there something I can use in defense? A piece of furniture that could double as a club or a spear? Since she's a jumbie, it probably won't hurt her, but maybe it might slow her down. But there's nothing, not even a sliver of wood to act as a stake.

She laughs, her maniacal cackles filling the room.

"Give up yet?"

I scowl. "Never."

My bravado is all I have. People have always told me I don't know how or when to ask for help, but when I'm finally ready to, there's no one around to ask. Go figure, right? The moment you realize you're not an island is the soul-gutting moment when you understand that you can't thrive alone.

"Mom, Granny, if either of you can hear me, I sure could use a little help right now."

Ushara screams and dashes toward me, and as her tattered skirts fly apart, I see it. Not the sight of the cloven foot that makes me shudder, but the velvet pouch at her waist. The one that Nox had touched, the one that had made her afraid and leap back from him at the market. It's something she treasures.

Just before she crashes into me, I let myself drop and roll, my knees taking the brunt of the pain as I reach up and snatch the bag. Without stopping, I dart across to the other side of the room, my prize clutched in one palm. Her shriek is inhuman when she realizes what I've done.

"What's in this?" I ask her, holding it up.

"Give it to me," she whines.

"Release Piku," I counter.

She makes a fist over the pocket. "I'll kill him."

My heart quakes at the threat, but I hold my ground. Clearly I have the upper hand now. "Touch one frill on his body, and I will destroy this with every ounce of magic inside of me. Now let him out." She doesn't have to know that I have no attack magic to speak of, so I keep my head high and my stare confident. Ushara eyeballs me as if trying to see how serious I am. Losing my patience, I shake the bag and pretend to hold it upside down. "Don't test me!"

"Wait." Trembling, she passes a hand over the cinched pocket and a disgruntled Piku scrambles free and scampers over to me.

I smirk at the utter rage on her face. "What do you have in this, anyway?"

She actually drops to the ground in an imploring position as I tug open the laces on the sack. I nearly puke at the foul scent that's even worse than the sewage smell earlier in the maze. Imagine the odor of a graveyard with the underlying stench of days'-old roadkill. I don't have to do a deep dive before I realize that inside, there are human and animal teeth, locks of hair, including the dark-brown one she'd stolen from me, and what appears to be pieces of old bones, picked clean. The dirt at the bottom of the pouch reeks. My mouth fills with bile.

I don't want to touch the bones or the teeth, but I don't want her to have a lock of my hair either. Who knows what she'll do with it. Fishing it out, I close the bag. "Piku, what do I do now?"

"You cannot let her have it," he says grimly. "The conjure bag is her totem and the source of her power."

"How do I get rid of it?" I lower my voice to a whisper. "You know, without magic?"

"You *have* magic, Rika," Piku says, his head cocked and eye intent on me.

I shake my head. "Yes, but spirit doesn't really do anything."

"Creation magic starts with a seed. A seed of thought. A whisper of an idea. Spirit blossoms and blooms when inspiration strikes."

"Nothing's striking."

Ushara lets out a hiss and a slow, knowing smile crawls over her face. Crap, maybe she heard me mention that my magic's useless. Panic slicks through my veins when she stands and saunters toward us.

"Don't come any closer!" I say and hold the bag aloft. "Or else!"

"Or else what?"

Crap. She definitely overheard. I close my eyes shut and focus everything I have on the pouch in my hand. *Create, magic, create.* I silently beg for help. I offer up all the promises I can think of to anyone listening . . . but nothing happens. Piku is wrong. The only sound in the room is Ushara's mocking laughter. "Poor little broken witchen."

"Dig deep, Rika," Piku says. "Reach for it."

Reach for what? Because the only thing inside me right now is the fear that we're probably—*okay, most likely*—going to lose. Grinding my teeth, I shake my head. If I could paint myself in this moment, it would be in colors of red and black, and maybe some yellow. Fear, darkness, and fading hope. The conjure bag in my hand would be a blot of purple at the center . . . swallowed up by another swirl of black.

Suddenly, as if fed by the images, the moonstones and abalone shells on the remaining bracelet start to blaze. I feel a warmth travel up my wrist to my arm, and then over my chest. My entire core warms with a pale, blushing pink light. Is this Granny's protection magic? It must be. I concentrate, letting the magic shift until the shine of the stones glistens so bright I have to squeeze my eyes shut. My palm grips the conjure bag as it explodes into sparkly black dust.

"No!" Ushara shrieks, but I can't even part my eyelids to see. Wind lifts the ends of my hair and the ground rumbles beneath my feet.

After a moment, the light dims.

I crack open one eyelid. My palm is empty. And la diablesse is gone.

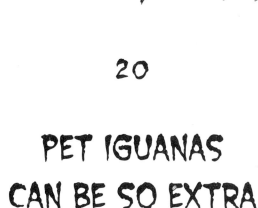

20

PET IGUANAS
CAN BE SO EXTRA

After Ushara vanished into nothingness, thanks to what I'm
positive was Granny's intervention, another doorway appeared.
Piku and I made haste getting through it in case it disappeared
too. But since then, we've been trapped on another level. This
one reminds me of the white room in Granny's house, only
this one has no windows and no doors. I'm starting to sense
a pattern with this whole setup.

"Do you think this is the next trial?" I ask Piku,
who has explored every corner and crevice of the
room. I still don't know if the everlasting
staircase counted as the seventh or
if the fight against Ushara counted
as eight. I bet both of those were
Monique's doing, which puts us squarely at
level seven. Two to go after this, and the team has
dwindled to just Piku and me.

"There's nothing here," he replies.

"Every mystery has an answer, right?" I say. "We just have to solve it."

But I have to admit that I am disheartened. There's nothing like a plain room with four white walls to make you lose hope. I'd joked about the island being my prison, but this is the real deal. Claustrophobia starts to set—like the walls are closing in.

Holy Skittles. They *are*! Or at least, one might be.

"Piku," I say. "Notice anything weird about this room?"

He tilts his neck and gives me a lizard eye roll. "The walls are white and we're stuck here until we find a stupid key."

I swallow my laugh. He sounds more like me every day. "Yes, but did it get smaller or is that my imagination?"

He looks doubtful as he surveys the area, but then he scuttles off, walking the full circuit of each of the four sides. "You're right," he says. "Those two sides got smaller, so one is moving."

"So, for argument's sake, does that mean we could get squashed soon?"

"That would be an excellent deduction."

We resume our search, peering at every corner and crack. But we're essentially caged in a perfect white cube—no, rectangle now—with no seams. I walk the perimeter several times. Piku and I time each rotation and manage to work out that the wall shifts inward two inches every count of sixty Mississippis, which means we don't have much time before neither of us can move. Every minute means two inches, and though my math is terrible, I'm estimating in a room that's ten feet square with one wall on the move, we're looking at less than an hour before squishville.

Frustration spikes. "I don't know where the key is, Piku. There's nothing here."

"Seems like it," he says. "But we've come too far to give up now, haven't we?"

I squat in the middle of the space and drop my head between my knees. "Yes, but we always had help." I caress my bracelet, my fingertips tracing each of the three stones and interlocking shells, I'm guessing one for each of us—me, my mom, and my grandmother. "Even with Ushara, I had help from Granny. She knew I was a dud so she lent me some of her magic."

"Magic doesn't work like that."

I frown. "What?"

"I could give you a crystal full of magic and it would never work for you. It would just be a pretty crystal." He hops up to my knee. "What exactly do you think happened in the other room?"

"Granny's magic took out the lajabless."

"Rika, that was your magic."

I shake my head. "No, the bracelet saved us. I know what I felt, Piku, and that light came from these stones."

"Okay, what were you thinking when the bag exploded?"

"About painting myself right before we died."

He chuffs. "See?"

"Okay, riddle me this, O Brilliant One: if I can do magic, then how come I can't do any now?" I wiggle my fingers for good measure. "I'm a flop."

Piku blinks. "Is that what you think?"

"That's what I know. Monique said so, remember?"

The little iguana gets right up in my face, his dewlap flaring, letting me know that he's all kinds of frustrated with me. "Let me set the record straight. The only reason the Minders were able to get in this tree was because of you. So if you're going to sit around and grumble like a spoiled little brat, whining about being a flop and not having any magic, boo hoo, then we might as well give up and let these four walls grind us to pulp. Because none of the others are here." He hisses in my face. "*You* are our only hope. So what are you going to do?"

He's right. While Piku's harsh words sting a bit, his defense of me feels nice, even though it's couched in a heavy dose of tough love. Self-pity isn't going to get us anywhere. Monique might have awesome fire powers and could easily be cast as a Disney child actor, but I've got a few things she doesn't.

I'm stubborn. And I'm stubborn.

Fine, I have one thing going for me.

"You're a good friend, Piku. Thank you." He scrambles up my arm and nuzzles my jaw. It actually feels good . . . at least until one of his dorsal spines pokes me in the chin. "Okay. We have four walls, which we've checked for weaknesses." I empty my pockets. "Plus some coins, a key chain, lip balm, and this jar of paint Granny gave me."

Seriously, why would she give me paint? I stare at it. Duh, unless I'm holding *magic* paint. My skin buzzes as though in agreement, wonder unfurling through me. I remove the lid and stare at the iridescent liquid, which is no doubt magical in nature. No paint I've ever found in a hobby or art store looks like this. I poke at the little brush in the lid and then swirl it into the liquid. "I think Granny meant for me to paint something. But what?"

Piku brightens and gives it an experimental sniff. "Try it, then."

"And paint what? There's only one color."

"So? You used creation magic when you painted a portal with ordinary paint back at the house," he points out, and I blink in surprise. I did do that. "Maybe you can get us out of here with that."

I frown at him, feeling the first stirring of excitement in my veins. In the place with fruit trees, Nox had said I had creation magic woven from spirit. "You think I should paint on the wall?" He nods with a flick of his tongue. "There's not a lot in here and I don't know if this will last." The pot is tiny like the size of a nail polish bottle.

The question is, what should I paint? I could paint the outside of the tree—if Piku's right, maybe it could portal us outside, but that won't help my mom. If I paint something in my bedroom or a flower from the garden outside my room, it could take me to Granny's house and maybe she could help us. But we would have the same issue of her being blocked from entering and I don't know where Monique is to remove whatever spell she set. Besides, she could be anywhere in this tree, along with Nox and the twins.

No, there's only one thing I can paint.

And that's something from my mom's room. *Here.*

I envision it as clearly as I can, when I'd touched her face in my tree—the small cot, the lump on the bed, the view of her dark curls spilling over the woolen blanket. I only have to pick one object, so I go with the thing that's most unlikely to change. The bed. With a deep breath, I stand and approach one of the walls. This is either going to be a brilliant idea or really, really, *really* foolish.

At the first lift of the brush, something breaks loose within me. It's weird, almost as if a surge of energy swirls in the pit of my stomach.

Here goes nothing!

With a confident stroke, I edge out the frame of the bed, wondering what color will show up on the wall, and I huff a disbelieving breath. I'm reminded of those coloring books for little kids that you use water to paint in the pictures and then the color magically appears? Well, that's happening now, only the colors appear as if transcribed directly from my mind.

The brown knotted wood of the bedposts, the linen sheets and scratchy wool blanket . . . everything comes vibrantly alive with each careful brushstroke. And the clearer I imagine it in my head, the more tangibly it appears. Every detail, down to the pulled threads of the blanket and the threadbare edges, come to life on the wall.

"Rika?"

"Yes, Piku?" I answer distractedly as I gnaw on my lip, trying to get the edge of the headboard just right. In my mind's eye I can see some intricately carved swirls in the wood, and I want to make sure I get everything.

"You're glowing."

My hand freezes and I stare down. Sure enough, the same blushing pink that I'd seen a hint of when I'd used Granny's bracelet envelops my fingers. Only, the petal pink glow is not coming from the moonstones on her bracelet, but from *me*!

My magic.

The sight's so beautiful that my breath catches. I'm not a flop or a dud. I just have a different kind of magic than the Minders do, one rooted in creativity. Thinking back, it makes so much sense. Like my mom, I've always had this power. To my surprise, the paint in the pot hasn't gone down a bit. I close the jar tightly and stick it in my pocket.

I blink and step back, only to nearly crush Piku underfoot. He squeals and darts out of the way. "Sorry."

After a quick look around, and given the much tinier, cramped area I'm now creating in, I realize that the room has shrunk. Correction: *is* shrinking! If this doesn't work, we're dust. Literally.

"Why didn't you say something?" I ask, my heart trying once more to crash out of my chest.

Piku chuffs. "This is our one shot, and no one messes with the muse."

We let the paint dry a little while I study the miniature bed. It's not to scale, of course. That would have taken forever. But even sized so much smaller, the level of detail really is something to be proud of . . . down to the soft, worn folds of the blanket and the crumpled appearance of warmth as if someone has only just rolled out of the sheets.

I scoop up Piku. "Ready?" he asks.

"What's the worst that can happen?" I say with a wink and then burst out laughing. "Don't answer that."

In this tree, the worst that can happen will probably end

up being the worst thing in the world, and that's the last thing either of us wants.

"To not ending up in a latrine somewhere," I say.

Piku snorts. "Yuck. Let's hope not."

I exhale and press my fingers to the painting of the bed.

As before, magic tugs on my belly button, the unearthly sensation of suction yanking me toward an unknown destination. I should be used to it by now, but the impression is not one that is normal on any level. A buzzing sound fills my ears and the top layer of my skin feels like it's pulling off my body. I'm totally fine, of course, but time and space portal travel is as though your body is flipping inside out and being drained through a straw.

We come to a stop in my mom's cell, the tiny room that I'd seen with the tree in Granny's house what seems like forever ago, landing squarely in the middle of the bed with a squeaky bounce.

And we're not alone.

"Darika?" my mom mumbles, her voice coming out raspy.

Scrambling off the bed, I fling myself into her arms, her familiar scent of sweet orange and cocoa butter curling around me. I burst into tears, sobbing. "Oh my gosh, Mom, I've missed you! Are you okay? Are you hurt?"

"I've missed you too," she says, squeezing me and peppering my sweaty forehead with kisses. "I'm fine. Is this real? Are you truly here, sassy-pea?"

I smile at the old nickname. Dad calls me sweet-pea and Mom always used to say that I was much too sassy to be sweet. The memory makes me cry harder. "Yes, Mom. I'm real. I was stuck in a weird white room and somehow I managed to find you. I didn't even know I could, but Piku did."

"Who's Piku?"

"My friend. Piku, say hi."

I release her just enough so the iguana can poke out of my hoodie. "My lady," he says in such a proper, worshipful voice it makes me want to giggle. "What an honor."

"Oh, hello there," she says with a fond smile, her eyes flicking back to mine after Piku's deferential address. "I suppose you know about the trinity."

I huff a laugh.

"Mom, why didn't you tell me you were a witch?" I scold but then hug her close again. I never want to let her go, not even to yell at her for not telling me who I really am. "Like with magic and stuff?"

"I wanted you to have a normal life."

I'm holding her so tightly, I nearly crack a rib. "I needed you, Mom."

"I know, and I'm so sorry. I didn't mean to be gone so long; I just got stuck in this tree." Her eyes widen as she holds me away from her with a scowl, concern crossing her beautiful brown gaze. "Wait, how *did* you get in?"

"Granny gave me special paint and I drew your bed, and it made some kind of magic portal, so here I am."

She tugs on one of my dark-brown strands with a proud smile. "Because you have a gift, love. Is Mama with you?"

"No, Granny got stuck outside."

Mom's eyes narrow. "You're here alone?"

"Well, I wasn't," I say. "I was with the Minders, but we

got separated. Nox got locked out, Monique lost her mind, and the twins got stuck on one of the levels with a stinking soucouyant, bloodsucking ball of fire. It's a long story, I can tell it to you later. We need to leave."

"But *I* want to hear it now. Do share your adventures, little witch."

The deep, scary voice I hear doesn't belong to my mom. Then I see him—a massive green devil stalking into my mom's room, dwarfing me with his hulking presence. Mom throws herself in front of me, hands spread wide in a protective stance, and I peek around her.

Bazil.

He looks really, really, *really* mad.

21

SKITTLES SAVE THE DAY (DUH)

At the sight of Bazil, Piku squeals and dives down into my hood. I get his reaction—we're in the devil's tower, after all, and the king of the silk cotton tree himself just walked in. Moving around my mom, I narrow my eyes at the new arrival, unwilling to show fear even though the sight of him makes my limbs tremble. I could have sworn there was a glass barrier I'd seen in my earlier visions.

I make a hurried glance around the room, which I hadn't done before. A vase of fresh flowers sits on a desk that's covered with writing materials, paints, and sketch pads. A soft rug rests below my seat, and on the walls are paintings that have the same look as my mom's in Granny's house. That's weird . . . this room is like any other, not a cell. My brows knit together. Is this some messed-up illusion?

"I got here fair and square, Bazil," I say, trying to make myself bigger than I am, even though a tiny, sensible voice inside of me is screaming *That won't work, he's not a bear* and *Run, Rika, run.* "Let my mom and Papa Bois go."

"Rika," my mom says, gently grasping my elbow.

I shake off her hand. "No, he made a bargain and he has to honor his vow. I won. I crushed the final challenge. I'm here."

"How did you get here?" Bazil asks in a conversational tone that reminds me of the Dr. Facilier–looking man at the well, though his appearance is completely different now. He wears the same bark-like skin from when I first entered the tree, his body huge and muscled and intimidating. That spindly crown is bigger than before, too. But his eyes are the same—a murky, sludgy green that reminds me of pond scum. Oddly, I'm not afraid, which I put down to sheer adrenaline. There's something about him that seems strangely familiar again. Maybe that's because we've spoken a few times throughout this whole thing.

"Turns out there's magic in art," I say with a smug smile. "Who knew?"

A dark glance spears me. "Explain."

"I painted a portal." I throw my hands out. "What does it matter? I beat your stupid maze. Release my mom, Papa Bois, and my friends, while you're at it. I won. I got here in time in one piece."

His laugh fills the room, making me want to clamp my hands over my ears. It sounds like fracturing thunder. The devil laughs so hard, he bends over clutching his sides. "Clever,

clever girl, but that little trick doesn't count. You see, Rika dearest, you didn't actually best the trials."

"I did!" A horrid feeling comes over me. What if he doesn't let my mom go? What then? It's not like I can take on a supernatural monster that's probably thousands of years old. Creation magic might be cool, but what am I going to do if he doesn't honor our deal? Paint him to death? I stick my hand in my pocket and grab hold of my little pot for courage. "This is over, Bazil."

"So feisty. I admire your mettle in the face of incredible odds, young one." Still smiling with a patronizing look, the devil cants his head. "However, if we are being fair, you completed seven levels at most, and the challenge is over when I say so." He glances up, his amused gaze fastening on my mom. "And besides, your mother is not a prisoner. Are you, Dulcie?"

I blink at the shocker of all shockers. Wait, what?

Turning, I meet my mother's even stare. "What's he saying, Mom?"

"Yes, Dulcie, shall we tell her?" Bazil says, clasping his hands together as if we're having a teatime chat and not a life-or-death discussion about freedom from magical bonds.

"Don't," she says softly, coming up behind me.

I pause at the hesitation in her voice as well as the complete lack of fear or anger or resignation. In the face of the devil's refusal to let her go, my mom is . . . unnaturally calm. A thread of anxiety creeps down my spine. Something's off. Did he put some kind of spell on her?

"Mom, what does he mean?"

She turns me around to face her, those gentle eyes fastening on me with so much love and devotion I want to throw myself into her arms again. "I'm not a prisoner, Rika."

"I don't understand."

"I'm here of my own accord. It was the only way for me to stop Pa"—she chokes and coughs as though something had tightened around her throat, which reminds me of the time I couldn't speak after Monique made me swear to secrecy in the woods—"Bazil from sending Ushara after your dad, your stepmom, and your baby brothers. And you, especially." Her fingers cup my cheek, a soft smile curling her mouth. "But you, my darling, you're so resilient and so brave. Most kids would have run the other way."

"I couldn't leave you here," I say. "I also got rid of Ushara."

Her eyes flash as she glares at the devil. "You tricked me. You showed me that Darika had given up and was returning to Colorado."

"A necessary illusion," he replies without an ounce of remorse.

Indignation followed by understanding floods me. One, I'd *never* give up on my mom. And two, of course he never intended for me to conquer the maze or even see her. If she had agreed to be here willingly, he wouldn't have wanted to give her any reason to leave. And if she thought I was in danger, she would.

He spreads his palms wide. "It delighted me to see her thrive in my maze."

Worry and regret fill her expression. "What were you thinking? She could have been killed in your twisted games, you liar!"

"And yet, she stands before you." Bazil shrugs as she gasps, her hands skimming my arms and hesitating over faint scratches. In wonder, I stare at them—they'd been bleeding profusely and oozing fluid only a short while ago. I've healed! I add that to my short list of magical accomplishments.

"You're hurt. What caused these?" she asks, fingers grazing over splotches of dried blood that didn't mysteriously disappear.

"Nothing serious, Mom."

She glowers over my shoulder. "I've seen your monstrous maze. It's lucky she even survived. Most don't." Electricity hums over her skin, transferring into mine, and I gasp at the feel of so much power. So that's what the magic of an elder witch feels like.

"Careful, Dulcie," Bazil warns. "Any harm you visit upon me will affect you just the same."

"The pain will be worth it," she growls.

"The trials weren't so bad," I tell my mom, not wanting her to get hurt because of me. Clearly, their agreement means she can't use magic against him. "And besides, I had help."

"I knew she would come," Bazil crows. "Once I set out enough bait."

I scowl. "You wanted me here, right?"

"Alas, while I secured your mother's promise to remain here with me of her own free will, I am still bound by the tree's magic, and I long for my freedom. Your mother's sacrifice has not done what she'd hoped. Humans must pay."

He'd said that before at the well. "And this payment means their destruction?"

261

"Yes."

"Because they somehow infected you?" He nods, a deep sadness flickering in his eyes. It's such an odd emotion to see from a monster that it makes me pause. For a moment, they shimmer from sludge-gray to a deep moss green filled with laughter and tenderness. I've seen those eyes before. . . .

"You are the key to releasing me, Darika," he says. "You must break the spell."

I press myself into my mom, taking comfort in her presence. "I'll never free you, even if I have to lock myself in here too."

"No, Rika!" My mom gasps.

"You did it," I say without taking my eyes from Bazil's. Admiration swirls in their depths. They're still green, I notice with some surprise, and still warm.

"I'm your mom. Keeping the world safe for you is my duty."

I smile. "And it will be mine as well, one day. Why not get a head start?"

"Oh, Dulcie, I do like her," Bazil says with a deep laugh that sounds less like breaking thunder and more like the booming resonant laugh of a grandfather. "She has such spirit! In fact, she reminds me of you when you were a girl. I thought you would say something like that, which is why I have one more trick up my sleeve."

His words fill me with instant horror.

"What did you do?" my mother and I both demand.

He holds out a deceptively smooth hand. "Shall we see?"

You can't resist a monster.

"Mom," I say, reaching behind me for her fingers. "Don't let go of me, okay? I need you to hold tight."

"I'll never let you go, love," she says.

I take his hand.

The minute his huge palm closes around mine, I'm assaulted by images. I brace for ugliness, but they're not what I expect, like scenes of mayhem and brimstone. Instead, they're filled with the scents and sights of spring, or what would be the wet season here, of flowery growth and rich tilled earth, of children's laughter and nursery rhymes, of a chubby baby boy with dark hair and a mischievous grin that seems so familiar. Magic fills the vines and the soil, shimmers along the branches of the trees, and I can hear the very heartbeat of the mountain.

And then it changes so fast that I'm left reeling. Smells shift into rot, reminding me of the scent at the base of the silk cottonwood tree, and the trees are bleeding into the dry, cracked dirt. The rivers shrink to trickles, their bubbly music cut short. The laughter of children fades. Without a doubt, I know the earth is dying. And *he* is dying, too . . . the bearded man with the skin of bark, deep compassionate eyes, and that quirky smile. A smile I know . . . one I've seen before. Nox's smile. Oh my gosh. Was that Nox's dad?

I blink as the images waver.

What was *that*?

Are they his dreams or his memories? And who was that man there at the end? Could it truly be Nox's father? As soon as I think it, that makes sense. Bazil is draining Papa Bois. Where is he? I have to find him too, for Nox's sake.

The visions abruptly stop as if a television has been switched off in my head.

"Next time, ask permission, little witch," Bazil murmurs.

263

"Why?" I retort. "You're always in *my* head when I don't want you there."

His laugher rumbles out. "Touché."

People are staring at us as I dimly realize that we're no longer inside the tree. Namely the Minders. Well, three of them, since Monique is nowhere in sight. But Fitz is there, and Hazel too. And Granny! Her eyes are bright and her spine is ramrod straight. She doesn't look sallow or weak, so maybe Monique's bargain did work. At least that's one good thing.

I register that we're at the bottom of the cottonwood tree in the clearing in Granny's orchard. My heart sinks as I take in the threat. Douens surround my friends and grandmother. I'm really starting to loathe those little beasts. My eyes meet Nox's tortured gaze, and I remember what I'd seen in Bazil's visions.

"Nox! He's got your dad somewhere, and he's sick!" I blurt. "But I don't know where. I don't think he has much time."

My mother makes a strangled noise as though she's trying to speak and can't. Granny does the same, and it strikes me that they might both be under another spell. My skin tingles. Suddenly, I'm jostled from my mom's hold as a dozen douens snatch her away and lead her over to the others.

It's just me and the devil now.

Bazil laughs. This one is cold and vicious. "Your mother or your grandmother. Choose one of the two, witchen. One lives and one . . . well . . ."

I shake my head. "That's an impossible choice."

"Shall we throw your friends into the mix? Which one shall it be? Let's see . . . roses are red, violets are blue, sugar is sweet, but certainly not you."

His finger lands squarely on Nox. My vision swims as I sway on my feet with fear. "Don't hurt him," I hear myself beg.

He pauses. "Choose, Darika."

"What difference does it make? You'll destroy us all anyway."

"Because I want you to see how difficult it is. No one wants to hurt their loved ones, but sometimes you have to for the greater good. Life comes with a cost, one that someone needs to pay." His voice hardens. "Sacrifice is required."

"This isn't sacrifice!" I scream. "You're asking me to sentence my mom or my grandmother or my friends to an eternal prison. To feed their souls to your dreadful tree. I won't. Take me instead."

Confusion flicks over his face. And I see that ragged pulse of empathy again.

But the moment is lost as a huge explosion rocks the clearing, the heat of fire searing into my skin. I'm thrown to the side as more flames break out, scattering the douens guarding my family and friends. Bazil roars in rage, but I take the moment to dive and roll toward them.

I notice the hulking form of Becks in the clearing, and in his arms are a half-dozen sharing-sized bags of Skittles. My mouth waters, but I watch with a combination of approval and resentment—*I won't lie*—as he throws handfuls of the candy into the midst of the reeling douens. As they had in the maze, they disperse with cries of delight.

"Yes!" I fist-pump with glee. Skittles to the rescue again.

A huge river of flame beats down upon Bazil and he hunkers down, his shoulders shaking. Is he *weeping*? And where is that fire coming from? I get my answer as I see Monique standing behind him, her face fierce, and I throw her a grateful glance. Whatever happened in the maze, I'm glad she was able to escape and that she's on my side now. Though I suspect that Bazil only wanted to trap *me*.

My elation is short-lived, however, when I hear an agonized whimper. Bazil looks up and he's not crying. He's *laughing*, loud raucous peals of laughter that make his entire body shake. Why, though? That doesn't sound like he's in pain. His minions are gone and he's on fire! He should be screaming.

"Hurt me and you hurt *her*," he cackles.

I frown as another anguished whimper echoes through the glade. What?

Piku yelps and dives off my shoulder to the ground. "Rika, your mother!"

No, no, no. Terror hits me right in the gut as I turn, only to see the suffering on my mom's face, her blistered skin red and raw as she falls into a pained crouch that mirrors the devil's. "Stop! Monique!"

Monique shoots me a doubtful look, but the flames quiet and recede. Loathing fills my veins at the sight of my mother's charred, burned flesh. Not toward the Fire Minder, but toward the devil who has somehow tied his survival to *my* mom's.

"They're connected. We hurt him, she feels the brunt of it."

A look of horror crosses Granny's face as she falls to the ground beside Mom, gathering her gently in her arms and whispering words of healing. They work, but unfortunately, they also heal the devil a few feet away. Becks, bless his protective heart, doesn't waste any time in sprinkling a thick barrier of salt around us in a circle.

"Thanks, Becks," I tell him.

He smiles. "Good to see you, Miss Darika." His face warms as he stoops next to my mom. "And you, too, Miss Dulcie."

My mom manages a smile of her own. "Becks to the rescue," she croaks.

"Just doing my job."

I stare at him in wonder. "Where'd you get the Skittles?"

"Monique told me what you did, and I bought some at the store."

Shut the front door and throw away the key. They sell my favorite candy in Trinidad? Becks's grin widens at the look on my face and he reaches into the satchel at his side. "Doh fret, I saved you a bag."

"You are my absolute favorite, Becks!"

I stare at Granny. "Are you okay?"

Her eyes twinkle. "Never better, doux-doux."

After we check on my mom and I leave Granny with her, Nox crushes me in a bear hug. "What about me?"

"Did *you* bring me any Skittles?" I ask, tears filling my eyes. "Seriously, Nox, I thought I was never going to see you again. And you too, Fitz." Fitz and Hazel slam into our group huddle and I gather my new friends close. "Where did you go? What happened?"

"Locked in a box. Hazel found me and then we located Nox." He glares at Monique, who is staring at the ground with a morose look on her face. "He told me what *she* did."

I reach out a hand to her, calling her over. Her mouth twists but she shuffles over and stands there uncertainly. "It was a misunderstanding," I say. "Right, Monique? If it wasn't for her, Granny would still be sick. She made Ushara do a binding promise to heal her, so it all worked out in the end. We are in this together."

"I do feel better than I have in months," Granny pipes up.

Monique wrings her hands. "I really messed up, and I'm sorry."

"Two Minders once told me everyone makes mistakes. It's what comes after that makes the difference. And you more than made up for that by showing up now. You also saved Granny. Now get in here!"

With a grateful smile, she joins our group huddle. I can see the expressions on the other Minders' faces, particularly Nox's, that it's probably going to take a while for any of them to come to terms with what she did, breaking Minder code and all, but hopefully this is a step in the right direction.

"This is endearing, but we're at a stalemate." Bazil's voice is jeering. "I have spent years imprisoned in this tree. Standing outside of it will make little difference. I will wait for as long as it takes for you to give me what I want. Release me from the curse of the tree or we stand here forever."

"Forever?" I roll my eyes. "Do you ever stop being such a drama llama?"

He grins amid the gasps around us at my sass, but it's all teeth and no humor. "And don't forget, your mother's fate is tied to mine, so don't get any stupid ideas."

I can't help noticing that our salt circle is surrounded by

shadow jumbies, slinking in from the gloom like ugly bits of darkness. Unlike the douens, these monsters won't go for a candy distraction. Huge with horns and tusks and sharp teeth, they look mean and forbidding.

"What do you want, Bazil?" I ask.

"You know what I want."

He wants his freedom to wreak destruction. But I can stop this . . . maybe.

The first step is to save the world from a maniacal devil on a power trip. And you can bet this girl has a plan.

a. Figure out how to break the bonds tying him to my mom.

b. Get everyone to safety.

c. Banish him back inside the tree where he belongs.

Second, inhale this bag of Skittles currently burning a hole in my pocket.

The quicker I get to step two, the better for everyone. "Fine, new deal. Let them go, cut ties with my mom, and I'll do what you ask."

"Rika, no!" The ragged plea is from my mom. "You don't understand. If he gets out, it will be chaos. He's not who you think he is."

"Who is he?" Nox asks.

But once more, she opens her mouth and nothing comes out. My gaze pans to Nox's, and I freeze in delayed shock. Those *eyes* . . . they're exactly the same! Forest green and alive with forest magic and warmth. I knew I'd seen them before!

I swivel back to Bazil, certainty settling over me.

I whisper, "*You're* Papa Bois."

22

ART MAGIC
SAVES THE DAY

Nox's face is stunned. "No, it can't be. This creature is not . . . my dad."

Everything is starting to make sense now. The approval in my mom's eyes bolsters me that I've guessed right. "He said he was infected by people," I say aloud, remembering the images I'd seen and the things I'd felt when I'd inadvertently crossed into his memories. "The damage to the earth is what everyone has done to the land right? They're destroying it. People are the ones who have been killing the magic of the wood."

"I don't understand," Nox says, brows furrowed. "There was always a jumbie tied to the silk cotton tree."

I reach for his hand and squeeze. "I think that's why your dad turned into this. It was how the silk cotton tree devil was able to corrupt him. He got weaker and weaker as the forests died and somehow the evil spirit got into him like a deadly virus." I stare at him. "But your dad is still in there, Nox. I've seen him."

Poor Nox's face is twisted in horror.

Light glitters in Bazil's eyes, and I can see the struggle as he fights to keep Papa Bois buried, Dr. Jekyll and Mr. Hyde–style. I have no idea how Nox's dad became entwined with the original demon of the tree. Maybe he was captured because of his sickness.

My heart clenches as I realize that we might be too late. Regardless of how his fall came to be, Papa Bois *is* Bazil now. All the devil spirit has done in the last few years is corrupt Papa Bois's soul and grow in strength and rage . . . because of humanity. And since the father of the forests is an almighty being, the creature he's become is more than a threat. He is a danger to life as we know it, the sure harbinger of the apocalypse.

Please don't let it be too late to save him.

"Humans don't deserve the earth," Bazil says.

"They can change," I say. "*We* can change."

His smile is condescending. "How can you do anything to slow the decay, little witch?"

My spirit deflates. He's right. What can any one person do?

And then I remember what I'd told myself with Ushara in that attic room: in scary situations, small steps are the answer. No matter how little, it's better than nothing. *Small steps.* I swallow hard and nod.

"I can do something about how I treat my own spaces

271

because change starts with me," I say, my voice soft at first and then stronger. "Give us a chance, please. It's not too late to correct the course."

Everyone waits with bated breath from where we stand in our small group. Even the forest has stopped breathing. Bazil howls and the jumbies around us roar with displeasure, making the hairs on my arms stand up. "Darika Lovelace, I accept your offer for my freedom from this tree."

My heart sinks, but I should have known beating him wasn't going to be easy. I'd offered that new deal before I'd guessed who he was. *New deal. Let them go, cut ties with my mom, and I'll do what you ask.*

"Rika, don't do it," my mom urges.

I hug her. "Trust me, Mom. I've got this."

And then I turn to Nox and the other Minders. I don't say anything, but our eyes meet in turn. If they've learned anything about me in the maze, it's that I really don't like losing. And if I've learned anything about me, it's that I'm stronger and smarter than I give myself credit for.

I lower my voice to a whisper as I pull Nox close. "We're going to get your dad back, I promise."

We face Bazil as a team, and then I step out of the circle. "Sever the ties with my mom, and tell your jumbies to back off."

Bazil whispers a word and nods to the jumbies, who melt back into the shadows where they came from until the glade is empty. He stares me down; the only thing in that malevolent gaze is retribution. There's nothing of Nox's dad in there now.

"Make the oath." Bazil's gaze is cruel even as he takes a

threatening step forward, but I stand strong, despite my wobbly knees. He's not going to risk his freedom by attacking me, not when it's so close, and my power has to be freely given.

"I agree to release you from the silk cottonwood tree"— I hold my ground when his chest rattles like a snake—"on one condition. Let my mom go."

A shimmer of magic glides through the grove as part of my promise is sealed.

"Feel that? Your turn," I say. "Break the spell or we're done here."

He's delaying to torment me, not because he's worried I won't hold up my end of the bargain. I know it doesn't matter—the vow made in the glade and bound in magic will hold. I couldn't break my promise even if I wanted to.

He growls a single word of power, and I hear my mom's answering gasp. Through the vow, I can feel the tether between them snap.

Monique leaps forward, her hands raised and ready to rage war in fire, but I lift my palm. Bazil is too powerful. Making the wrong move could cost us dearly. Mom is safe from harm for the moment, but my part of the deal still hangs in the balance. If I renege now, who knows what will happen?

"Nox, knife."

"Rika," he cautions as he huffs a shattered breath. "Why are you doing this? The cost of letting him loose is too high, even if you're right about him being . . . my dad."

I stare at my friend, heart melting when his voice chokes on that last word. I think about my own dad. "No, we don't give up now. We battled poisonous fart-bats and flesh-hungry spiders. We're saving him."

"Not if you get hurt."

"Sometimes a skinned knee is worth the lesson." I take the knife from Nox and squeeze my fist around the edge, wincing at the sting. Okay, maybe this is a little worse than a skinned knee. *Ouch!* Note to self: don't play with sharp knives—they hurt!

"Mom, Granny," I say.

The other two making up the trinity of Lovelace witches approach me, and I'm humbled by their trust. My plan might be clumsy and depend on a whole lot of luck, but it *has* to work.

"You've gotten us this far, Rika-love," Granny says, her brown eyes twinkling. "Keep going. We have your back."

I'm boosted by her faith in me. "Thanks, Granny."

Kneeling, I cup my palm and place it on the ground, connecting with the roots of the silk cottonwood tree. Mom and Granny kneel with me, whispering words of power, weaving a song of our magic through the earth and the roots. In my mind's eye, I see the intricate threads of the spell binding the devil to the tree unravel and fall, until they're nothing but a golden mass at the base.

"There, all done," I say in a snarky tone in spite of the sourness in my stomach. "Happy now?"

Bazil's power rockets through the woods, and I quail as the sheer strength of it nearly knocks me to the ground. I hadn't planned on him being *that* strong. But of course he is—he's the king of the wood and one of the strongest magical creatures in existence. In full monster I'm-going-to-pulverize-the-earth-to-dust mode, he reminds me of Te Kā in the movie *Moana*, only this isn't as simple as giving Te Fiti back her stolen heart.

Bazil has no heart that I can see, which leaves me only one option.

Fight for my life. Fight for *all* our lives.

Reaching into my pocket, I grab hold of Granny's paint and twist the lid open with my thumb. The fate of the world lies in a tiny bottle of iridescent hope, but amazing things can come in small packages. I know the Minders are with me no matter what, but this is either going to be awesome or really, *really* bad.

Bazil rolls his neck, his grin wide and full of fangs, power pulsing from him in bursts so strong they shake the branches of the surrounding bush. "Three little witches will rue the day they tried to trap me in this tree."

"Hey, jerkface!" I call out. "Won't you ever learn?"

Cracking his knuckles, he sends me a patronizing look. "What's that, witchen?"

"Never mess with a Lovelace!"

With that, I fling the gourd of paint with all the pent-up emotion I have bubbling inside me. To his credit, he knocks the flying projectile away at the last second of collision, but not before shimmer splatters his chest. The magical paint sinks in and begins to spread along his green skin.

"What is this?" he thunders, clawing at his chest, but the pigment only spreads to his fingers.

"You're not afraid of a little paint, are you?" I taunt.

He roars with rage, shaking the entire clearing. I feel the slightest warning in my bones before an eruption of power bursts from his body, punching outward in an unforgiving wave. Leaves rip from trees, earth lifts in chunks, and bodies go flying. Including mine.

Struggling to get to my feet, I blink the grit out of my eyes. I might be imagining it, but he seems to have grown in size. Thunder booms overhead as lightning splits the sky in frightening forks. Even though early morning has come, it could be nighttime.

"In what world did you think you could defeat me?" he growls.

"Mom? Granny?" I ask, unable to see through the tornado of dirt that blows around the grove. "Nox? Anyone?"

But everyone is down, except for me.

The moonstones in Granny's bracelet at my wrist glow with power, and I realize that they are the only reason I'm still standing right now. I send out a wish that the others are safe, and I square my shoulders. Time to finish this.

I brace against the billowing wind and shade my eyes. Bazil is still splotched in paint. I sink to the ground and clear my mind, letting it connect with the earth and life around me. I count backward in my head from ten, controlling my breathing, getting my brain to go blank from all the noise and the chaos around me. In and out, and in and out, each time growing calmer. Only then do I reach for the magic in my middle.

My gift . . . the spark of creation.

And I paint. I paint in my head, imagining thick powerful vines of gold spreading out from the center of Bazil's body and winding around him. I paint away the dark hollows filled with hate and despair and replace them with vibrant color—the colors of springtime and hope and renewal. Every hue I've ever painted in my life, I reimagine now.

Brilliant hibiscus flowers in full bloom, lush purple bougainvillea, bright green leaves with thick healthy stems, and I fill the brown beautiful earth enriching them all with seeds of love and life. Magic spreads over me, like sunshine on a warm summer day.

In my head, I'm painting the monster away.

In real life, I'm in a glade locked in battle with a being much stronger than me.

My body trembles with exhaustion, but Piku is there cheering me on, and then I hear the Minders. I sense Mom, Granny, and Becks at my back, and feel their combined energies pouring into me and giving me strength. But it's not enough. A corrupted Papa Bois, now the fiendish Bazil, is too strong. My focus falters and the colors dim.

"Don't give up, Rika," my mom whispers. "You're the bravest girl I know. I'm so very proud of you."

"Me too, doux-doux," Granny says.

Suddenly, I'm filled with so much warmth I want to cry. I feel my tears wet on my face and my mom's lips on my hair. Magic and power from them stream into me, filling up my well. From the Minders too.

White for air, blue for water, red for fire, brown for earth. Nox, Hazel, Monique, Fitz.

Silver for Granny, gold for my mom, and my own blushing pink. We each have different uniquely expressed forms of spirit. Mine is through my art.

277

Even a splash of green for Piku. I grin. Pure dragon power.

The colors of the rainbow rip through the darkness. I feel it. I feel them all, and I know just what to do. I take every ounce of that magic and I send it toward my creation, imbuing it with everything inside of me. I understand now. Bazil is empty: he's a parasite feeding off of Nox's dad and a wall blocking Papa Bois from connecting with the lifeblood of the forest. If I give Bazil a taste of our magic—the beating heart of the forest and the souls of all of us—it might be enough to rip them apart. To break the devil's darkness and let the light back in.

I open my eyes and laugh. "Time to taste the rainbow, turd sniffer."

"Good one!" Piku says.

Bazil drops to his knees. "Impossible! You are not this strong!"

"Maybe," I say, feeling the magic humming in my veins, "but I'm never alone."

The devil spirit–slash–Papa Bois tries one last-ditch effort, appealing to the boy standing at my side. "Son, join me. We can burn this world together."

Nox shakes his head. "Nope, I'm with her. Do it, Rika!"

Once more, the light burns so brightly that it's almost blinding. I feel hot, like my entire body is blazing. I take all my colors and imagine a wall in front of me . . . a wall that needs to be broken, and I blast my magic into it. The explosion shakes the ground, and a shower of sparkles rains down upon us.

I hold my breath.

A dark shadow lingers, reaching for me. *No!*

But as ghostly tendrils touch my aura and I brace for pain, they waver and dissipate like ash on the wind. When the last of the dark finally fades, the skies clear to a beautiful blue color with golden rays piercing through the trees.

Bazil—or whatever that evil infection was—is gone, and in his place sits a bearded man with kind eyes and brown weathered skin.

"Father!" Nox yells and runs toward him.

Papa Bois smiles and catches him in an embrace. "It's good to see you, my boy."

"You too, Dad, you too." He frowns. "Is Bazil truly gone?"

"The essence of the devil is back in the silk cotton tree where it belongs." Papa Bois sighs with his whole body. "I let my anger weaken me and it gave him a chance to taint my spirit with his. When you let bad things inside your spirit, they can contaminate you. After that, all I knew was rage. But I'm free now, thanks to you, thanks to the Minders, and thanks to the Lovelace witches."

Overwhelmed, I rest my head on my mom's shoulder and tuck my grandmother in on my other side. And then we're bombarded by the Minders. Fitz, then Hazel, then Monique. Granny pulls her close and kisses her head, and I can only smile. There's more than enough of my granny to go around, and I'm glad Monique has her.

"Lennox," my mom says as he joins the group hug. "Thank you for looking out for my girl. Thanks to all of you."

Fitz grins. "Mango don't fall far from the tree."

That boy and his quirky sayings, but I guess mangoes are

sweeter than apples. I'm like Mom, and like Granny. We're the Lovelace trinity. I grin and give him a high five.

We leave Nox and the other Minders to bring Papa Bois up to speed, and start the trek home. Piku scrambles up my arm and settles himself in my hood. I wonder if you can take iguanas back to the States. He'd probably despise the Colorado winters.

"Granny," I say, brightening when I see the house come into view and feeling my belly rumble.

"Yes, Rika-love?"

"What's for breakfast?" It's past dawn. No wonder I'm starving.

We share a laugh as she assures me she will cook up a feast once everyone takes a good, long, hot shower. No one wants to have devil guts in their hair.

As we climb the porch steps, I squeeze Mom's arm and feel a residual tingle of power. "Hey, Mom, since I'm a witch and I technically just saved the world from major destruction and a possible apocalypse, does that mean I can skip eighth grade?"

She ruffles my hair with a smile like pure sunshine. "Not a chance."

23

IT'S ONLY GOODBYE FOR NOW

Who knew summer in the islands could be so fun? I'm already planning my return trip, maybe for winter break. Then every summer after. And maybe Dad and Cassie will come with the boys and we can make it a true Lovelace-Rose family holiday. My brothers would love Trinidad and have a blast in Granny's orchard.

I'm packing up my stuff in my bedroom, making sure nothing's missing from my backpack. A beautiful purple emperor butterfly with iridescent blue wings flutters through the open window, and I catch my breath, remembering Granny's saying. *A butterfly in the house means good luck.* I smile as Piku, who is sunning himself at his usual spot near the windowsill, cracks an interested eye. "Don't you dare eat that!"

He goes for a lazy eyeball lick instead and pins me with a stern glare. "As if, human."

I giggle. Granny and Mom decided it would be better for him to stay here in his natural habitat, and while I'm sad I can't take him with me, I know they're right. I'm going to miss the cranky, know-it-all reptile, though. I glance over to where my mom is folding some of my freshly laundered clothes and tucking them into my suitcase.

"Mom, do you promise you'll video-call me with him?"

"Of course, honey," she says.

She's going to stay here with Granny, just to make sure things stay on track with the witches on the island and the restoration of the magic in the forest. She and I finished clearing out her old room together. Granny's ploy worked—the past always informs the present and impacts the future. If I hadn't been in this room, I wouldn't have known what I could do or found out who my mom was. I wouldn't have believed I was a Lovelace witch.

Or still a baby witchen, as Piku loves to remind me.

When I showed them the grimoire I'd found, Mom, Granny, and I had a long chat about the history of our family line. It's important to know where you come from to know where you're going to go. I'm a witch, like my mom and like her mom. And with great supernatural power comes revenge-on-anyone-who-has-ever-crossed-me.

Just kidding! I'm a good witch. I know that great power comes with great responsibility. Way back when, I remember Mom telling me some old French dude named Voltaire said that. Then Dad had to chime in that it was most definitely Spider-Man. They're both right, of course.

Still, it had been good to learn more about magic in a much calmer, I'm-not-going-to-die setting. I have to start honing my creative gifts. Granny and Mom even showed me how to make my own set of jet-bead bracelets with protections over the gems to ward off maljo, or any kind of evil eye. I've made ones for myself and for Max and Theo. No bad energy or jumbie mischief for us, thank you very much. And they've gifted me with my very own grimoire. I can't wait to fill its pages with my own drawings and notes about any growth in my creation magic!

Honestly, I don't want to leave the country, after just having been reunited, but Mom's and Granny's obligations as witch leaders of these beautiful islands don't end with us saving the world. Meanwhile, I have to start eighth grade and make things right at home. I have to earn my Dad's and stepmom's trust back. If I paint a wall, I'll get permission first.

I meant it when I said it to Bazil: change starts with me.

"Chill out, bae," Piku drawls. "I won't ghost you."

I snort. "I regret teaching you slang."

"I'm awoken and I like it."

"It's *woke,* but please stop." I can't stop laughing and collapse onto the floor in giggles.

A singsong voice filters in from the back garden. "There's a brown girl in the ring, tra la la la la . . ."

"That's Nox and the others. Do I have time to go say goodbye?"

My mom smiles. "Of course you do. You have a few minutes, just don't be too long or we'll be late to the airport. I'll get Becks to grab your things."

"Thanks, Mom, I won't." I kiss her cheek and glance over at Piku. "You coming?"

"Without me watching out for you, you'll probably fall down a hole or something before your flight."

I feel him nuzzle my cheek as he climbs into his spot. "I'm going to miss you sitting on my shoulder. What if I get another pet iguana to keep me company?"

"Bite your tongue, girl. No one can replace the great Piku."

I give his tail an affectionate tug. "I'm only joking!"

We make our way outside and I breathe in the soft balmy air. We're well into the wet season now, and the trees are thick in foliage and fruit. The drought that had plagued the landscape has essentially receded. I gaze fondly at my grandmother's clotheslines where she's hanging out fresh laundry, and I wave. "Hi, Granny!"

"Hey, Rika-love." Brown eyes twinkle. "Don't go past the tree line into the woods."

"The devil's locked in his tree, Granny."

"Doesn't mean he can't come back."

I send her a wicked look. "Invite Papa Bois over for some cascadoux. You know he'll be like putty in your hands."

"Cheeky girl!"

With a laugh, I run outside and catch up with my friends in the same grove where I'd met them weeks ago. Nox is waiting with a ripe mango in hand.

"It's like you can read my mind," I tell him, and take the yellow fruit.

"Are you packed?"

"Glomph, shortoof," I reply with a mouthful.

"Huh?" he says with a laugh.

I chew and swallow, trying not to let any juice dribble from my chin to my clothes. "So good. Yes, I'm pretty much done."

Hazel squeals and runs over to me. "I'm going to miss you."

"I'll miss you too." She takes my hands in hers and rinses them with a stream of water that appears out of nowhere. I grin. "Especially that handy bit of water magic."

"What about mine?" Fitz asks. A bright green vine twines up my leg to offer up a pretty pink flower at the end. I take it with a smile and tuck it behind my ear.

"Yours too, my friend." I pull him in for a hug and rumple his braids. "Stay out of trouble and no more mudslides without me, okay?"

"Bet." Turning red, he swipes at his eye and ducks his face. "Sorry, I have some dirt in my eye."

"Hey, Rika." I turn around to see Monique and smile. Hard to think that at the start of the summer, we were enemies, and now we're practically besties. Just goes to show that you never know about people. I like Monique. She's smart and has a wicked sense of humor. She walks over to me, glossy hair in a long braid and her honey-colored eyes bright. One day, I'll get used to how pretty she is and not feel so much envy. Or is it admiration? Between her and Nox, my poor heart might be in for a battle. "I made you something."

"Oh yeah?" I say.

She hands out a handmade necklace that has a red stone woven into it. "I made two, one for you with a red stone to remind you of me, and one for me with a pink stone." She pats her throat where a matching necklace sits.

"Wow, Monique, this is beautiful. Thank you." I loop it twice and fasten it right next to Granny's bracelet, which she insisted I keep. "I'll treasure it."

We had also finally spoken to Granny about the broken totem, and it turns out that Granny had only asked another witch to step in with Monique's training because she was advancing so much faster than the other students and she didn't want Monique to be held back in her studies and lose momentum. In truth, Granny didn't even remember the broken bracelet. She gave Monique another one made of red and black jumbie beads that wards off malevolent spirits. Monique was thrilled. She felt special, and I love that for her.

"You'll message me?" she asks.

"Every day," I say and give my friend a hug. "Now that we have a group chat for the Minders on Insta, there's no getting rid of me."

That had been Monique's brilliant idea. Since they don't have reliable internet access, Granny has agreed to get a dedicated line and a computer that doesn't use "old floppy disks"—*what even are those?*—which really is for us to stay in touch.

Granny's steps into the twenty-first century aren't just for me to keep up with my friends, but also to launch her new website on homegrown organic fruits and veggies as well as homemade witchy remedies and poultices. Sustainable living with a touch of magic, she says. My granny, queen of the small business. Good thing we all pitched in the last week to clean out the rest of Mom's room and the entire old wing of the house. That will now be converted to supply space for her new venture.

"I'll walk you out to the truck," Nox says after I give

Monique another hug and squeeze Hazel and Fitz in for one last goodbye.

I get a bit tongue-tied and teary-eyed when Nox takes my hand in his. I know I'll never hear the end of it from Piku, who has already started his incessant teasing, but for now, the little imp stays blessedly quiet.

"You'll take care of the others, right?" I say when we get to the courtyard. Becks is loading my suitcase into the truck and Mom has my backpack. Granny isn't out yet, so we have a couple more minutes.

Nox smiles. "You know I will. Dad says bye, by the way."

"Oh, tell him I'll come back soon."

Papa Bois turned out to be an older version of Nox— serious, kind, with a quirky sense of humor. At first it was strange talking to him, knowing that he and the devil that had named himself Bazil were so entwined and determined to destroy the world. But after I got to know him a little, my fear went away—not all the way, just enough to not lose my cool.

"I'll miss you," Nox says and tugs on a lock of my hair.

I grin at my friend. "Still think I'm a pest?"

"The worst menace ever," he says with a smirk. "Practice your magic daily, okay? And remember that shield. Don't let your guard down just because it seems like the worst is over. Bad things are always lurking in the shadows."

I roll my eyes. "I won't forget, Nox."

"Come on, Darika," Granny calls out and hops into the truck. "Or we'll be late."

"I guess I have to go," I tell Nox. We hug, awkwardly at first, and then tighter. I didn't feel my eyes burning until now.

I don't want to let him go. . . . I don't want to leave, even though I know I have to. But I'll be back.

"Safe travels, Rika."

"Bye, Nox." Pushing to my toes, I kiss his cheek and duck my face to hide my blush.

I pass the old wishing well in the courtyard on the way to the truck, and then stop to peer down into the depths. I smile as I see evidence of Fitz's stone ladder. On instinct, I fish in my jeans pockets for one of my coins and find a quarter. I make a silent wish. Exhaling, I twist the coin in my fingers and flick it off my thumb, watching as it flips in a silver arc down to the bottom where it plops with a small splash.

"Hey, did you make a wish?" Nox calls out.

"You bet my glorious Skittles rainbow I did."

"Good. I hope it comes true." Then he gives me a sweet-eye, as Fitz calls it—which is a special saucy kind of wink—that makes my blush deepen and says, "Until we meet again, Lovelace!"

Cheeks on fire, I grin, my heart warming with delight. I'm not going to say my wish out loud because then it won't come true, but I know for a fact that it's going to be bright and iridescent like a bubble caught in the biggest ray of sunshine. I think about all those coins I'd thrown in before, like wishing for my mom to be here, while not truly imagining they could come true. Without hope, what's the point of having big dreams?

No more lost wishes for me.

Because magic is real, and I *believe.*

DARIKA LOVELACE-ROSE
WILL RETURN SOON
IF THAT WISH KNOWS
WHAT'S GOOD FOR IT.

AUTHOR'S NOTE

I've always loved reading and making up stories. I remember carrying around a small notebook that I wrote in almost daily when I was nine. Those pages held everything—stories cooked up by an often overactive imagination fueled by other novels I devoured. I read anything and everything, from Grimms' fairy tales to Greek mythology. The darker and spookier, the better! The lure of the unknown, the combined beauty and horror of the supernatural, and the intrigue of all things magic were mental candy for me.

Having spent the first seventeen years of my life in Trinidad and Tobago, a country rich in occult folklore, I had more than enough fuel for imagination. Growing up, I had my share of spooky or "jumbie" (monster) stories—word-of-mouth tales of voodoo or West Indian sorcery called obeah, myths about la diablesse or the soucouyant, a supernatural beast disguised as an old woman by day and a bloodsucking creature by night. Fingers crossed you had a spine-chilling introduction to both creatures in *Bumps in the Night*!

The silk cotton tree in the story is a real tree and can be found in many areas of the Caribbean. The tree itself can be taller than two hundred feet, with sprawling buttresses beneath its roots, and takes nearly eighty years to fully grow! It's surrounded by superstition. In Caribbean countries, it is called the "god tree" or the "devil tree." In Guyana, it's referred to as the "jumbie tree."

There are many scary stories surrounding the silk cotton trees: they're possessed by spirits, they house the souls of the dead, they're sentient and vengeful, they cause curses. Considered the source of obeah and magic, many people were afraid to even cut down a silk cotton tree, for fear of unleashing all those dead souls on people or suffering blights. One man in Trinidad claimed he had a stroke after cutting down some branches. Another said he saw the spirits of dead children near his home when a tree fell. Creepy, right?

Speaking of creepy, I got my inspiration for Bazil from an old Trinidadian story I read while doing research on which supernatural characters I wanted to include. There was a devil named Bazil, who was known as the visitor of death and reaped the souls of men outside Sangre Grande, a town in Trinidad. According to legend, Bazil was lured to a silk cotton tree by an elderly carpenter who had carved seven locked rooms in the tree and trapped the devil inside so the man could cheat death. I couldn't stop thinking about a Dr. Facilier–type creature ensnared in the tree as well as these escape-type rooms . . . which is how I came up with the maze. I loved the idea of having challenges for each level, and conquering the maze meant beating the resident devil.

Growing up and reading C. S. Lewis, I was fascinated by the world of Narnia and by reaching other magical places through portals, and when this plot started coming together, I knew I wanted the tree to be something similar. I also wanted the tree maze to be a challenge. Darika and her friends have to navigate each level inside this unearthly realm loaded with traps and tricks . . . then face the consequences if mistakes are made. But *everyone* makes mistakes! Besting the maze is about courage and resilience. It's about getting up if you fall and giving it your best no matter what.

Themes of trust, friendship, and found family are important to me, and while delving into those in this novel, I wanted to bring a lot of my culture to the page, including the food, landmarks, and traditions. I have Indian, Middle Eastern, and French Creole roots, and the people of Trinidad are a diverse mix of Amerindian, African, Asian, and European ancestry. Each group includes its own rich tapestry of folklore and customs. The world is a very big, broad place, so I encourage you to expand your horizons and read books from other cultures written by authors of different backgrounds. You'll discover whole new worlds and mythologies to explore!

Hope you had a fun, hair-raising time reading *Bumps in the Night*!

XO,

ACKNOWLEDGMENTS

Firstly, to my incredible editor, Bria Ragin, this is our second book together, and as with the first, working with you has been such a great experience. I could not ask for better partners for my middle-grade debut than you and Delacorte Press! Thank you for all your notes and suggestions and for asking all those questions that really made me drill into the mythology and significance of this story. Our vibe is chef's kiss! You deserve *all* the juiciest mangoes!

To my rock-star agent, Thao Le, how is it that I really never have enough words for how phenomenal you are and how ridiculously lucky I feel to have you in my corner? Seriously, it's like all the adoration wants to come out at once in a glitter explosion. Thank you so much for your hard work, your guidance, your insight, and everything you do to manage and advocate for my career. I would not be here without you.

Huge thanks to the powerhouses: Wendy Loggia, Beverly Horowitz, and Barbara Marcus! I'm so honored to make my middle-grade debut with such an incredible imprint! Being with PRH for my middle-grade and young adult books has been a dream come true, and I'm more grateful than you can imagine. Thank you.

Big thanks to my cover artist, Matt Rockefeller, who nailed the creepy magical concept and those douens, and to Jen Valero, who designed the amazing interior and the cover . . . you both absolutely crushed it! Special thanks to Tamar Schwartz, Colleen Fellingham, Marla Garfield, and Tracy Heydweiller for your hard work on getting this book into shape. So much gratitude goes to everyone in the production, design, sales, marketing, and publicity teams at Delacorte for your efforts behind the scenes—I'm so very appreciative of all you have done to give this book the best chance for success.

To all the readers, reviewers, booksellers, librarians, educators, writer friends, extended family, and close friends who support me and spread the word about my books, an enormous thank-you for all you do! I adore you. Last but never least, to my family, Cameron, Connor, Noah, and Olivia, thanks for loving me and for always making life such an adventure.

ABOUT THE AUTHOR

AMALIE HOWARD is a bestselling, critically acclaimed author of several novels for teens and adults. *ALA Booklist* called her young adult historical romance, *Queen Bee,* "a true diamond of the first water." Her books have been featured in *Entertainment Weekly, Cosmopolitan Magazine, Oprah Daily,* and *Seventeen.* When she's not writing, she can usually be found reading, being the president of her one-woman Harley Davidson motorcycle club, or power-napping. Born in Trinidad, where *Bumps in the Night* is set, she has always dreamed of discovering a portal to a world full of monsters and magic. She now lives in Colorado, a magical place, with her family and three little monsters to call her own. She still hopes to find a portal someday.

amaliehoward.com